22 Dead Little Bodies
and Other Stories

Stuart MacBride is the *Sunday Times* No. 1 bestselling author of the Logan McRae and Ash Henderson novels. He was crowned World Stovies Champion in 2014 and was awarded an honorary doctorate by Dundee University in 2015.

Stuart lives in the northeast of Scotland with his wife, Fiona, their cats, hens, horses, and a vast collection of assorted weeds.

For more information visit StuartMacBride.com
Facebook.com/stuartmacbridebooks
@stuartmacbride

By Stuart MacBride

The Logan McRae Novels
Cold Granite
Dying Light
Broken Skin
Flesh House
Blind Eye
Dark Blood
Shatter the Bones
Close to the Bone
22 Dead Little Bodies
The Missing and the Dead

The Ash Henderson Novels
Birthdays for the Dead
A Song for the Dying

Other Works
Sawbones (a novella)
12 Days of Winter (short stories)
Partners in Crime (Two Logan and Steel short stories)
The 45% Hangover (a Logan and Steel novella)
The Completely Wholesome Adventures of Skeleton Bob
(a picture book)

Writing as Stuart B. MacBride
Halfhead

STUART MACBRIDE

22 DEAD LITTLE BODIES

AND OTHER STORIES

HARPER

HarperCollins*Publishers*
1 London Bridge Street
London SE1 9GF

www.harpercollins.co.uk

First published as an anthology by HarperCollins*Publishers* 2015
5

A catalogue record for this book
is available from the British Library

ISBN: 978-0-00-814176-9

Set in Meridien by Palimpsest Book Production Limited, Falkirk, Stirlingshire.

Printed and bound in Great Britain by Clays Ltd, St Ives plc

Contents

The Introduction

in which the writer drones on about the stories in this collection

Believe it or not, *22 Dead Little Bodies* started life as a subplot in *The Missing and the Dead*. Well, half of it did, anyway. We trimmed seven subplots in total from *The Missing and the Dead* in order to slim it down to the chunky 160,000-word book that came out in January 2015 – so you can imagine how huge it was before. Loathe to throw this one away, I reworked it into what was meant to be a 10,000-word short story … and it ended up being 42,000 words long instead. Officially that makes it a novel. A short one, but a novel nonetheless. But while it made a nifty, and pretty sexy, little hardback, it was just a bit too small to turn into a full-length paperback. So we decided to bundle it in with two short stories and a novella, all set in Logan's happy-go-lucky world.

'Stramash' was originally published as part of the Isle of Jura Distillery's Writers' Retreat project. 'DI Steel's Bad Heir Day' appeared as a Christmas story in the *Evening Express* for charity, and later got bundled into an ebook with 'Stramash' under the title *Partners in Crime*. *The 45% Hangover* was a very rude ebook, then a lovely mini paperback in its own right. And now all of these stories live together, here, in one Steel-infested lump.

If you're the kind of crazy mixed-up kid who likes to know how the tales in this book fit in with the rest of Logan's timeline, it goes like this:

'DI Steel's Bad Heir Day'
Shatter the Bones
'Stramash'
Close to the Bone
The 45% Hangover
22 Dead Little Bodies
The Missing and the Dead

And that's it, except to say that I hope you enjoy these. Some are a bit dark, some are a bit violent, and one contains scenes of gratuitous nudity that any right-minded reader will find highly offensive. And if you're not highly offended, there's probably something wrong with you. Seek help.

All the best,

Stuart MacBride

22 Dead Little Bodies

For Brucie

Without Whom

As always I relied on a lot of clever people while I was writing this book, so I'd like to take this opportunity to thank: Sergeant Bruce Crawford and everyone in B Division; Sarah, Jane, Julia, Louise, Oli, Laura, Roger, Kate (E), Oliver, Lucy, Damon, Charlie, Tom, Kate (S), Eleanor, Dom, Marie, the DC Bishopbriggs Pure-Dead-Brilliant Brigade, and everyone at HarperCollins, for doing such a great job; Lee, Graham, Angie, Pete, Lizzy, Chuck, Toby, Wayne, Liza, Kevin, Lorraine, Sarah, Charlie, Joe, Steph, David, Ann, Ross, James, Maggie, Susan, Chris, Joe and all the excellent booksellers and librarians out there – every one of you, most certainly, rock; Phil Patterson and the team at Marjacq Scripts, for keeping my cat in shoes all these years.

More thanks go to Allan, Lola, and Rudi for the feedback and input; Twinkle, Jean, Brenda, and Dolly Bellfield for the eggs; and Gherkin for the mice.

And saving the best for last – as always – Fiona and Grendel.

— one small step (one giant leap) —

1

Oh dear *God* … it was a long way down.

Logan shuffled along the damp concrete ledge.

His left shoe skidded on something, wheeching out over the gaping drop. 'Aaagh…'

He grabbed at the handrail, heart thumping as the carrier bag from Markies spiralled away, down … down … down … fluttering like a green plastic bat on a suicide run.

All the saliva disappeared from his mouth, leaving the taste of old batteries behind.

Thump.

The bag battered into the cobbled street: prawn-and-mayonnaise sandwich exploding, the bottle of Coke spraying foam out at the circle of onlookers. The ones nearest danced back a couple of paces, out of reach of the sticky brown foam. Then stared up at him again: a circle of pale faces and open mouths. Waiting.

One or two of them had their mobile phones out, filming. Probably hoping for something horrible to happen so they could post it on YouTube.

Had to be at *least* sixty feet down.

Why couldn't jumpers leap off bungalows? Why did the

selfish sods always threaten to throw themselves off bloody huge buildings?

Logan inched closer to the man standing at the far edge of the roof. 'You...' He cleared his throat, but it didn't shift the taste. 'You don't have to do this.'

The man didn't look around. One hand gripped the railing beside him, the skin stained dark red. Blood. It spread up his sleeve – turning the grey suit jacket almost black.

His other hand was just as bad. The sticky scarlet fingers were curled around a carving knife, the blade glinting against the pale grey sky. Black handle, eight-inch blade, the metal streaked with more red.

Great.

Because what was the point of slitting your wrists in the privacy of your own home when you could do it on top of a dirty big building in the east end of Aberdeen instead? With a nice big audience to watch you jump.

And it was a *long* way down.

Logan dragged his eyes away from the slick cobblestones. 'It isn't worth it.'

Another shrug. Mr Suicide's voice trembled, not much more than a broken whisper. 'How could she *do* that?'

'Why don't you put down the knife and come back inside?'

The distant wail of a siren cut through the drab afternoon.

'Knife...?' He turned his head and frowned. Little pointy nose, receding hairline, thin face, watery eyes lurking above bruise-coloured bags. A streak of dried blood across his forehead. The front of his shirt was soaked through with it, sticking to his pigeon chest. The sour stink of hot copper and rotting onions radiated out of him like tendrils.

Logan inched closer. 'Put it down, and we can go inside and talk about it, OK?'

He looked down at the carving knife in his hand, eyes

narrowing, forehead creasing. As if he'd never seen it before. 'Oh...'

'What's your name?'

'John.'

'OK, John: I'm Logan, and I'm going to— Bollocks.' His phone rang deep in his pocket, blaring out the Imperial March from *Star Wars*. He fumbled it out with one hand, the other still wrapped tightly around the railing. 'What?'

A smoky, gravelly voice burst from the earpiece. *'Where the hell are you?'* Detective Chief Inspector Steel. She sniffed. *'Supposed to be—'*

'I'm kinda busy right now...'

'I don't care if you're having a foursome with Doris Day, Natalie Portman, and a jar of Nutella – I'm hungry. Where's my sodding lunch?'

'I'm *busy*.' He held the phone against his chest. 'What's your last name, John?'

'What does it matter?' John went back to staring at the ground, blood dripping from his fingertips. 'Skinner. John Skinner.'

'Right.' Back to the phone, keeping his voice down. 'Run a PNC check on a John Skinner, IC-one male, mid-thirties. I need—'

'Do I look like your mum? Lunch, lunch, lunch, lunch—'

For God's sake.

'Just for *once*, can you think about someone other than your sodding self?' Logan pulled on a smile for the blood-soaked man teetering on the edge of the roof. 'Sorry, my boss is a bit...' He curled his lip. 'Well, you know.'

'And another thing – how come you've no' filled out the overtime returns yet? You got any idea—'

'I'm *busy*.' He thumbed the off button and stuck the phone back in his pocket. 'Come on, John, put the knife down. It'll be OK.'

11

'No.' John shook his head, wiped a hand across his glistening eyes, leaving a thick streak of scarlet behind, like warpaint. 'No it won't.' He held the knife out and dropped it.

The blade tumbled through the air then clattered against the cobbled street below.

A uniformed PC turned up, pushing the crowd back, widening the semicircle, looking up over her shoulder and talking into her airwave handset. With any luck there'd be a trained suicide negotiator on scene in a couple of minutes. And maybe the fire brigade with one of those big inflatable mattress things in case the negotiator didn't work. And this would all be someone else's problem.

'It'll never be OK again.' John let go of the railing. 'How could it?'

'Don't do anything you'll—'

'I'm sorry.' He crouched, leaned backwards … then jumped, springing out from the roof. Eyes closed.

'NO!' Logan lunged, hand grasping the air where John Skinner wasn't any more.

Someone down there screamed.

John Skinner's suit jacket snapped and fluttered in the wind, arms windmilling, legs thrashing all the way down. Getting smaller, and smaller, and smaller, and *THUMP*.

A wet crunch. A spray of blood.

Body all twisted and broken, bright red seeping out onto the dark grey cobblestones. More screaming.

Logan crumpled back against the railing, holding on tight, and peered over the edge.

The ring of bystanders had flinched away as John Skinner hit, but now they were creeping closer again, phones held high to get a decent view over the heads of their fellow ghouls.

The wailing siren got closer, then a patrol car skidded to

a halt and four officers clambered out. Pushed their way through the amateur film crew. Then stood there staring at what was left of John Skinner.

Logan's mobile burst into the Imperial March again. Steel calling with the PNC check on their victim. He pulled the phone out. Pressed the button. 'You're too late.'

'Aye, see when I said, "Get your bumhole back here", I meant now. No' tomorrow, no' in a fortnight: now. *Sodding starving here.'*

2

'Where the hell have you been?' DCI Steel had commandeered his seat, slouching there with both feet up on his desk. A wrinkled wreck in a wrinkled suit, with a napkin tucked into the collar of her blue silk shirt. Tomato sauce smeared on either side of her mouth; the smoky scent of bacon thick in the air. She took another bite of the buttie in her hand, talking and chewing at the same time. 'Could've starved to death waiting for you.'

She'd made some sort of effort with her hair today – possibly with a garden strimmer. It stuck out at random angles, grey showing through in a thick line at the roots.

Logan dumped his coat on the hook beside the door. 'Feel free to sod off soon as you like.'

She swallowed. Pointed. 'You owe me a smoked-ham-and-mustard sandwich and a bottle of Coke. And change from a fiver.'

'They didn't have ham, so I got you prawn instead.' He scrubbed a hand over his face, then dug in his pockets. Dumped a couple of pound coins on the desk. 'Don't suppose there's any point asking you to get out of my seat?'

'Nope. Come on: make with the lunch.'

14

He settled into the visitor's chair, and slumped back, arms dangling loose at his sides. Frowning up at the ceiling. 'He's dead, by the way. In case you cared.'

'I'm still no' seeing any sandwiches here, Laz.'

'Ambulance crew say it'd be pretty much instantaneous. Flattened his skull like stamping on a cardboard box.'

'What about crisps?'

'Got you salt-and-vinegar. I slipped on the rooftop, almost went over myself. Lunch hit the deck instead of me. You can fight the seagulls for it.' He closed his eyes. 'They're probably busy eating leftover bits of John Skinner anyway.'

She sighed. 'See when they call it "talking a jumper down", they mean by the stairs, no' the quick way.'

'Funny.' He put both hands over his face. 'That's really, really funny.'

'Laz, you know I love you like a retarded wee brother, but it's time to pull up your frilly man-panties and get over it.' Steel's voice softened. 'People jump off things. They go splat. It happens. Nothing personal. Wasn't your fault.'

Raised voices thundered past in the corridor outside, something about football and beer.

'So...' A click, then a sooking noise. 'You got anything exciting on?'

He let his hands fall away. 'It's CID. There's *never* anything exciting on.'

Steel made a figure of eight with the e-cigarette in her hand. 'What did Aunty Roberta tell you?'

'Don't, OK? I'm not—'

'"Come join the MIT," I said. "These new specialist teams will hoover up all the interesting cases," I said. "All you'll be left with is the GED crap no one else wants to do," I said. "It won't be like it was when we were Grampian Police," I said. But would you listen?'

A rap on the door, then Constable Guthrie stuck his head

in. With his pale eyebrows, blond hair, and pink eyes he looked like a slightly startled rabbit. 'Sorry, Guv, but I need a word. Inspector?'

Steel popped the fake cigarette between her teeth. 'What?'

'Er, not you, Guv – DI McRae.'

She sniffed. 'No' good enough for you, am I?'

'It … I…' He pulled his mouth into a dead-fish pout. Then held out a sheet of A4 towards Logan. 'Did that PNC check you wanted: John Skinner, fourteen Buchanan Street, Kincorth. Married, two kids. Conviction for speeding eighteen months ago. Drives a dark blue BMW M5, registration number X—'

'Who cares what he drives?' Logan slumped further in his seat. 'We're not setting up a lookout request, Constable. We know fine well where he is.'

Pink bloomed on Guthrie's cheeks. 'Sorry, Guv.' He shuffled his feet a bit. 'Anyway, couple of people at the scene got the whole thing on their phones, you want to see the footage?'

'I caught the live show, I *really* don't need to see the action replay.'

'Oh…'

Steel polished off the last of her buttie, then sooked the sauce and flour off her fingers. 'Well, if you minions of CID will forgive me, I've got to go do some proper grown-up police work. Got a serial rapist on the books.' She stood and stretched, arms up, exposing a semicircle of pale stomach. Then slumped a bit. Had a scratch at one boob. 'Still hungry though.'

Guthrie pointed at his own cheek. 'You've got tomato sauce, right here.'

'Thanks.' She wiped it off with a thumb. 'And as a reward, you can get your pasty backside over to Buchanan Street, let the Merry Widow know her bloke's died of cobblestone poisoning. Offer her a shoulder to cry on – perchance a quickie, or kneetrembler up against the tumble drier – then wheech her down the mortuary to ID the body.'

Logan gritted his teeth. 'Do you have to be so bloody—'

'Oh come off it, Laz – the boy Skinner topped *himself*, no one made him do it. He jumped, leaving a wife and two wee kiddies to cope with the sticky aftermath. What kind of selfish scumbag does that?' Steel hoiked up her trousers. 'It's always some poor cow that's left picking up the pieces.'

And that's exactly what the Scenes Examination Branch had to do. Pick up the pieces before the seagulls got their beaks into what was left spread across the cobbles of Exchequer Row.

'… so I wondered if there was any news.' Logan paused in the middle of the corridor, one hand on the door through to the main CID office.

A sigh came from the mobile's earpiece. *'I'm sorry, Mr McRae, but Mr and Mrs Moore feel it's not really big enough for them.'*

'Oh.' His shoulders dipped an inch. He cleared his throat. 'Any other viewings coming up?'

'Sorry. Mrs Denis called to cancel Wednesday. They've bought a new-build out by Inverurie instead. The market isn't all that buoyant for one-bedroom flats right now.'

Great. Just – sodding – great.

'Yeah, thanks anyway.' The line went dead and he slipped the phone back in his pocket.

Eighteen months, and they'd achieved exactly bugger all.

He deflated a little further, then thunked his forehead off the CID door three times.

No reply. So Logan let himself in.

The main CID office wasn't anywhere near as big as the one they'd shared before the change to Police Scotland: no big fancy flatscreen TV for briefings; no sink for making tea and coffee; no vending machine full of crisps, chocolate, and

17

energy drinks. Instead, it was barely large enough to squeeze in four desks – one on each wall – and a pair of whiteboards covered in low-level crimes and lower-level criminals. A motley patchwork of manky carpet tiles clung to the concrete floor. Ceiling tiles stained like a toddler's nappy. Ancient computers with flickering screens.

Even the filing cabinets looked depressed.

Logan wandered over to one of them and checked the kettle perched on top: half empty. He stuck it on to boil. 'Where's everyone?'

DS Baird looked up from her screen. Pulled the earbuds out. 'Sorry, Guv?' Her short blonde hair formed random spikes on top of a rectangular face with heavy eyebrows. A pair of thick-framed glasses in black magnified her eyes to twice the size they should have been. Her smile was like a wee shiny gift. 'Coffee with two, if you're making.'

He pulled two mugs out of the top drawer. 'Where's Stoney and Wheezy Doug?'

She pointed at one of the empty desks. 'DC "couldn't find his own backside with both hands" Stone's off trying to find who's been vandalizing cars in Mannofield, and DC "just as useless" Andrews is off taking witness statements for that fire-raising at the Garthdee Asda.'

'You going to forgive them any time soon?'

'No. You need something?'

'Just interested.' The kettle rumbled to a boil.

'Hear you caught a jumper this afternoon.' Creases appeared between those thick black eyebrows. 'Well, not "caught" caught, but you know what I mean.'

'Guthrie's delivering the death message.'

A nod. 'I hate doing suicides. Don't mind telling someone their loved one's died in a car crash, or an accident, or they've been stabbed, but suicides...' Baird shuddered. 'It's the look of betrayal, you know?'

18

Logan dug a spoon into the coffee, breaking the kitty-litter clumps back into their individual grains. 'How many times do I have to tell people *not* to put damp spoons in the jar?'

'Like you're making it up to spite them.' A sigh. 'Can't really blame the family, though, can you?'

The office phone rang, and she picked it up. 'CID: DS Baird.' Then her expression curdled. 'Not *again*... Really? ... Uh-huh...'

Two sugars in one mug, milk in the other.

'No. I can't... He's not here.'

Logan put the black coffee on her desk. She looked up and gave him a grimace in return. Put the phone against her chest, smothering the mouthpiece. 'Sorry, Guv, but Mrs Black's downstairs again.'

He took a sip of his own coffee. 'Which brave soul doth possess the Nutter Spoon of Doom upon this dark day?'

Baird scooted her chair over to DC Andrews's desk and pulled a wooden spoon from the top drawer. It had a photo of a woman's face stuck to the bowl end: grey hair, squinty eyes, long nose, mouth stretched out and down, as if she'd taken a bite out of something foul.

'Ooh...' Logan sooked a breath in through his teeth. 'Looks like it's not your lucky day, Denise, for whomever wields the Nutter Spoon of Doom must—'

'I'm on the no-go list. Apparently I'm in collusion with McLennan Homes and the Planning Department to launder drug money for the Taliban.' She held out the spoon with its glowering stuck-on face. 'Sorry, Guv.'

Logan backed away from it. 'Maybe someone in uniform could—'

'They're all banned from talking to her. She's got complaints in against everyone else.'

'Everyone?'

'Yes, but…' Baird waggled the spoon at him. 'Maybe she'll like you?'

Logan took the Nutter Spoon of Doom. It was only a little bit of wood with a photo Sellotaped to the end, but it felt as if it was carved from lead.

Oh joy.

3

Logan stopped outside the visiting-room door. Took a deep breath. Didn't open it.

The reception area was quiet. A bored PC slumped behind the bulletproof glass that topped the curved desk, poking away at a smartphone. Posters clarted the walls, warning against drug farms in cul-de-sacs and walking home alone at night. An information point cycled through views of Aberdeen. And a strange smell of mouldy cheese permeated the room.

No point putting it off any longer.

He shifted his grip on the thick manila folder tucked under his arm, opened the door, and stepped inside. It wasn't much bigger than a cupboard, with a couple of filing cabinets on one wall and a small opaque window that didn't really overlook the rear-podium car park.

Mrs Black was sitting on the other side of the small table that took up most of the available space. She narrowed her eyes, tugged at the hem of her skirt, and sniffed – turning that long nose up towards the ceiling. Her short grey hair shimmered as if it had been conditioned within an inch of its existence. Then the glasses came out of the bag clutched to her chest. Slipped on with all the pomp and circumstance of a royal wedding. Voice clipped and dark. 'I have been waiting here for nearly an *hour*.'

Logan suppressed a sigh. Did his best to keep his voice polite and neutral. 'Mrs Black.' Stepped inside and closed the visiting-room door. 'I'm sorry if my trying to catch criminals and keep the streets safe has inconvenienced you in any way.'

Her lips pursed. Pause. Two. Three. Four. 'He's doing it again.'

Of course he is.

Logan thumped the manila folder down on the little table. It was about as thick as a house brick, bulging with paperwork; a red elastic band wrapped around it to keep everything in. Then he settled into the room's remaining seat and took out his notebook. 'Right, we'd better take it from the beginning. You said, "He's doing it again." Who is?'

Mrs Black folded her arms across her chest and scowled. 'You know very well, *"Who"*.' A small shudder. 'Justin Robson.' The name came out as if it tasted of sick. 'He's... He's covering my cherry tree with ... *dog mess*.'

'Dog mess.'

'That's right: dog mess. I want him arrested.'

Logan tapped his pen against the folder. 'And you've seen him doing it?'

'Of course not. He's too careful for that. Does it in the middle of the night when Mr Black and I are sleeping.' Another shudder. 'Up till all hours listening to that horrible rap music of his, with all the swearing and violence. I've complained to the council, but do they do anything? Of course they don't.'

'You do know that we can't arrest someone without proof, don't you?'

Both hands slapped down on the desk. '*You* know he did it. *I* know he did it. Ever since I did my *public duty* and reported him he's been *completely* intolerable.'

'Ah yes.' Logan removed the elastic band and opened the folder. Took out the top chunk of paperwork. 'Here we are.

22

On the thirteenth of April, two years ago, you claimed to have seen Mr Robson smoking cannabis in the garden outside his house.'

The nose went up again. 'And did anyone arrest him for it? Of course they didn't.'

'This isn't a totalitarian state, we can't just—'

'Are you going to arrest him or not?'

'We need evidence before—'

She jabbed the desk with a finger. 'I *had* thought you might be different. That you'd be an *honest* policeman for a change, unlike the rest of these corrupt—'

'Now hold on, that's—'

'—clearly in the pocket of drug dealers and pornographers!'

Logan shuffled his chair back from the table an inch. 'Pornographers?'

'Justin Robson posted an obscene publication through my door; a magazine full of women performing the most revolting acts.' Her mouth puckered like a chicken's bum. A sniff. 'Mr Black had to burn it in the back garden. Well, it's not as if we could've put it in the recycling, what would the binmen think?'

'Mrs Black, I can assure you that neither I, nor any of my team are being paid off by drug dealers *or* pornographers. We can't arrest Mr Robson for smoking marijuana two years ago, because there's no evidence.'

She hissed a breath out through that long raised nose. 'I saw him with my own eyes!'

'I see.' Logan wrote that down in his notebook. 'And how did you determine that what he was smoking was actually marijuana? Did you perform a chemical analysis on the roach? Did you see him roll it?'

'Don't be facetious.'

'I'm not being facetious, I'm trying to understand why you think he was smoking—'

23

'You're not going to do anything about him putting dog mess on my cherry tree, are you? You're going to sit there and do nothing, because you're as corrupt as all the rest.'

Slow, calm breaths.

Logan opened the folder and pulled out the thick wad of paperwork. 'Mrs Black, in the last two years, you've made five hundred and seventeen complaints against Mr Robson; the local council; the Scottish Government; the Prince of Wales; Jimmy Shand; Ewan McGregor; the whole Westminster cabinet; our local MP, MSP, *and* MEP; and nearly every police officer in Aberdeen Division.'

'I have a moral obligation, and a *right*, to report corruption wherever I find it!'

'OK.' He reached beneath the desk and pulled a fresh complaint form from the bottom of the pile. Placed it in front of her. 'If you'd like to report me for taking money from drug dealers and pornographers, you should speak to someone from Professional Standards. I can give you their number.'

She curled her top lip. 'What makes you think they're not all corrupt too?'

Logan pushed through the double doors, out onto the rear-podium car park. The bulk of Divisional Headquarters formed walls of concrete and glass on three sides, the back of the next street over closing the gap, turning it into a sun trap. Which meant the pool car was like a sodding oven when he unlocked the door.

Then froze.

Scowled.

Leaned back against the bonnet and crossed his arms as a dented brown Vauxhall spluttered its way up the ramp and into the parking space opposite.

The driver gave Logan a smile and a wave as he climbed out into the sunshine. Broad face with ruddy cheeks, no neck, greying hair that wasn't as fond of his head as it had been twenty years ago. A proper farmer's face. 'Fine day, the day, Guv. Do—'

'Wheezy! Where the bloody hell have you been?'

DC Andrews's mouth clicked shut, then his eyebrows peaked in the middle. 'I've been taking witness—'

'I had to interview Marion Sodding Black!'

'It's not my fault, I wasn't even here!' He cleared his throat. Coughed. Covered his mouth and hacked out a couple of barks that ended with a glob of phlegm being spat against the tarmac. Leaving his ruddy farmer's face red and swollen. 'Gah...' Deep, groaning breaths.

Then Logan closed his eyes. Counted to three. Wheezy was right – it wasn't his fault he was out working when Mrs Black turned up. 'OK. I'm sorry. That was unfair.' He straightened his jacket. 'Did you find anything out at Garthdee?'

'Oh, aye.' Wheezy Doug locked his pool car. 'Fiver says it was Bobby Greig. Security camera's didn't get his face, but I'd recognize that manky BMX bike of his anywhere.'

'Good. That's good.' Logan went for an innocent smile. 'So you're free right now?'

'As I can be. Need to get a search warrant and...' Wheezy Doug pulled his chin in, giving himself a ripple of neck wrinkles. Narrowed his eyes. 'Wait a minute: *why*?'

'Oh, just asking.'

He backed off a pace. 'No you're not. You've got something horrible needs doing, don't you?'

'Me? No. Not a bit of it. I want you to go visit Pitmedden Court for me. Take a look at a cherry tree for me.'

Wheezy Doug's face unclenched. 'Oh, that's OK then. Thought for a moment there you...' And then it was back again. 'Pitmedden *Court*? Gah...' He covered his eyes with his hands. 'Noooooo ... It's her, isn't it?'

The innocent smile turned into a grin. 'Mrs Black says

her neighbour's sticking dog poo in her tree. And you're officially in possession of the Nutter Spoon of Doom.'

'Mrs Black's a pain in the hoop.'

'Yup, but right now she's *your* pain. Now get your hoop in gear and go check out her tree.'

Logan tucked his phone between his ear and his shoulder, then locked the pool car's door. 'Nah, same nonsense as usual. Everyone's corrupt. Everyone's out to get her. Her neighbour's hanging bags of dog crap in her cherry tree.'

On the other end, DS Baird groaned. *'Dog crap? I must've missed that issue of* Better Homes and Gardens. *Stoney's back – says are you coming to the pub after work?'*

Quick check of the watch: five to four.

'Depends how long I am here. Yeah. Well, probably.'

Wind rustled through the thick green crown of a sycamore tree, dropping helicopter seed pods onto the pool car's bonnet to lie amongst the dappled sunlight. Buchanan Street's grey terraces faced each other across a short stretch of divoted tarmac. Eight houses on each side in utilitarian granite, unadorned by anything fancier than UPVC windows and doors. Most of the gardens had been converted into off-street parking, bordered by knee-high walls and the occasional browning hedge.

Number Fourteen's parking area was empty, but a useless Police Constable and his patrol car idled outside – blocking the drive.

The house didn't look any different to its neighbours. As if nothing had happened. As if the guy who lived there hadn't jumped off the casino roof and splattered himself across Exchequer Row.

Logan hung up and wandered over to the patrol car. Knocked on the driver's window.

Sitting behind the wheel, PC Guthrie gave a little squeak and sat bolt upright, stuffing a magazine into the footwell before Logan could get a good look at it. He turned and hauled on a pained smile, pink blooming on his cheeks as he buzzed down the window. 'Sorry, Guv. Frightened the life out of me.'

Logan leaned on the roof of the car, looming through the open window. 'That better not have been porn, Sunshine, or I swear to God…'

The blush deepened. 'Porn? No. No, course not.' He cleared his throat then grabbed his hat and climbed out into the afternoon. 'I've been round all the neighbours: no one's seen Mrs Skinner since she took the kids to school this morning.'

Logan turned on the spot. Sixteen houses, all crushed together. 'It's Saturday, why was she taking the kids to school?'

'Ballet classes for the wee boy, and maths club for the girl. He's six, she's seven.'

Made sense. 'You tried the school?'

A shrug. 'Closes at two on a Saturday.'

Well, it wasn't as if they'd still be there anyway. Not now. 'OK. Any of the neighbours got a contact number for Mrs Skinner?'

Guthrie pulled out his notepad and flicked through to the marker. Passed it over. 'Mobile: goes straight to voicemail.'

Logan tried it anyway.

Click. 'Hello, this is Emma, I can't do the phone thing right now, so make messages after the bleep.' Beeeeeep.

'Mrs Skinner, this is Detective Inspector Logan McRae of Police Scotland. Can you give me a call when you get this, please? You can get back to me on this number, or call one-zero-one and ask them to put you through. Thanks.' He hung up. Put his phone away.

Guthrie sniffed, then slid the back of a finger underneath his nose, as if trying to catch a drip. 'Shame we can't deliver the death message by text, isn't it?'

Logan stared at him, until the blush came back. 'For that little moment of compassion, you can stay here till she comes home.'

27

His shoulders dipped. 'Guv.'

'And stop reading porn in the patrol car!'

Logan pulled in to the kerb and swore his mobile phone out of his pocket. Checked the display. No idea who the number belonged to. Might be Mrs Skinner calling back?

He hit the button. 'DI McRae.'

Harlaw playing fields lay flat and green behind their high wire fence. Three cricket matches, and a game of rugby, grunting and thwacking away in the afternoon light.

Logan tried again. 'Hello?'

A familiar dark, clipped female voice sounded in his ear: *You were supposed to be investigating my tree.*

'Mrs Black.' Oh joy.

I'll be putting in a formal complaint. I know my rights! You have to—'

'We *are* investigating, Mrs Black.' Keep it calm and level. No shouting. No swearing or telling her what she can do with her sodding complaints. Don't sigh. 'I've sent an officer round there. He will be taking statements. He will be photographing any evidence. OK?' You vile, rancid, old battle-axe.

Silence.

Outside, a scruffy man with a beard down to the middle of his chest and hair like a diseased scarecrow lurched along the pavement. Scruffy overcoat, suit trousers, hiking boots, trilby hat. Not the best fashion statement in the world.

A carrier bag swung from one hand, like a pendulum. Something heavy in there. And from the look of him, it was probably cheap and very alcoholic.

Then Mrs Black was back. *'That* man *is making my life a living hell and you're doing nothing to prevent it. What about my human rights? I demand you* do *something!'*

Seriously?

Deep breath. 'We are doing something. We're *investigating.*'

Logan coiled his other hand around the steering wheel. Strangling it. 'Mrs Black, if Mr Robson's done something illegal under Scottish law, we'll arrest him. Putting dog mess in someone's tree is antisocial, but it isn't illegal.'

'Of course it's illegal! How could it not be illegal?' She was getting louder and shriller. *'I can't sleep, I can't breathe, I can't … Mr Black…'* A deep breath. *'It's the law. He's harassing me. He's putting dog mess in my cherry tree!'*

Captain Scruffy stumbled into the path of a large woman wheeling a pushchair along the pavement.

She flinched to a halt, detoured around him. Shuddering as she marched off.

He wobbled in place, plastic bag clutched to his chest, yelling slurred obscenities after her.

'I demand you arrest that Robson creature!'

'Mrs Black, this is a *civil* matter, not a criminal one. You need to get yourself a lawyer and sue him.'

'Why should I spend all that money on a lawyer, when it's your job to arrest him? I demand you do your job!'

Captain Scruffy shook his fist at the escaping woman. The motion sent him off again: one step to the right. One to the left. Two to the right. And on his backside in three, two…

'Are you even listening to me?'

The next stagger took him backwards, off the kerb and into the traffic.

Sodding hell.

A blare of horns. An Audi estate swerved, barely missing him with its front bumper. A Range Rover slammed on its brakes.

Captain Scruffy pirouetted, carrier bag swinging out with the motion.

BANG. A bright-orange Mini caught the bag, right on the bonnet, spinning him around and bouncing him off the windscreen. Sending him clattering to the tarmac like a bag of dirty laundry.

'Why won't anyone there take me seriously? I pay my taxes! I have rights! How dare you ignore me!'

Logan clicked off his seatbelt.

'I have to go.'

'Don't you dare hang up on me, I—'

He hung up on her and scrambled out into the warm afternoon.

The Mini was slewed at thirty degrees across both lanes, its driver already out of the car staring at the bonnet. 'Oh God, oh God, oh God...' She had a hand to her mouth, eyes wide, knees trembling. Didn't seem to be even vaguely interested in the man lying on his back in the middle of the road behind her.

Then she turned on him. 'YOU BLOODY IDIOT! WHAT'S MUM GOING TO SAY?' Two fast steps, then she slammed a trainer into the fallen man's stomach. 'SHE'S ONLY HAD IT A WEEK!' Another kick, this one catching him on the side of the head, sending that stupid little hat flying.

The other drivers stayed where they were, in their cars. No one helped, but a couple dragged out their mobile phones to film it, so that was all right.

Logan ran. Grabbed her by the arm and spun her around. 'That's enough!'

She swung a fist at Logan's head. So he slammed her into the side of her mum's car, grabbed her wrist and put it into a lock hold. Applying pressure till her legs buckled. 'AAAAAAAAGH! Get off me! GET OFF ME! RAPE! RAPE! HELP!'

He pulled his cuffs out. 'I'm detaining you under Section Fourteen of the Criminal Procedure – Scotland – Act 1995, because I suspect you of having committed an offence punishable by imprisonment—'

'RAPE! HELP! SOMEONE HELP ME! RAPE!'

No one got out of their car.

'You are not obliged to say anything, but anything you do say—'

'HELP! HELP!'

Deep breath: 'WOULD YOU SHUT UP?'

She went limp. Slumped forward until her forehead was resting on the new Mini's roof. 'It's only a week old. She'll never let me borrow it again.'

Logan clicked the cuffs over her wrists. 'But anything you do say will be noted down and may be used in evidence.' Then steered her over to the pool car and stuffed her into the back. 'Stay there. Don't make it any worse.'

He got out his phone again and dialled Control. 'I need an ambulance to Cromwell Road, got an … Hold on.'

Captain Scruffy had levered himself up onto his bum, wobbling there with blood pouring down his filthy face. Eyes bloodshot and blinking out of phase with one another.

Logan squatted down in front of him. 'Are you OK?'

An aura of rotting vegetables, BO, and baked-on urine spread out like a fog.

It took a bit, but eventually that big hairy head swung around to squint at him. 'Broke my bottle…' He clutched the carrier bag to his chest. Bits of broken glass stuck out through the plastic. 'BROKE MY BOTTLE!' The bottom lip trembled, then tears sparked up in those pinky-yellow eyes, tumbled down the filthy cheeks. 'NOOOOOOOO!'

'You're a bloody idiot, you know that, don't you?' Back to the phone. 'We've got an IC-One male who's been hit by a car and assaulted.' Logan nodded at him, trying not to breathe through his nose. 'What's your name?'

'My bottle … My lovely, lovely, bottle.' He hauled in air, showing off a mouth full of twisted brown teeth. 'BASTARDS! *MY* BOTTLE!'

Yeah, it was definitely one of those days.

4

'Logan, we don't normally see you here during the day.' Claire stuck her book down on the nurses' station desk and smiled at him, making two dimples in her smooth round cheeks. 'To what do we owe the honour?'

Logan pointed over his shoulder, back along the corridor. 'Got a road-rage victim in A-and-E. Thought I'd pop past while they were stitching him up.'

Claire squeezed one eye shut. 'It's not a hairy young gentleman with personal hygiene issues, is it? Only Donald from security was just in here moaning about being bitten.'

Yeah, probably. 'How's Samantha today?'

'Getting up to all sorts of hijinks.' She stood and smoothed out the creases in her nurse's scrubs. 'You got time for a cup of tea?'

'Wouldn't say no.'

'Oh, and this came for you this morning.' Claire reached into a drawer and pulled out a grey envelope. 'Think it's from Sunny Glen.'

'Thanks.' He took it and wandered down the corridor to Samantha's room.

The blinds were drawn, shutting out most of the light, but it was still warm enough to make him yawn.

He sank onto the edge of the bed, leaned in and gave her a kiss on the cheek. Cold and pale. 'Hey, you.'

She didn't answer, but then she never did.

Something about the gloom and her porcelain skin made the tattoos stand out even more than usual. Jagged and dark. Like something trying to crawl its way out of her body.

He brushed a strand of brown hair from her face. 'Got a reply from Sunny Glen.' Logan held up the envelope. 'What do you think?'

No reply.

'Yeah, me too.' He ripped it open. '"Dear Mr McRae, thank you for the application for specialist residential care on behalf of your girlfriend Samantha Mackie. As you know, our Neurological Care Unit has a worldwide reputation for managing and treating those in long-term comas…" Blah, blah, blah.' He turned the letter over. 'Oh sodding hell. "Unfortunately we do not have any spaces available at the current time." Could they not have said that in the first place?' He crumpled the sheet of paper into a ball and lobbed it across the room at the bin. Missed. Slouched over and put it in properly. 'Place is probably rubbish anyway. And it's all the way up on the sodding coast, not exactly convenient, is it? Traipsing all the way up there. You'd have hated it.'

Still felt as if someone had used his soul as cat litter, though.

'Doesn't matter. We've got another three applications out there. Bound to be one who'll take a hell-raiser like you.'

Nothing.

A knock on the door, and Claire stuck her head into the room. 'I even managed to find a couple of biscuits for you. So…' She frowned as Logan's phone launched into its anonymous ringtone. 'How many times do we have to talk about this?'

'Only be a minute.' He pulled it out and hit the button. 'McRae.'

A man's voice, sounding out of breath. *'You the joker who brought in Gordon Taylor?'*

Who the hell was Gordon Taylor? 'Sorry?'

'The homeless guy – got hit by a car. Someone gave him a kicking.'

Ah, right. *That* Gordon Taylor. 'What about him?'

'He's bitten two security guards and punched a nurse.'

Wonderful. Another dollop added to the cat litter. 'I'll be right down.' He put his phone away. Took the mug of tea from Claire and kissed her on the cheek. 'Don't let Samantha give you any trouble, OK? You know how feisty she gets.'

The elevator juddered to a halt, and Logan stepped out into the familiar, depressing, scuffed green corridors. No paintings on the walls here, no community art projects, or murals, or anything to break the bleak industrial gloom. He followed the coloured lines set into the floor.

Here and there, squares of duct tape held the peeling surface together. And everything smelled of disinfectant and over-boiled cauliflower.

A porter bustled past, pushing a small child in a big bed. Drips and tubes and wires snaking from the little body to various bags and bits of equipment.

Logan pulled out his phone and called Guthrie. 'Any sign of Mrs Skinner yet?'

'Sorry, Guv. I've checked all the neighbours again, but no one's heard from her.'

'OK.' He stepped around the corner, and stopped outside the doors to Accident and Emergency. 'Get onto Control and see if you can…' A frown. 'Have you been round the house? Peered in all the windows? Just in case.'

'*Yup. Even got her next-door to let me through so I could climb the garden fence and have a squint in the back. She's not lying dead on the floor anywhere.*'

At least that was something.

'Get Control to dig up the grandparents. They might know where she is.'

'*Will do.*' A pause. '*Guv, did I ever tell you about what happened last time Snow White—*'

'Yes. And *no more* porn in the patrol car.'

Logan hung up, pushed the door open, and stepped inside.

It wasn't difficult to find Gordon Taylor, not with all the shouting and swearing going on. He was in a cubicle at the far end – *crash*, *bang*, *wallop*. A nurse squatted outside the curtains, head thrown back, a wad of tissues clamped against her nose stained bright red.

'*Hold still, you little sod…*'

'*Ow!*'

'*Can someone hold his head so he won't bite?*'

'*Ow! Ow, ow, ow… Bloody hell…*'

Logan slipped through the curtains and stared at the human octopus wrestling with itself on the hospital bed. Arms, legs, hands, feet, all struggling to keep the figure on the bottom from getting up.

One of the nurses yanked her arm into the air. 'OW! He bit me!'

'Don't let go of his head!'

Logan reached into his pocket, pulled out the little canister of CS gas, and walked over to the bed. 'Let go of him.'

A doctor turned and glared. 'Are you off your head?'

Click, the safety cover flipped off the top of the gas canister. 'Then you probably want to cover your nose and mouth.'

Gordon Taylor's filthy, blood-caked face rose from between the medics' arms, teeth snapping.

Logan jammed the CS gas canister right between his eyes.

35

Raised his voice over the crashing and banging, the grunting and swearing. 'You've been gassed before, right, Gordon? Want to try it again?'

A blink. Then he froze.

'Good boy. Now you let these nice people examine you, or I'm going to gas you back to the Thatcher era, OK?'

Gordon Taylor went limp.

The doctor bowed his head for a moment. 'Oh thank God...' Then straightened up. 'Right, we need blood tests and a sedative. Then get these filthy rags off him.'

The nurses bustled about with needles and scissors, faces contorted with disgust every time a new layer of clothes came off revealing a new odour.

Logan kept the CS gas where Taylor could see it. 'You're an idiot, you know that, don't you? Staggering about, blootered, abusing passers-by, falling into the road. Lucky you didn't kill yourself.'

Taylor didn't move. Kept his eyes fixed on the gas canister.

One of the nurses gagged, holding out a filthy shirt with her fingertips.

Gordon Taylor's arms were knots of ropey muscles, stretched taut across too-big bones. No fat on them. But the left one had a Gordon Highlanders tattoo, the ink barely visible beneath the filth. His torso was a mess of bruises – some fresh and red, some middle-aged purple-and-blue, some dying yellow-and-green.

He jerked his chin up. 'She broke my bottle.' The slur had gone from his voice, but his breath was enough to make Logan back off a couple of steps.

'You're a drunken sodding menace to yourself and others, Gordon. What the hell were you thinking, staggering out into the road? What if a car swerves, trying to avoid your drunken backside, hits someone else and kills them? That what you want?'

'A whole bottle of Bells that was!' No wonder his breath was minging – his teeth looked like stubbed-out cigarettes.

'I've arrested the woman who assaulted you. She'll—'

'Tell her! Tell her I'll not press charges if she buys me a new bottle...' Gordon Taylor's eyes widened. 'No, *two* bottles. Aye, and litre bottles, not tiny wee ones.'

Nothing like getting your priorities straight.

'That's not how it works, Gordon. She has to—' Logan's phone burst into song in his pocket. 'Sodding hell.'

The doctor narrowed his eyes. 'You're not supposed to have your phone switched on in here.'

'Police business.' He pulled it out and hit the button, killing the noise. 'For God's sake, what *now*?'

There was a moment of silence, then a deep voice rumbled out of the speakers. *'I think you mean, "Good afternoon", don't you, Acting Detective Inspector McRae?'*

Oh no. Not this. Not now.

Logan closed his eyes. 'Superintendent Young. Sorry. I'm kind of in the middle of—'

'I think you and I need to have a chat about a complaint that's landed on my desk. Why don't we say, my office? Any time in the next fifteen minutes is good.'

Wonderful.

5

Superintendent Young was all dressed up in Nosferatu black – black T-shirt with epaulettes, black police-issue trousers, and black shoes. He sat back in his seat and tapped his pen against an A4 pad. Tap. Tap. Tap. 'Are you denying the allegations?'

The Professional Standards office was tombstone quiet. A wooden clock ticked away to itself on the wall beside Young's desk. The chair creaked beneath Logan's bum. A muffled scuffing sound as someone tried to sneak past outside – scared to make a noise in case someone inside heard them and came hunting. And the sinister sods didn't burst into flame when exposed to sunlight *or* holy water, so you were never safe.

Trophies made a little gilded plastic parade across the two filing cabinets in the corner, all the figures frozen in the execution of their chosen sport – clay-pigeon shooting, judo, boxing, ten-pin bowling, fly-fishing, curling. A framed print of *The Monarch of the Glen* above the printer.

Tick. Tick. Tick.

Quarter past five. Should be in the pub by now, not sitting here.

Logan dumped the letter of complaint back on Young's desk. 'With all due respect to anyone unfortunate enough

38

to suffer from mental illness, Marion Black is a complete and utter sodding nutter.'

'You didn't answer my question.'

Logan shifted in the creaky chair. 'While I do *know* a pornographer, he's never offered me a bribe.'

Young raised an eyebrow. 'You actually know someone who makes dirty movies?'

'Helps us out from time to time cleaning up CCTV footage. Moved into mainstream film a couple of years ago. Ever see *Witchfire*? That was him.'

'And he used to make porn?'

'You should ask DCI Steel to show you – she's got the complete collection.'

A tilt of the head, as if Young was considering doing just that. 'What about drug dealers?'

'Guv, Marion Black has accused nearly everyone in a three hundred mile radius of corruption at some point. She's a menace. You *know* that.'

'It doesn't matter how many complaints an individual makes, Logan, we have to take every one of them seriously.'

Logan poked the letter. It was a printout from a slightly blotchy inkjet, the words on the far left of the pages smudged. Densely packed type with no line breaks. 'I met her at ten past three today, and spoke to her on the phone a little after four. And in that time she managed to write a three-page letter of complaint and deliver it to you lot. She's probably got a dozen of them sitting on her computer ready to go at any time. Insert-some-poor-sod's-name-here and off you go.'

Young swivelled his chair from side to side a couple of times. 'It's not going to work, you know.'

'What isn't?'

'This.' Young spread his hands, taking in the whole room. 'You think the easiest way to get shot of Mrs Black is to ignore her. You do nothing about her concerns, she makes a complaint about corruption, and you get to pass the Nutter Spoon of Doom on to the next poor sod without having to do any work.'

Warmth prickled at the back of Logan's neck. He licked his lips. 'Nutter Spoon of Doom, Guv? I don't think I've ever heard of—'

'Oh don't be ridiculous, we know all about it.' He sat forward. 'Let me make this abundantly clear, *Acting* Detective Inspector McRae: you have the spoon, and you're going to personally deal with Mrs Black whether you like it or not.' A finger came up, pointing at the middle of Logan's chest. 'Not one of your minions: you.'

Logan threw his arms out, appealing to the ref. 'I met her today at three o'clock! I've got a suicide, a road-rage incident, a spate of car vandalism, petty thefts, fire-raising, a shoplifting ring, three common assaults, and a bunch of other cases to deal with. When was I supposed to go visit her poo tree?'

'*Make* time.'

'I delegated the task to DC Andrews.'

'I don't care.' Young sat back again. 'And make sure you never speak to Mrs Black without another officer present. Preferably someone who can film it on their body-worn video.'

Logan stared at the ceiling tiles for a moment. They were clean. New and pristine. 'I'm not even supposed to be holding the spoon – it's Wheezy Doug's turn.'

'My heart bleeds.' Superintendent Young prodded the complaint file. 'What about this man Mrs Black complained about in the first place…?'

'Justin Robson. She claims to have seen him smoking cannabis in his garden two and a bit years ago. Says he's now festooning her cherry tree with what she calls "dog mess".'

'I see.' Young narrowed his eyes, tapped his fingertips against his pursed lips. 'And how has CID investigated this unwelcomed act of garden embellishment?'

Logan shrugged. 'I told Wheezy Doug to go take a look this afternoon. Haven't had time to catch up with him yet.'

'Hmm...'

Silence.

Young pursed and tapped.

Logan just sat there.

Tick. Tick. Tick.

More pursing and tapping. Then: 'I think it's about time someone looked into Mrs Black's neighbour. I want you to have a word with this Justin Robson. Ask him, politely, to defuse his feud with Mrs Black. And tell him to *stop* decorating her tree with dog shit. Or at least wait until Christmas. It's only August.'

Wonderful. Make-work. As if they didn't have enough to do.

'Guv, with all due respect, it—'

'Get cracking this evening; I'll authorize the overtime. Let's see if we can't at least *look* like we're taking her seriously.'

'Sorry, Guv, still no sign of Mrs Skinner or the kids.' Guthrie sniffed down the phone. *'You want me to hang on some more?'*

'Does she have her own car?' Logan unbuckled his seat-belt, as DC Wheezy Doug Andrews parked the pool car behind a Volvo Estate.

Pitmedden Court basked in the evening light. A long collection of grey harled houses, some in terraces of three or four, some semidetatched. Some with tiny portico porches, some without. A nice road. Tidy gardens and knee-high garden walls. Speed bumps. Hello, Mrs McGillivray, I hope your Jack's doing well the day.

'Hold on ... Yes: dark-green Honda Jazz.'

'Get a lookout request on the go. And make sure the Automatic Number Plate Recognition lot are keeping an eye out. Enough people filmed her husband jumping off the roof

41

on their phones; I don't want the poor woman seeing him splattered across the cobbles on the evening news.'

'*Guv.*'

'What about the grandparents?'

'*Got an address in Portlethen, and one in Stoneywood. You want me to pack it in here and go speak to them? Or hang about in case she comes home?*'

Logan checked his watch: five past six. 'Abandon ship. Better give his parents the death message first, then see if either set knows where she is. And get on to the media office too – we need a blanket ban on anything that can ID John Skinner till we've spoken to the wife.' Logan put his phone back in his pocket. Turned to Wheezy Doug. 'We ready?'

His bottom lip protruded an inch as he tugged the fluor-escent yellow high-viz waistcoat on over his suit jacket. 'Feel like a right neep.'

'It's what all the stylish young men about town are wearing this season. And if you'd looked into it when I sodding well *told* you to, we wouldn't be here now.'

A blush darkened Wheezy's cheeks. 'Sorry, Guv.' He fiddled a BWV unit onto one of the clips that pimpled the waistcoat's front, like nipples on a cat. The body-worn video unit was about the same size and shape as a packet of cigarettes; with a white credit-card style front with the Police Scotland logo, a camera icon, and the words 'CCTV In Operation' on it. 'Don't see why you couldn't have got some spod from Uniform to do this bit, though.'

'Because she's filed *complaints* against all the spods from Uniform. No more whingeing.' Logan climbed out into the sunshine. 'Come on.'

The street's twin rows of tidy gardens were alive with the sound of lawns being mowed. Gravel being raked. Cars being washed. The screech and yell of little children playing. The bark of an overexcited dog. The smell of charcoal and grilling meat oozing its way in through the warm August air.

Wheezy Doug sighed, then joined him. Pulled out the keys and plipped the pool car's locks. 'That's the one over there – wishing well, crappy cherry tree, and leylandii hedge.'

The hedge was a proper spite job: at least eight-foot-tall, casting thick dark shadows across the neighbouring property's lawn.

Logan puffed out a breath. 'Suppose we'd better do this.' He marched across the road to the garden gate. Stopped and looked up at the cherry tree.

It was thick with shining green leaves, the swelling fruits drooping on wishbone stalks. And tied onto nearly every branch was a small blue plastic bag with something heavy and dark in it. There had to be at least twenty of them on there. Maybe thirty?

Young was right – it did look … inappropriately festive.

'Right. First up, Justin Robson.' Logan walked along the front wall, past the thicket of spiteful hedge, and in through the gate next door. All nice and tidy, with rosebushes in lustrous shades of red-and-gold, and a sundial lawn ornament that was two hours out.

Honeysuckle grew up one side of the front door and over the lintel, hanging with searing yellow flowers. Scenting the air.

Wheezy Doug stifled a cough. 'Doesn't really look like a drug den, does it?' Then turned and nodded at the white BMW parked out front: spoiler, alloys, low-profile tyres. 'The *car*, on the other hand has Drug Dealer written all over it.' A howch and a spit. He wiped the line of spittle from his chin. 'Right, everyone on their best behaviour, it's Candid Camera time.' He slid the white credit-card cover down, setting the body-worn video recording. Cleared his throat. 'Detective Constable Douglas Andrews, twentieth August, at

43

thirteen Pitmedden Court, Kincorth, Aberdeen. Present is DI McRae.' A nod. 'OK, Guv.'

Logan got as far as the first knock when the door swung open.

A short man with trendy hair and a stripy apron stared up at them through smeared glasses. 'Yes?'

He held up his warrant card. 'Detective Inspector McRae, CID. Are you Justin Robson?'

'That was quick, I only called two minutes ago.' He stepped back, wiping his hands on the green-and-white stripes, leaving dark-red smears.

OK… That *definitely* looked like blood.

'Mr Robson?' Logan's right hand drifted inside his jacket, where the small canister of CS gas lurked. 'Is everything OK, sir?'

'No it's not. Not by a long sodding chalk.' Then he blinked a couple of times. 'Sorry, where are my manners, come in, come in.' Reversing down the hallway and into the kitchen.

Wheezy Doug's voice dropped to a whisper, a wee smile playing at the corners of his mouth. 'Was that blood? Maybe he's killed Mrs Black and hacked her up?'

They should be so lucky.

Logan gave it a beat, then followed Robson through into the kitchen.

It was compact, but kitted out with a fancy-looking oven and induction hob. Built-in deep-fat fryer, American-style double fridge freezer. A glass of white wine sat on the granite countertop, next to two racks of ribs on a chopping board.

Wheezy Doug reached for his cuffs as Robson reached for a cleaver. Pointed. 'Oh no you don't. Put the knife down and—'

'Knife…? Oh, this.' He wiggled it a couple of times. 'Sorry, but we've got friends coming round and I need to get these ready.' The cleaver's shiny blade slipped between the rib bones, slicing through flesh and cartilage as if they were yoghurt. 'I hope you're going to arrest her.'

Nope, no idea.

Logan let go of his CS gas. 'Perhaps you should start from the beginning, sir? Make sure nothing's got lost in translation.'

'That...' the cleaver thumped through the next chunk of flesh, '*bitch* next door. I mean, look at them!' He pointed the severed bone at a small pile of crumpled A4 sheets on the kitchen table. 'That's slander. It's illegal. I know my rights.'

Not another one.

Wheezy Doug picked a sheet from the top of the pile. Pulled a face. 'Actually, sir, slander would be if she *said* this to someone, once it's in writing it's libel.' He handed the bit of paper to Logan.

A black-and-white photo of Justin Robson sat beneath the words, 'GET THIS DRUG DEALING SCUM OFF OUR STREETS!!!'

Ah...

Logan scanned the paragraph at the bottom of the page:

This so-called "man" is **DEALING DRUGS** in Kincorth! He does it from his home and various establishments around town. How will *YOU* feel when he starts selling them outside the school gates where *YOUR* child goes to learn? Our **CORRUPTION-RIDDEN** police force do nothing while *HE* corrupts our children with **POISON**!

Robson hacked off another rib. 'I mean, for God's sake, it's got my photo and my home address and my telephone number on it. And they're all over the place!' Hack, thump, hack. 'I want that woman locked up, she's a bloody menace.'

'I see.' Logan took another look around the room. Wheezy Doug was right, it didn't really look like a drug dealer's house. Far too clean for that. Still, belt and braces: 'And *are* you selling drugs to schoolchildren, Mr Robson?'

'This isn't *Breaking Bad*.' Hack. Thump. Hack. 'I don't deal drugs, I programme distributed integration applications for the oil industry. That's quite enough excitement for me.' He pulled over the second rack of ribs. 'You can search the place, if you like? If it'll finally shut *her* up.'

A nod. 'We might take you up on that.' Logan folded the notice and slipped it into a jacket pocket. 'Mr Robson, Mrs Black tells me that you've been putting "dog mess" in her cherry tree. Is that true? We checked, and the thing's covered in poop-scoop bags.'

Hack, hack, hack. 'I don't have a dog. Does this look like a house that has a dog? Nasty, smelly, dirty things.'

'I didn't ask if you *had* a dog, Mr Robson, I asked if you were responsible for putting ... dog waste in her tree.'

He stopped hacking and stared, face wrinkled on one side. 'Are you seriously suggesting that I prowl the streets of Aberdeen, collecting other people's dog shit, just so I can put it in her tree? Really?' Hack. Thump. Hack.

'Everyone needs a hobby.'

'Trust me, I've got better things to do with my spare time.' The second rack of ribs ended up a lot less neat than the first. He dumped them all in a big glass bowl. 'All she ever does is cause trouble. Like she's so perfect, with her screaming and crying at all hours of the night. Her and her creepy husband. And her bloody, sodding...' A deep breath, then Robson slopped in some sort of sauce from a jug. Dug his hands in and mixed the whole lot up. Squeezing the ribs like he was strangling them. 'Have you ever had to live next door to three hundred thousand nasty little parakeets? Squawking and screeching and flapping at all hours. Not to mention the *smell*. And will the council do anything about it? No, of course they sodding won't.'

46

He thumped over to the sink and washed his hands. 'I swear to God, one of these days—'

'Actually,' Logan held up a hand, 'it might be an idea to remember there's two police officers in the room before you go making death threats.'

Robson's head slumped. Then he dried his hands. 'I'm sorry. It's ... that woman drives me *insane*.' He opened the back door and took his bowl of glistening bones and meat out onto a small decking area, where a kettle barbecue sat. The rich earthy scent of wood-smoke embraced them, not quite covering the bitter ammonia stink coming from the other side of another massive leylandii hedge that blotted out the light.

Squeaking and chirping prickled the air, partially muffled by the dense green foliage.

Wheezy Doug stared up at the hedge. Sniffed. Then clicked the cover up on his body-worn video, stopping it recording. 'You know, I remember this one terrace where ... well, let's call them "Couple A" put up a huge hedge to spite "Couple B". So "Couple B" snuck out in the middle of the night and watered it with tree-stump killer for a fortnight. Not that Police Scotland would advocate such behaviour. Would we, Guv?'

'Don't worry.' Robson creaked up the lid of the barbecue and put down a double layer of tinfoil on the bars. 'That hedge is the only thing between me and those revolting birds, there's no way I'm sabotaging it.' He laid out the ribs in careful bony rows.

Logan nodded back at the house. 'Sorry to be a pain, but can I use your toilet?'

'Top of the stairs.' More ribs joined their comrades.

'Won't be a minute.'

Back through the kitchen and into the hall. Quick left turn into the lounge.

Well, Robson did say they could search the place if they

liked. Fancy patterned wallpaper made up a single swirly green-and-black graphic across one wall. A huge flatscreen television was hooked up to a PlayStation, an X-Box, and what looked like a very expensive surround sound system. Black leather couch. All spotless.

Cupboard under the stairs: hoover, ironing board, shelves with cleaning products arranged in neat rows.

Upstairs.

The master bedroom had a king-sized bed against one wall, with a black duvet cover and too many pillows. Both bedside cabinets were topped with a lamp and a clock radio. No clutter. The clothes in the wardrobe arranged by colour.

The spare room was kitted out as a study. Shelves covered one wall, stuffed with programming manuals and reference books. Fancy desk, big full-colour laser printer, ergonomic chair. Framed qualification certificates above a beige filing cabinet.

Two big speakers rested against the adjoining wall, with their backs to the room and their fronts against the plasterboard. Both were wired into an amplifier with an iPod plugged into the top. The perfect setup for blasting rap music through the bricks at your neighbours in the dead of night.

So Justin Robson wasn't exactly the put-upon innocent he pretended to be.

A quick check of the linen cupboard – just to be thorough – then through to the bathroom for a rummage in the medicine cabinet. Nothing out of the ordinary. Well, except for two packs of antidepressants, but they had chemist's stickers on the outside with dosage instructions, Robson's name, and the prescribing doctor's details. All aboveboard.

Might as well play out the charade properly.

Logan flushed the toilet, unused, and washed his hands. Headed back downstairs.

'Well, thank you for your time, Mr Robson. In case you're wondering: we'll be keeping an eye on Mrs Black's tree from now on. I'd appreciate it if you'd help us make sure there are no more decorations on there.'

Next door, Wheezy Doug leaned on the doorbell. 'What do you think? Is Robson our Phantom Pooper Scooper? The Defecation Decorator. The...' A frown. 'Christmas Tree Crapper?'

'Hmmm...' Logan turned towards the thick barrier of leylandii hedge – tall enough and thick enough to completely blot out all view of Justin Robson's house. 'He's a neat freak – the whole place is like a show home. Is someone that anal going to collect other people's dog shit to spite their neighbour? Don't know.' Stranger things had happened. And then there were those two heavy-duty speakers up against the wall in the study ... 'Possibly.'

Mrs Black's garden wasn't nearly as tidy as her neighbour's. Dandelions and clover encroached on the lawn. More weeds in the borders. The cherry tree with its droopy blue plastic decorations.

Even if you removed every single one of them, would you *really* want to eat the fruit that had grown between those dangling bags?

Wheezy Doug sniffed, then stifled a cough. 'Can't really blame him though, can you? Living next to the Wicked Twit of the West would drive anyone barmy.' Another go on the bell. 'Maybe she's not in?'

'One more try, and we're off.' Superintendent Young could moan all he liked, they'd done their bit. Wasn't their fault Mrs Black was out.

The *drrrrrrrringgggg* sounded again as Wheezy ground his thumb against the button.

Then, finally, a silhouette appeared in the rippled glass panels that took up the top half of the door. A thin wobbly voice: 'Who is it?'

Logan poked Wheezy. 'You filming this?'

A quick fiddle with the BWV. 'Am now.'

'Good.' Logan leaned in close to the glass. 'Mrs Black? It's the police. Can you open up, please?'

She didn't move.

'Mrs Black?'

'It's not convenient.'

'We need to talk to you about a complaint.'

A breeze stirred the blue plastic poo bags, making them swing like filthy pendulums.

'Mrs Black?'

There was a *click* and the door pulled open a couple of inches.

She peered out at them, her short grey hair flat on one side, crusts of yellow clinging to the corners of her baggy eyes. A flash of tartan pyjamas. 'Have you arrested him yet?'

'Mrs Black, have you been putting these up around town?' Logan reached into his pocket and pulled out the folded flyer. Held it up so she could see it.

She stiffened. Her nose came up, and all trace of tremor in her voice was gone. 'The people here have a right to know.'

'If you have proof that Mr Robson is dealing drugs, why didn't you call us?'

'He's a vile, revolting individual. He should be ... should be *castrated* and locked up where he can't hurt anyone any more.'

Logan put the flyer back in his pocket. Closed his eyes and counted to three. 'Mrs Black, you can't go making accusations like that without proof: it's libellous. And Mr Robson's made a formal complaint.'

Her face hardened. 'I should have known...'

'Mrs Black, can we come in please?'

'I've been complaining about him for *years* and did you

50

do anything about it?' She bared her teeth. 'But as soon as he says anything, you're over here with your jackboots and your threats!'

Don't sigh.

'No one's threatening you, Mrs Black. Do you have any proof that Mr Robson is dealing drugs?'

Her finger jabbed over Logan's shoulder. 'HE PUT DOG MESS IN MY TREE!'

'Do you have any proof? If you have proof we'll look at it and—'

'HE DESERVES TO DIE FOR WHAT HE'S PUT ME THROUGH!'

Wheezy Doug stepped forward, palms out. 'Mrs Black, I need you to calm down, OK?'

'HE'S SCUM!' Her voice dropped to a hissing whisper. 'Sitting in there with his drugs and his pornography and his filthy rap music. I *demand* you arrest him.'

The sound of whirring lawn mowers. A child somewhere singing about popping caps in some gangbanger's ass. A motorbike purring past on the road. All as Mrs Black stood there, trembling in her pyjamas, lips flecked with spittle.

Logan kept his voice low and neutral. 'I need you to stop putting up these posters. And if you *have* any evidence that Mr Robson is dealing drugs, I want you to call me.' He pulled out a Police Scotland business card with the station number on it. Held it out.

She stared at the card in his hand. Curled her lip. Spat at her feet. 'You're all as corrupt as each other.'

Then stepped back and slammed the door.

Not the result they'd hoped for, but no one could say they hadn't tried.

'So...' Wheezy Doug dragged the toe of his shoe along the path. 'Pub?'

Logan popped the business card through the letterbox. 'Pub.'

51

6

Sodding keyhole wouldn't hold still... The key skittered around the moving target, until finally it clicked into place.

Hurrah.

Logan picked up his fish supper again, and pushed through into the flat. Floor was a bit shifty too.

Deep breath.

He eased the door closed and shushed the Yale lock as it clunked shut. Wouldn't do to wake the neighbours. They wouldn't like that. Got to be a good neighbour. 'Shhhh...'

Then he dumped his keys on the little table by the radiator. 'Cthulhu? Daddy's home.'

Silence.

Little sod.

Logan grabbed the salt, vinegar, mayonnaise, and a tin of Stella from the kitchen and escorted his supper through into the pristine living room.

Whole place was unnaturally tidy, everything superfluous hidden away in various cupboards and the loft, leaving nothing behind but estate-agent approved set dressing. Like the two glossy magazines lined up perfectly with the edge of the coffee table. Or the line of candles on the windowsill. The photos in the wooden frames lined up where the books used to be. Everything dusted and hoovered with OCD fervour. All so some pair of picky sods could take a quick sniff around then decide the flat wasn't 'big enough for them'. Scumbags.

He slumped into the couch then clicked the ring-pull off the Stella. Gulped down a mouthful. Stifled a burp.

Why? Who the hell was going to complain about it?

He took another swig, then let his diaphragm rattle.

Better.

The batter was a bit thick, but the fish was moist and meaty. The chips limp in a way that only chip shops could get away with. How come a chip shop couldn't get chips crispy? You'd think they'd be chip experts. Clue's in the name.

The light on the answering machine winked at him, like a malevolent rat with one glowing red eye.

He stuck two fingers up at it and went back to his flaccid chips.

Cthulhu finally deigned to put in an appearance, padding in on silent fuzzy feet, tail held high. All grey and brown and black and stripy, with a huge white ruff and little white paws. She popped up onto the arm of the couch, then sat there, blinking slowly at him.

'Oh, you love me when there's food in it for you, don't you?' But he blinked back and gave her a nugget of haddock anyway.

Cue purring and chewing.

And still the answering machine glowered with its ratty eye.

Tough. Whatever it was, it could wait till morning.

Fish for Logan. Fish for Cthulhu.

The answering machine didn't care.

He stuffed down a mouthful of chips, followed by a swig of Stella.

It kept on glowering.

'Oh for God's sake.' He levered himself to his feet and

lurched across the rolling deck. Propped himself up with one hand on the shelf. Pressed the button.

'*You have three new messages. Message one:*' Bleeeeeep.

'*Logan? It's your mother. Why do I always—*'

'Gah!' He poked the machine.

'*Message deleted. Message two:*' Bleeeeeep.

'*Hello? Mr McRae? It's Marjory from Willkie and Oxford, Solicitors. I know Mr and Mrs Moore said they weren't interested, but they've come back with an offer for the flat. It's twenty thousand less than the valuation though…*'

'Pair of wankers.' Poke.

'*Message deleted. Message three:*' Bleeeeeep.

'*Hello, Logan? It's Hamish.*' The voice was a gravelly, breathless mix of Aberdonian and public school. Rattling at the edges where the cancer was eating him. '*I've been thinking about mortality. Yours. Mine. Reuben's. Everyone… Give me a call back and we can talk about it.*'

The chip fat congealed at the back of Logan's throat. Crept forward and lined his mouth. Made his teeth itch. Wee Hamish Mowat. Not exactly the kind of message anyone wanted lying about on their answering machine where Professional Standards could find it.

And tell me, Acting DI McRae, would you care to explain why Aberdeen's biggest crime lord is phoning you for a chat, like an old mate?

No Logan sodding wouldn't. Poke.

'*Message deleted. You have no new messages.*'

Mortality.

With any luck, Wee Hamish had decided to save everyone the bother, and shot Reuben in the face.

Yeah, well. Probably not.

But a boy could dream, couldn't he?

— dearly beloved —

7

'… OK, let me know what you come up with. And for God's sake, someone give Guthrie a poke!'

The CID office had a full contingent of grey faces and wrinkly eyes. The four office chairs were lined up along two sides, turned towards the whiteboard for the morning briefing. Their occupants nursed tins of Irn-Bru and greasy bacon butties. Well, all except for PC Guthrie – slumped so far back in his seat that any further and he'd be on the floor. Gob open, head hanging to the side.

DS Baird leaned over and gave him a poke. 'You're snoring!'

Blinking, Guthrie surfaced, mouth working like a drowning fish. 'Mwake…'

Logan folded his arms and leaned back against the filing cabinet. 'Are we boring you, Constable?'

Wheezy Doug rolled his eyes. 'He wasn't even in the pub last night! No excuse.'

'Yeah.' DC Stone took another bite of buttie, talking with his mouth full. 'Should change your nickname from "Sunshine" to "Lightweight".' A little tuft of hair clung to the tip of Stoney's forehead, combed forward, backward, and sideways trying to hide a bald patch the size of a dinner plate. To be honest, Stoney's head was more bald patch than hair. As if trying to draw attention away from it, a huge moustache lurked beneath his nose like a hairy troll under a bridge. 'That right, Lightweight?'

Guthrie ran a hand over his face, scrubbing it out of shape. 'Just knackered from shagging your mum all night.'

That got him a collective, 'Oooh!'

Logan thumped a hand against the filing cabinet, setting it booming. 'All right, that's enough.' He pointed at the yawning constable. 'Where are we with Mrs Skinner?'

A shudder. Then Guthrie yawned. Pulled himself up in his seat. 'Still nothing from the lookout request. And she's not been back to the house since yesterday morning.'

'So where is she?'

Shrug. 'Neither set of grandparents had any idea. But, it's Sunday, right? Maybe she's gone to church? Or she stayed over at a friend's house? Slumber party for the kids?'

Logan frowned out of the window. Early morning sunlight painted the side of Marischal College, making the cleaned granite glow. They'd done their best – waited for her, put out a lookout request, contacted the next of kin. Sort of. What else were they supposed to do? If Mrs Skinner didn't want to be found, she didn't want to be found.

Maybe she knew her husband was working up to jumping off a dirty big building and decided to get out of town before he hit?

'Better get onto the Mire, Tayside, Highland, Fife, and Forth Valley – tell them to keep an eye out for her and the kids. Him diving off the casino roof's going to make the news sooner or later, and...' Logan closed his mouth.

Guthrie was shaking his head.

'What?'

The constable stood and crossed to one of the ancient

computers. 'I wasn't really shagging Stoney's mum all last night, I was checking the internet.' He thumped away at the keyboard. 'Three people loaded the footage up onto YouTube by midnight. I reported them, but it's already out there. See?' The screen filled with shaky cameraphone footage, looking up from Exchequer Row. The casino was five storeys of darkened windows, separated by strips of grey cladding. A figure stood on the roof – too far away to make out any detail on his face – arms by his sides, head down.

Muffled voices crackled from the speakers, *'Oh my God...'*, *'Look at him...'*, *'Is he going to jump?'*, *'Where? What are we looking at?'*, *'Oh my God...'*, *'Is that a knife?'*, *'Someone call the police!'*, *'Oh my God...'*

The scene swirled left, capturing the crowd. Most of them had their phones out, cameras pointing up at John Skinner as he wobbled on the edge.

Bloody vultures. Whatever happened to good Samaritans?

'There's someone else up there!', *'Oh my God...'*

A seasick lurch and the screen filled with the casino again as Logan inched his way out onto the ledge.

In real life, Logan pointed at the video. 'I want this taken down.'

'Oh my God...' A collective gasp as the green plastic bag from Markies kamikazed down to the cobbles, a bomb of crisps and sandwiches that exploded on impact. *'Someone has to call the police!'*, *'Oh my God...'*, *'This is so cool, it—'*

Logan jabbed at the mouse and the image froze. 'Get it deleted off the internet.'

Guthrie screwed up one side of his face. 'It's kinda gone viral, Guv. Copies popping up all over the place.'

'Then get out there and find me John Skinner's wife. *Now!*'

*　*　*

'I see.' Superintendent Young folded his hands behind his head and leaned back in the visitor's chair. He'd forgone his usual Police-Scotland-ninja-outfit for a pair of blue jeans and chunky trainers. A red T-shirt with 'SKELETON BOB IS MY COPILOT' on it under a grey hoodie. As if he was fourteen instead of forty. Forty something. Probably nearer fifty. 'And is Justin Robson going to pursue this?'

Logan shuffled a mess of paperwork into a stack and popped it in the out-tray. 'You didn't have to come in on your day off, Guv. I'm sure we can cope till Monday.'

'It's this, or clearing out the garage.' A shrug. 'Call me dedicated. So: Robson?'

'Well, it's civil, rather than criminal, so he'd have to take her to court. But he's got her bang to rights for defamation. Posters up all over the area saying he's a drug dealer? No way she'll wriggle out of it.'

'Hmm...' Young stuck his legs out and crossed his ankles, head back, looking up at the stained ceiling. 'On the one hand, if he *does* sue her it'll serve her right. Maybe make her rethink her obsession. On the other hand, it could tip her off the deep end.'

'Either way she's going to end up a bigger pain in our backsides.'

'True.' A shrug. 'Anything else you need my help with? This suicide victim's missing wife thing?'

Logan bared his teeth. 'Thanks, Guv, but I think you've helped enough.'

'Ah well, if you're sure.' Young stood. Stretched. Slumped. 'Suppose I'd better go clear out the garage. No rest for the saintly.' He paused, with one hand on the door. 'I hear you had a run in with Gordy Taylor yesterday?'

'Wants to drop the charges in exchange for two litres of whisky.'

'And so we support those brave souls who fight in our

name…' A sigh. 'Right. Well, drop me a text or something.' Another pause. 'You're sure there's nothing else?'

Logan did his best to smile. 'Not unless you want to buy a one-bedroom flat?'

Logan licked his top lip. Stared down at his mobile phone. Couldn't put it off any longer. Well, he could, but it probably wasn't a great idea. He dug his thumbs into the back panel and slid the cover off. Prised out the battery and replaced the SIM card with a cheapy pay-as-you-go from the supermarket checkout loaded up with a whole fiver's worth of calls. Clicked everything back into place.

'Guv?'

When he looked up, Wheezy Doug was standing in the doorway, clutching a manila folder to his chest.

'Is it quick?'

A nod. Then a cough. Then a gargly clearing of the throat. 'Got the lookout request extended across all of Police Scotland. And the Media Office want clearance on a press release and poster.' He dug into the folder and came out with two sheets of paper. 'You want to OK them?'

Logan gave them a quick once-over, then handed both back. 'If they can figure out how to spell "Saturday" properly, tell them to run it.'

'Guv.' He put the sheets away. 'You hear they turfed Gordy Taylor out of hospital last night? Shouting and swearing and making an arse of himself.'

What a shock. 'Nothing broken when he got himself run over, then?'

'Nah. Lurched out the door and found himself some more booze. Uniform got a dozen complaints from Harlaw Road about him staggering about, knocking over bins and doing pretty much the same thing he'd been doing up at the hospital.' Wheezy sooked on his teeth for a bit. Then shook his head. 'I knew his dad. Decent enough bloke. Bit racist, with a drink in him, but other than that...'

'OK. Let me know if anyone spots Mrs Skinner.'

'Guv.'

Soon as Wheezy was gone, Logan grabbed his phone and headed out.

Sunlight sparkled back from the white granity mass of Marischal College, caught the wheeling seagulls and set them glowing against the blue sky. A taxi grumbled by, followed by a fat man on a bicycle wearing nowhere near enough Lycra to keep everything under control.

Logan nipped across the road, past the council headquarters and along Broad Street. Kept going onto the Gallowgate. Nice and casual. Up the hill, and right into the council car park in front of the squat DVLA building.

Nice and out of the way.

He pulled out his phone and dialled Wee Hamish's number. Listened to it ring.

And ring.

And ring.

That brittle, gravelly voice: *'Hello?'*

'Hamish. It's Logan McRae.'

'Ah, Logan. Yes. Good. How are you? How's that young lady of yours?'

'Still in a coma.' Strange how it didn't hurt to say that any more. Perhaps four years was long enough for it to scab over? 'What can I do for you, Hamish?'

'Is she getting all the help she needs, do you think?'

Logan wandered across the car park. 'The doctors and nurses are very good.'

'Oh I've got nothing but admiration for the NHS, believe me. They were very kind to my Juliette those last few months. But ... Maybe a private hospital would provide a more individual service? Where there's not so much pressure to meet performance targets.'

A path ran along the back of the car park, bordered by a wall. Logan leaned on it, looking down the hill to the dual carriageway and the big Morrisons. 'We got knocked back from Sunny Glen. No places.' A small laugh clawed its way out of his throat. 'Not that we can afford it. Anyway, it's too far away. I couldn't get all the way up to Banff to visit her every day. What's the point of that?'

'Hmm … I hear you're still trying to sell the flat. Any luck?'

'Hamish, you said you wanted to talk about Reuben.'

'Are you in financial difficulties, Logan, because if you are I'd be more than happy to lend—'

'No. I'm fine. I just … felt like selling the flat, that's all.'

'I thought you loved it there. Nice central location. And it's very convenient for work.'

'It's got memories I don't need.' Down below, an ambulance skirled its way along the dual carriageway, all lights blazing. 'Time for a change.'

'I understand.' There was a small pause, filled with a hissing noise, as if Wee Hamish was taking a hit from an aqualung. *'Would you like me to put in a word for you? There are a couple of neurology specialists I know who could help you find a place. Somewhere Samantha can get the individual attention she deserves. Let me see what I can do.'*

Logan tightened his grip on the phone. Puffed out a breath. 'What about you? How are you feeling?'

'I've been thinking about us a lot recently. You, me, and Reuben. When I'm gone, he'll come after you. You're too big a threat for him to ignore.'

'I'm not a threat! I keep telling—'

'It doesn't matter if you turn down the mantle or not, Logan. To Reuben you'll always be a threat.' Another hisssssssss. *'Would you like me to kill him for you?'*

All the moisture evaporated from Logan's mouth. 'What?'

'It would pain me, of course – he's been my right-hand man for

a long, long time – but sometimes you have to sacrifice a rook to keep the game going.'

'Now, hold on—'

'Oh, it won't be until I'm gone. The least I can do is let him come to the funeral. But after that. Before he's had time to move against you...'

Logan turned away from the road. Squinted up at the DVLA's windows. No one looked back at him. Thank God. 'Hamish, I'm a police officer: I can't be part of a plot to *murder* someone! Not even Reuben.'

'Are you sure? He's more dangerous than you think.' This time, the hiss-filled pause stretched out into silence. Then: *'Well, perhaps that would be best. After all, if you're taking over the company, the staff will respect you more if you get rid of him yourself.'*

'That's not what I meant! It—'

'Don't leave it too long, Logan. When I die, the clock starts ticking.'

'You OK, Guv?' Guthrie lowered his pale eyebrows, making little wrinkles between them.

Logan sank into one of the CID office chairs. 'I nearly fell off a roof yesterday, my suit smells of drunk tramp, I'm dealing with a tree festooned with dog turds, I can't sell my flat, and I had an early-morning run-in with Professional Standards. I've had better days.'

A smile. 'Then I've got something that'll cheer you up.'

'Is it midget porn again? Because I've told you about that already.'

'Nope.' He held up his notebook. 'One dark-green Honda Jazz, parked on Newburgh Road, Bridge of Don. It's Emma Skinner's.'

Logan stood. 'Well, what are you sitting there for? Get a pool car!'

*   *   *

Newburgh Road was a twisting warren of identikit houses, buried away amongst all the other identikit housing developments on this side of the river. Some residents had added porches, or garages, but the same bland boxy stereotype shone through regardless.

Guthrie pointed through the windscreen at the blocky back end of a dark-green hatchback. 'Patrol car was out cruising for a pervert – been stealing knickers off washing lines – when the Honda pinged up on the ANPR.'

They parked behind it.

Logan climbed out into the sun and did a slow three-sixty. Nothing out of the ordinary. Just more beige architecture, the harling greyed by weather. 'Any idea which house?'

Guthrie locked up. 'Thought we'd door-to-door it. Can't be that far, can it?'

'Pffff...' Logan leaned back against a low garden wall and wiped a hand across his forehead. It came away damp. 'You *sure* that's her car?'

Guthrie took out his notebook and checked again. 'Number plate matches.'

'Then where the sodding hell is she?'

'Well, maybe—'

'Forty minutes! Wandering round like a pair of idiots, knocking on doors.' The scent of charring meat oozed out from a garden somewhere near, making his stomach growl. 'Starving now.'

Guthrie gave a big theatrical shrug. 'I don't get it. It's not like it'd be hard to find a parking space here, is it? You'd dump your car right outside the person you're visiting, right?'

'Unless you weren't supposed to be here. Didn't want people to see your car...' Logan pushed off the wall. 'We keep looking.'

*   *   *

'OK, thanks anyway.'

As soon as the auld mannie in the faded 'BRITAIN'S NEXT BIG STAR' T-shirt had closed the door, Logan stepped into the shade of a box hedge.

He ran a hand across the nape of his neck and wiped it dry on his trousers. Checked his watch. That was an hour they'd been at it now. Slogging their way along the road in the baking sun. Knocking on doors. Asking questions. Showing people the photo of Emma Skinner that Guthrie had found on Facebook. A selfie of Emma and her two kids, grinning away like lunatics, the background blocked out by the three of them. She had her blonde hair pulled back from her face, a half-inch of brown roots showing. A silver ring in her left nostril. An easy smile. Two small children with chocolate smudges covering half of their faces.

Logan loosened his tie.

A whole hour of shoving the photo under people's noses.

And still nothing.

Maybe she hadn't been visiting someone here after all? Maybe this was simply a convenient place to dump the car? Somewhere to keep it hidden.

Why? Why would she want to hide?

'Guv?' One house over, Guthrie was backing away from the door – a hand scrabbling at the Airwave clipped to his stabproof vest. 'Guv!'

Logan hopped the low garden wall and hurried across a manicured lawn ringed with nasturtiums. 'Someone spotted her?'

Guthrie stopped in the middle of the path and pointed at the house. 'In there…'

OK.

He walked over to the front window. It was too bright outside, and too dark inside to see anything other than the reflected street scene. Logan cupped his hands either side of his eyes and pressed his forehead against the glass.

A high-heeled shoe lay in front of a glass-topped coffee table. On its side. The foot it belonged to poked out from behind the couch. Skin pale, a thick line of purple running horizontal with the ground where the blood had settled. More blood on the oatmeal-coloured carpet. Little dots and splashes. Dozens of them. More streaking up the walls, making scarlet spatters across a print of the New York skyline.

Definitely dead.

8

'Got you ham-cheese-and-mustard, and a tin of Lilt.' Guthrie held out a Tesco carrier bag.

Sitting back against the pool car, Logan dipped into the bag. 'Crisps?'

'Cheese-and-onion.'

Better than nothing. 'Thanks.'

A cordon of blue-and-white 'Police' tape cut across Newburgh Road, keeping the scene secure – enclosing the house, a patrol car, and the Scenes Examination Branch's dirty transit van. At least someone'd had the brains to scrub a hand through the filthier bits of finger graffiti.

Guthrie got stuck into an egg-and-cress, making mayonnaise smears either side of his mouth. 'Starving...'

Logan clicked the ring-pull off his fizzy juice, and chased down a mouthful of sandwich. Then wiggled the can towards the house. 'Looks like we're on.'

A pair of figures stepped out of the front door, both done up in full SOC Smurf outfits – blue booties, white Tyvek suit, blue nitrile gloves, facemasks, and eye goggles. Smurf One was tall and lanky, Smurf Two shorter with an itchy bum. Smurf Two dug and scratched away at its backside as the pair of them made their way across to the pool car.

Logan took another bite, talking with his mouth full. 'Well?'

DI Steel peeled her suit's hood back, then pulled off the mask and let it dangle beneath her chin. 'Sodding roasting...' Her face was a florid shade of red, the skin streaked with glistening lines of sweat. She stuck out her gloved hands, groping for Logan's Lilt. 'Give.' Then glugged away at it as Smurf One unfurled his suit and tied the arms around his waist.

Detective Sergeant Simon Rennie puffed out his cheeks and sagged. Wafted a hand in front of his flushed shiny face. Being inside the hood had done something terrible to his hair, leaving the blond mop sticking out at all angles, like a confused hedgehog. 'Gah...'

Logan tried again. 'Is it her?'

Steel gulped. Puffed out a long breath. Then burped. 'God, that's better.'

Rennie held out the picture Guthrie found on Facebook. 'It's her. Multiple stab wounds to the chest and abdomen – and I mean *multiple*. Has to be at least forty.' He rubbed a forearm across his face, blotting away the sweat. 'Don't have another tin of juice, do you?'

Steel handed him whatever was left of Logan's. 'There's a naked bloke in the bedroom too. Throat cut from ear to ear. Place looks like something out of a B-movie slasher; it's dripping from the ceiling and everything.'

A sigh escaped from Logan's chest. 'Let me guess – she's naked too.'

'Nope: kinky bra with matching thong.'

Which explained why Emma Skinner had parked so far away. Didn't want anyone to see her visiting her lover.

Mr Suicide's voice trembled, not much more than a broken whisper. 'How could she do that?' It explained that as well.

The lover had to die, but the wife had to be *punished*.

'We've had the murder weapon since yesterday.' Logan pointed towards the house. 'Anyone want to bet you'll find John Skinner's fingerprints all over the place? He follows her here, he catches her in the act, slits the lover's throat, then goes berserk with the knife. Can't live with what he's done, so he chucks himself off the casino roof, still clutching the knife.'

'Aye, well done Jonathan Creek.' Steel snatched the Lilt back from Rennie and tipped her head back. Frowned. Shook the can a couple of times. 'You greedy little sod!'

'You didn't say I couldn't finish it.'

'You don't glug back the last of someone else's *drink*. Everyone knows that.' She unzipped her SOC suit. 'Idiot.' Then snapped off her gloves. 'Got sweat trickling right down the crack of my—'

'What about the kids?' Logan nodded towards the picture in Rennie's hand. Those two chocolatey faces. 'Mrs Skinner takes them to their school clubs, Saturday morning, drives over here to see her lover. Her *husband* follows her and kills the pair of them, then drives back into town and jumps off the casino roof. Where are the kids?'

Steel closed her eyes. 'Crap.' She massaged her forehead for a moment. Then straightened up. 'Right, finding the kids is now *everyone's* number one priority. I want lookout requests, I want posters, I want media appeals…' She frowned. 'What?'

Logan popped his half-eaten sandwich back in the packet. 'Already done it. Media office are holding off till you've delivered the death message, but other than that they're ready to go.'

'Oh.' A sniff. 'In that case: Laz, you get started on the paperwork, and I'll—'

'Oh no you don't.' Logan held up a hand. 'You took the case over, remember? Turned up here all lights blazing

70

and said it was too *complicated* for us thickies in CID – this was a job for the Major Investigation Team. Remember that?'

She shuffled her feet. Looked off into the distance. 'Yeah, well, I may have been a bit overenthusiastic with—'

'Do your own sodding paperwork.'

'You're no' *still* sulking, are you?' Steel leaned against Logan's office doorway, arms folded, a 'World's Greatest Lesbian' mug dangling from the fingers of one hand.

He turned back to the duty roster, typing in the team's work plan for the next shift. 'Away and boil your head.'

'You're going to have to learn to share, Laz.'

'Share?' He thumped away at the keyboard, making it suffer. 'You turn up, you tell us we're crap, then you take the case away – even though we've already *solved* it – and grab all the sodding credit.'

A sniff. 'Yeah, but I had to do all the paperwork.'

He stared at her. 'Did you really? Or did you get Rennie to do it?'

A little blush coloured her cheeks. 'I supervised.'

Back to the roster. 'Feel free to sod off any time you like.'

She did. But she was back three minutes later with a steaming mug in each hand, a packet of biscuits tucked under her arm, and a Jaffa Cake poking out of her mouth. 'Mmmnnphh, gnnnph, mmmmnph?'

One of the mugs got placed on the desk in front of him. Then the biscuits.

He scowled at them. 'What's this?'

'Peace offering.' She sank into one of the visitors' chairs. 'Between friends.'

'What are you after?'

'Me? Nothing.' A shrug and a smile. 'Can't two old friends share a cuppa and a digestive biscuit or two?'

He picked up the mug and sniffed. It smelled like tea, but it looked like coffee. 'What happened to the Jaffa Cakes?'

'Yeah, they're all gone.' She plonked her feet up on his desk. 'So, double murder solved in an hour and a half. Not bad going.'

'Are you seriously sitting there gloating about solving a case that *I* solved for you?'

'Moan, bitch, whinge.' She crunched a bite out of her digestive, getting crumbs all down the front of her shirt. 'You're such a princess.'

'I am *not* a sodding princess.'

'Whatever you say, Your Majesty.' More crumbs. Steel stared out of the window, then her shoulders dropped a little. 'Still no sign of the kids.'

'Early days yet.'

'Got a press conference at half six, going out live on the news. No' exactly looking forward to that. Come Monday morning, going to be like a siege out there.' She took a slurp of tea. Finished her biscuit. Offered him the packet. 'So … You busy Tuesday night?'

'Here we go.'

'Only it's Susan and me's anniversary, and if you're no' too busy sitting at home like a sad sack, you could look after Jasmine for the night. Be nice for you to spend a bit more time with your daughter.'

Logan saved the file, then closed down the computer. 'How come you only think I need to spend more time with Jasmine when you need a free babysitter?'

'Think of it – I'm going to wheech Susan off to a swanky hotel, get room service to deliver champagne and strawberries, put a bit of porn on the telly, then shag her brains out.' Steel flicked biscuit crumbs out of her own cleavage. 'Very romantic.'

'I'm busy Tuesday.'

'No you're no'.'

'Yes I am.'

'Doing what?'

'I've got … a viewing. Someone's coming round to look at the flat.'

'No they're no'. You're going to be sitting at home, watching *The Little Mermaid*, in your pants, with your cat. Nipping off for a touch of onanism when singing along to "Part of Your World" gets you a bit horny.'

A knock on the door and Wheezy Doug stuck his head in. Oh thank God.

'Guv? It's Mrs Black – just called nine-nine-nine.'

Maybe not. Logan folded forwards until his forehead rested on the keyboard. 'It's *home* time.'

'Yeah, but she says her neighbour's trying to kill her with a cleaver.'

The siren shredded the early evening air as their pool car slewed around onto Pitmedden Court.

Steel latched onto the grab handle above the passenger door as the front wheels hit a speed bump, wheeching them into the air like something off the *Streets of San Francisco*. 'Yeeeeeeee-ha!'

The car slammed down onto the tarmac again, with a grinding groan.

Sitting in the back, Logan reached out and slapped Wheezy Doug over the back of the head. 'What did I tell you?'

'Sorry, Guv, urgent threat to life and that.' He kept his foot down.

Mrs Black's thick leylandii hedge appeared in the middle distance, rushing up to meet them as Wheezy screeched the car to a halt, nose in to the kerb. He grabbed a high-viz waistcoat and jumped out, struggling into the thing as he ran across the pavement.

Logan scrambled after him, charging up the path to Mrs Black's house as Wheezy slid the front down on his body-worn video, setting it recording.

BANG – Justin Robson battered his bare foot into his neighbour's front door. 'YOU BITCH! YOU BLOODY VINDICTIVE BLOODY BITCH!' His Bagpuss sweat pants billowed as he drew back for another kick, camouflage T-shirt stained beneath the armpits. The same dirty big kitchen knife as last time, clutched in one hand. 'COME OUT HERE!'

Logan stopped, a good six foot shy of the huge blade. 'Mr Robson? I need you to calm down for me.'

BANG. Another kick. 'I'LL BLOODY KILL YOU!'

Wheezy dragged out a canister of CS gas. Held the other hand out in front of him, palm out. 'Mr Robson, it's the police. Drop the knife. *Now.*'

Robson turned. Chest heaving. Mouth a wet wobbly line. Glasses steamed up. 'Did you see what that BITCH did to my car? Did you?' Back to the house. 'YOU RANCID, VINDICTIVE, BLOODY BITCH!'

Wheezy raised the canister. 'Ever been gassed, Mr Robson? It's not nice. And you're going to find out what it feels like if you don't *drop the bloody knife*!'

He looked down at the cleaver, as if seeing it for the first time. Then let go. Backed up a pace, hands up as it clattered on the paving slabs. Cleared his throat. 'OK, OK, there's no need for that. This is all a big misunder— ulk!'

Wheezy grabbed him by the camouflage and spun him into the closed front door. Shoved his head against the UPVC. Stuffed the canister of CS gas back where it came from as he whipped out the cuffs. Snapped them on Robson's wrists. Dragged him away down the path.

'Get off me!' Robson shook his head left and right, like a dog with a rat. 'It's *her* you should be arresting, not me. Look what she did to my car!'

Logan pulled a blue nitrile glove from his pocket and snapped it on. Bent and picked up the fallen knife. Carried it out to the kerb.

'Look at my car...'

Justin Robson's white BMW wasn't so white any more. What looked like gloss paint Jackson Pollocked across the roof, windscreen, and bonnet in bright splatters of pink and yellow and blue, running in rainbow tears down the wings. The words 'Drug Dealer!!!' were scratched into the bodywork, over and over again, gouged deep enough to crease the raw metal underneath.

'Look at it...'

The sound of someone sooking on a tube appeared at Logan's shoulder, followed by a puff of vapour. Steel did a slow circuit of the vandalized BMW. 'No' the colour I would've chosen, but it makes a statement.'

Logan took the knife around to the pool car's boot, unzipped the holdall in there and pulled out a knife tube. He slipped the cleaver inside the clear plastic tube and sealed it. Marched back to where Wheezy held the sagging man. 'Right, Justin Robson, I'm arresting you for breach of the peace, possession of a deadly weapon, attempted breaking and entering, attempted—'

'We get it.' Steel worked her e-cigarette from one side of her mouth to the other. Nodded at Robson. 'You: Bagpuss. Tweedle Dum and Tweedle Dee here tell me you're on a feud with her next door.'

'She's *insane*.'

'Don't care.' A yellowed finger pointed in Logan's direction. 'Tweedle Dee – get this wifie...?'

He stared back at her. 'Marion Black.'

'Don't care. You get Wifie Black out here and we'll see if Saint Roberta of Steel can't pour some baby oil on these troubled waters. Amen, and all that.'

He didn't even try to suppress the groan. 'Seriously?'

'Finger out, Laz, got bigger fish to fry than this pair of idiots.' She checked her watch. 'Got to be on telly in an hour. Chop, chop.'

Fine. Wasn't as if they didn't have to take Mrs Black's statement anyway.

He turned and marched back up the path. Gave the front door the policeman's knock – three, loud and hard. 'Mrs Black?'

A thin voice came from the other side of the door. 'Who is it?'

'It's the police.' As if the pool car sitting out front with its blue lights flashing wasn't enough of a clue. 'I need you to open up.'

'Not if he's still out there. Is he still out there?'

'Mr Robson is in custody at the moment, so if...'

The door sprang open. Mrs Black stood on the threshold in her dressing gown and jammies, even though it couldn't have been much more than twenty past five. She had a fire iron in both hands, clutched against her chest. 'He's a menace. I *told* you he was dangerous!' She grinned up at Logan. The whites were visible all the way around her bulging eyes. 'I told you, but you wouldn't listen. Said there wasn't any proof.' The words rolled out on a cloud of second-hand alcohol. She shifted from one slippered foot to the other. 'Is this proof enough for you? *Is* it?'

'I need you to come talk to the Detective Chief Inspector.'

At that, Mrs Black pulled herself up straight, shoulders back. 'About time I got to speak to *someone* in authority.' She brushed past him, shuffling up the path.

Then froze as she reached the pavement and spotted DCI Steel. 'Where is he then? This Detective Chief Inspector?'

Steel sniffed. Howched. And spat into the gutter. 'Bit sexist, isn't it?'

Yeah, this was definitely going to end well.

Robson glowered out from behind his squint glasses. 'You vicious, scheming—'

Wheezy must have done something painful to him, because his eyes screwed shut and whatever word came next got replaced by a hiss.

A nod. Then Mrs Black's grin darkened. 'See? He's *dangerous*. He's a drug dealer and he tried to kill me and now you've got to lock him up for the rest of his perverted unnatural life, and—'

'She planned this! Can't you see she planned it? It's all a set-up—'

'—prison and that's where you belong you—'

'—vandalized my car! She *knew* I loved—'

A harsh, shrill whistle ripped the air and everyone went quiet.

A handful of neighbours had drifted into their front gardens. Suddenly consumed by an overpowering need to trim their hedges, or prune a rose bush. All of them frozen by the whistle.

Steel took two fingers from her mouth and wiped them on her rumpled suit jacket. 'Better.' She turned a shark smile on Mrs Black. 'Did you, or did you no', trash this man's car?'

The nose came up. 'I did nothing of the sort.'

'So, when I get my two colleagues here to search your property, they're no' going to find any paint tins? White spirit? Stained clothes or shoes?'

Mrs Black's mouth pursed at that last one. She looked out across the gardens. 'He tried to kill me.'

'Thought so: they never get rid of the shoes.' Steel turned the smile on Robson. 'And did you, Justin Robson, attempt to stab Mrs Black to death?'

Pink rushed up his cheeks. He stared down at his bare

feet. 'She trashed my car, I was … only trying to … was carving the Sunday roast when I saw what she did.' A shrug. 'Forgot I was holding the knife…'

'And does anyone here present have any just reason why I shouldn't throw the book at you pair of silly sods and let the courts decide?' Steel made a gun out of her fingers and shot Mrs Black in the face. 'Criminal damage.' Then did the same to Robson. 'Aggravated assault. Minimum eight months apiece. That what you want?'

Neither of them said anything.

'Because if I hear so much as a *whisper* that you've been sodding about like this again, I'm going to bury the Great Leather Shoe of God in both your arses.'

Silence.

She shot Robson again. 'Do you understand?'

He shifted his feet. Turned his head to the side. 'I do.'

Mrs Black got another finger bullet. 'You?'

A pause. Then she lowered her eyes and nodded. 'Yes. Fine. No more fighting.'

Steel raised her arms, as if delivering a benediction. 'Then by the powers vested in me by the High Heid Yins of Police Scotland, I hereby declare this feud *over*.'

— they never get rid of the shoes —

9

Stoney eased into the room, a folder balanced on the palm of one hand acting as a tray for a mound of tinfoil-wrapped packages. 'Three bacon, one sausage, and one booby-trapped. Get them while they're hot.'

The rest of the team swarmed him, snatching up their butties, then retreating to their seats to unwrap them. The air filled with the meaty smoky scents.

Early morning light oozed through the dirty office window, turning it nearly opaque, hiding the pre-rush-hour calm of a slowly waking Aberdeen.

Logan checked his watch: five past seven. Time to get going. He ripped a bite of sausage buttie and pointed at the whiteboard. 'Guthrie?'

At least he didn't look *quite* so much like an extra from *Night of the Living Dead* this morning.

'Mrs Skinner's boyfriend was a Brian Williams. Twenty-two. Engineer with TransWell Subsea Systems in Portlethen. Steel's MIT took over the investigation, but I still had to deliver the sodding death message to his fiancée. She wasn't too chuffed.'

Wheezy Doug picked at his teeth. 'There's a shock.'

'Here's a bigger one – the MIT are taking all the credit.'

DS Baird frowned at the whiteboard for a moment, then wiped a smear of tomato sauce from her cheek. 'Got a good write-up in the paper, though.' She picked a copy of the *Aberdeen Examiner* from her desk and held it up.

The front page had a more formal photograph than the one Logan and Guthrie had been showing around yesterday. A posed family portrait with a marbly background. Everyone in their Sunday best, hair combed, teeth shiny. 'FAMILY FEARS FOR MISSING CHILDREN'.

Baird cleared her throat and turned the paper back to face herself. '"It wasn't as if the Skinner family didn't have enough tragedy to deal with. On Saturday, John Skinner – thirty-five – jumped to his death, and on Sunday, his wife of eight years, Emma Skinner – twenty-seven – was found stabbed to death in a family home in the Bridge of Don. But what hurts most, say John and Emma's parents, is that Heidi – seven – and Toby – six – are missing…"' Baird wrinkled her top lip. 'Why are the papers obsessed with how old people are? What's the point?'

Wheezy stuffed down another bite of buttie, talking with his mouth full. 'They say anything about us?'

She skimmed the front page, lips moving silently as she went. 'Nope. "Detective Chief Inspector Roberta Steel…" See they haven't got *her* age. "…told a press conference yesterday that Police Scotland was very concerned for the children's safety. 'We will leave no stone unturned in our quest to find Heidi and Toby…'" Blah, blah, blah. Nothing about you, or the Guvnor.'

'Typical.'

A little yellow trail of yolk was making its way down Guthrie's chin. 'Guv, are you still interested in Gordy Taylor?'

'Wasn't interested in him in the first place.'

'Only the girl who gave him a kicking's up before the Sheriff at twenty past nine.'

'Pleading guilty?'

'Blaming it on PMS and starting university.'

Baird shuddered. '*Hate* women who do that. "Oh, I can't act rationally, because I'm a weak and feeble woman at the mercy of my hormonal uterus." Puts the whole cause back a hundred years.'

Logan held up his hand. 'Right, soon as everyone's finished their buttie, I want—' His phone blared out the anonymous ringtone that signalled an unknown caller. 'Give us a minute.' He pulled it out and hit the button. 'DI McRae.'

Screaming battered out of the earpiece and he flinched back.

Then tried again. 'Hello? Who is this?'

The screaming broke into jagged words, roughened by sobs. '*He's killed them all!*'

'There! Look what he did. LOOK AT THEM!' Mrs Black's trembling finger came up and pointed at the back fence.

The back garden stank of ammonia. It turned every breath into a struggle, caught the back of the throat, made the air taste of sour vinegar and dirt. Logan blinked tears from his stinging eyes.

Cages ran down one side of the long garden, backing onto the massive leylandii hedge between this side and Justin Robson's house on the other. Wooden frames with metal mesh inserts, full of perches and floored with sawdust and droppings. Every single door hung open.

But they weren't what Mrs Black was pointing at.

About twenty little bodies were frozen against the back fence – wings out. Most were blue with white faces, but some were green-and-yellow instead. And each one had a large nail hammered through its breast, pinning it to the wood. As if a butterfly collector had decided his hobby just wasn't creepy enough and it was time to upgrade to something bigger.

83

Blood made spattered patterns on the fence behind and beneath them.

Mrs Black sobbed, tears coating her cheeks, gulping down air only to cry it out again. 'My *babies*...'

'OK.' A nod. 'Is Mr Black—'

'Don't you ... don't you *dare* mention ... mention that *bastard's* name.' She ground the heel of her hand into her eye sockets. 'He walked out on me. On ME! Packed his bags like *I* was the one being unreasonable.' She threw her arms out. 'LOOK AT IT! LOOK WHAT HAPPENED!' The arms drooped by her sides. 'My babies...'

Logan puffed out a breath. Then patted Wheezy Doug on the shoulder. 'Constable Andrews, maybe you should get Mrs Black inside and make a cup of tea, or something. I'm going next door.'

Justin Robson folded his arms and leaned back against the kitchen counter. 'Nope. Nothing to do with me.' His face was pale with greeny-purple bags under the eyes, his breath stale and bitter. Hair slicked back and wet. Dark-blue dressing gown.

Behind him, the garden was in darkness, the early morning sunshine murdered by Mrs Black's spite hedge. A curl of smoke twisted up into the gloom.

Logan pulled out his notebook. 'Come off it: she trashes your car, and you decide to turn the other cheek? *Really?*'

'Wasn't even here: out all night at a friend's house. You can check if you like.'

'Oh we will.' The pen hovered over the pad. 'Name?'

'Can do you better than that. Hold on, I'll call him.' Robson picked the phone out of its cradle and fiddled with the buttons. The sound of ringing blared out of the speaker.

Then, *click*. *'Hello?'*

'Bobby? It's Justin. Sorry to call so early, but can you tell this guy where I was last night?' He held out the phone.

'What? Yeah, Justin came round about six-ish? We watched a couple of films. Had a bit too much wine and a moan about girls till about three in the morning. Justin was so blootered he could barely stand.'

'Cheeky sod. No I wasn't.'

'Were. So I put him in the spare room. Set the alarm. And went to bed.'

Logan wrote it all down. At least that explained the pallor and the smell. 'And he didn't leave the house?'

'No way Justin could've got out without deactivating the alarm and he doesn't know the code. Didn't go home till about half an hour ago? Forty-five minutes? Something like that? Told him he should cop a sicky and crash here all morning, but blah-blah work etc.'

A nice tight alibi. Very convenient. 'OK, I'm going to need your full name and address.'

Wheezy Doug snapped off his blue nitrile gloves and stuffed them into a carrier bag. 'What kind of dick does that to harmless wee birds?'

Logan nodded back towards the house with the decorated cherry tree. 'How is she?'

'Mangled. Says that after her husband stormed out, she hit the vodka. Staggered off to bed about eleven after checking the birds were all fine. Gets up at seven this morning and finds *that*.' Wheezy puffed out his cheeks. 'Poor wee things. I had to lever them off the fence with a claw-hammer. That's why some are a bit squashed.' He pulled out a pen and printed the evidence label for twenty parakeets, all sharing a big evidence pouch. Each one individually zip-locked into its own tiny plastic bag. 'What about laughing boy?'

'Says he had nothing to do with it. Got himself an alibi.'

'That's convenient.' Wheezy closed the pool car's boot.

'Exactly what I thought.' Logan led the way back to the house.

Robson had moved through to the lounge, a bowl of Rice Krispies in his lap. Breakfast News burbled away on the widescreen telly as he tied a tie around his pale neck. He'd swapped the dressing gown for trainers, jeans, and a pale-yellow shirt.

'... *double murder in Aberdeen yesterday have been identified as Emma Skinner and Brian Williams*...'

He straightened his tie, then dipped a spoon into his cereal. 'You forget something?'

'... *committed suicide on Saturday.*' The screen filled with amateur mobile-phone video of John Skinner preparing to jump.

Logan stepped between Robson and the TV as the anchor handed over to Carol for the weather. 'You do understand that we can take DNA from the parakeets, don't you? Whoever killed them will have left their DNA on their feathers. We'll get it from the nails too. *And* fingerprints.'

'Isn't science marvellous.'

'We can match contact traces of metal between the nail-heads and a specific hammer. We can match the nails with ones from the same batch.'

'OK.' He killed the TV, then put his breakfast on the coffee table. 'Tell you what, if you don't believe I was with Bobby all night, why don't you search the house again? Do the garden too. You can even try the shed.'

Little sod was either innocent, or arrogant enough to believe he could get away with it.

Wheezy Doug tucked his hands into his pockets and nodded at Robson's feet. The trainers were bright white, without so much as a scuff on them. 'They're nice. Look new.'

'Cool, aren't they? Fresh on today.'

'Where are the old ones?'

He smiled. 'Yeah, they were getting all stinky and dirty.

Plus, someone *might* have been sick on them last night. So I got rid of them.'

What a surprise. Nothing quite so incriminating as a pair of blood-stained Nikes.

Logan took out his notebook. 'And where, *exactly*, are these sick-drenched shoes now? In the bin?'

'Ah...' Robson bared his top teeth in a rabbit grin. 'I burned them soon as I got home. Was doing some garden rubbish anyway.' He stood and walked through to the kitchen. Pointed out through the window to a stainless-steel bin, hidden away in the shadows at the bottom of the garden. The thing had holes in its sides and a chimney lid. Coils of smoke drifted away into the morning sky. 'Never had one before, but it's *really* efficient. Burns everything.'

Definitely arrogant. And probably right.

Robson frowned. 'You know, now I think about it, if I'd been nailing live parakeets to a fence, I'd be all covered with scratches and pecks, wouldn't I?' He held up his hands. Not a single mark on them. 'I mean, they're going to put up a fight, aren't they?'

Logan stepped in close. 'This stops and it stops here. No more. Understand?'

The smile didn't slip an inch. 'Nothing to do with me. You'd have to speak to the bitch next door.'

Yeah, there was no way this was over.

'We'll be watching you, Mr Robson.' Logan turned and marched from the room, down the hall and out the front door.

Wheezy Doug hurried after him. Unlocked the pool car and slipped in behind the wheel. 'He did it, didn't he?'

'Course he did. He doesn't have scratches on his hands, because he wore gloves. And then he burned them. So no fingerprints on the nails or the birds. And odds on he'd wear a facemask too.'

'So no DNA, or good as.'

'Bet he even burned the hammer.' Logan stared back at the house.

Robson was standing in the living room, smiling through the window. He gave them a wave.

Logan didn't wave back. 'This is going to get worse before it gets better.'

Wheezy pulled away from the kerb. 'And last time we were here, I distinctly remember DCI Steel making a big thing of how no one ever gets rid of their shoes. The wee turd listened and learned.'

Logan took his Airwave handset from his jacket pocket. 'Should've arrested them both when we had probable cause.' Too late for that now though, it'd been no-crimed. He pressed the talk button. 'DI McRae to Control. I need a Wildlife Crime Officer, or whatever it is we're calling them these days.'

Twenty dead parakeets.

Yeah, this was definitely going to get a *lot* worse.

10

Baird dipped into the big evidence bag and came out with a wee, individually wrapped, dead parakeet. Wrinkled her nose. 'Poor thing.'

Logan's office was warmer than it had any right to be. He cracked open the window, letting in a waft of stale air tainted by cigarette smoke. 'Killed all twenty of them.'

She placed it back in the bag with the others. 'Twenty dead little bodies.'

'If you were Mrs Black, what would you do?'

'Me?' Baird scrunched her lips into a duck pout. 'If I was a total nutjob, what would I do? Cut his knackers off. No, not cut, I'd *hack* them off. With a rusty spoon.'

Logan sank into his seat. 'That's what worries me.' He pointed at the big bag. 'Get it off to the labs. I want anything they can get linking the birds to Justin Robson before this goes any further. At least if one of them's banged up they can't kill each other.'

'Guv.' She picked it up. 'What about the Skinner kids?'

'No idea.'

'Seems a shame, doesn't it? Wasn't their fault their mum was screwing around.'

'Never is.' Logan pulled his keyboard over. 'If the lab gives you stick about analysing a bunch of parakeets, tell them I'll be round to insert a size nine up their jacksy next time I've got a minute. It's—'

A knock on the door and there was Guthrie, face all pink and shiny, out of breath as if he'd been running. 'Guv ... It's ... It's...' He folded over and grabbed his knees for a bit. 'Argh ... God...'

Baird patted him on the back. 'That's what you get for eating so much cheese, Sunshine.'

He shook her off and had another go. 'Guv, it's ... Gordy Taylor...'

Logan groaned. 'What's he done now?'

'Dead...'

Baird dumped the evidence bag back on Logan's desk. 'I'll get a pool car.'

Baird tucked her hair into the SOC suit's hood, then pulled the zip up all the way to her chin. Grabbed a handful of material around the waist and hoiked it up, setting the white Tyvek rustling. 'You ready?'

Behind her, a double line of blue-and-white 'Police' tape cut off a chunk of Harlaw Road, tied between trees on opposite sides of the street, casting a snaking shadow. A crime scene dappled with light falling through the leaves.

The houses on the opposite side of the street didn't look all that fancy – detached granite bungalows with attic conversions and dormer windows – but they overlooked the green expanse of the playing fields, so probably cost an absolute fortune.

Logan snapped a second set of blue nitrile gloves on over the first. 'Might as well.'

They ducked under the outer cordon and rustled their way across the tarmac to the inner boundary of yellow-and-black – 'Crime Scene – Do Not Cross' – where a spotty uniform with huge eyes demanded to see their ID then wrote their names in the log before letting them past.

Two large council bins were lined up against the kerb, and behind them someone in the full Smurf outfit was squatting beside the body. He had a bony wrist in one hand, turning it over, letting the attached filthy hand flop one way, then the other.

Logan sank down next to him, blinking at the stench of alcohol and baked sewage. 'Doc.'

The figure looked up and nodded – more or less anonymous behind the facemask and safety goggles. 'Well, it's official: this gentleman's definitely dead.'

He let go of the wrist and shuffled back, letting them get a proper look at the body.

Gordon Taylor lay curled up on his side; knees drawn up to his chest; one arm thrown back, the hand dangling against his spine; the other reaching out in front. Head twisted back, mouth open. Eyes glazed. Beard and hair matted with twigs and vomit.

A bluebottle landed on Gordon's cheek, and the Duty Doctor wafted it away. 'Well, there's no sign of serious trauma. He's not been stabbed, or bludgeoned to death. The only sign of blood is that...' The doctor pointed at the grubby bandage wrapped around Gordon's right hand. It was stained with dark-scarlet blobs.

'You want to guess at time of death?'

'Very roughly? Sometime between him getting chucked out of hospital, and the bin men finding him here this morning.' A shrug. 'Anyone who gives you anything more precise is a liar.'

'Any sign of foul play?'

'Doubt it: your friend here choked on his own vomit. If you want *my* opinion, you're looking at what happens when you spend your life downing litre bottles of supermarket vodka, whisky, and gin. Sooner or later it catches up with you.' He straightened up with a groan and rubbed at the small of his back. 'And with that, the brave Duty Doctor's work was done, and he could get back to treating hypochondriac morons who think they know better than him because they've looked leprosy up on the internet.'

The uniform with the spots held up the barrier tape and the undertaker's plain grey van eased back out onto Harlaw Road. The driver nodded to Logan and drove off.

Wheezy Doug was in conversation with a middle-aged man with a walking stick, two houses down. Stoney was at the far end of the street, nodding and taking notes as a mother of two waved her arms about, a pair of red-haired kids running screaming around her legs. DS Baird wandered up the road, hands in her pockets.

She stopped beside Logan and nodded at the departing van. 'That him off, then?'

'You get anything?'

'Far as we can tell, Gordon Taylor's been hanging around here for about a fortnight. I got Control to pull anything relating to Harlaw Road and three streets either side. There's been an increase in breaking and enterings: low-level stuff, shed padlocks forced, meths and white spirit nicked kind of thing. One stolen handbag – owner put it on the roof of her car while she unloaded the shopping, came back: no handbag. Loads of complaints of anti-social behaviour.' She pulled out her notebook and flipped it open at the marker. 'And I quote, "There's a smelly tramp staggering up and down the street at all hours, singing filthy rugby songs and rummaging through the bins."' Baird turned the page. 'Eight counts of public urination. No one ever caught him at it, but in the morning people's doorways would smell of piddle. That lot,' she pointed at a tidy house with an immaculate garden, where a little old lady was pruning a rosebush, 'called the police eight times in the last week.'

Well, the old dear wasn't so much pruning the bush as nipping *tiny* bits off the one branch, probably using it as an excuse to have a nosy. She wasn't the only one. At least half a dozen others were out, taking their time washing cars or raking the lawn. Pretending not to snoop.

A glazier's van sat outside the old lady's house. The driver and his mate were in the cab, stuffing down chocolate biscuits and pouring tea from a thermos. Staring as if this was the most interesting thing to happen all day. An episode of *Taggart*, playing out right there in front of them.

Logan turned his back on the gawkers. 'So what happened?'

Baird shrugged. 'Patrol car did a drift by a couple of times, but you know what it's like. Don't have time to attend every moaning numpty.'

True. But if they'd *actually* done something about it – if they'd turned up and arrested him – Gordon Taylor would probably still be alive today. Hard to drink yourself to death in a police cell.

Something heavy settled behind Logan's eyes, pulling his whole head down.

And if *he'd* arrested Gordon Taylor on Saturday for being drunk and incapable, or done him for biting two security guards and a nurse, or for punching that other nurse on the nose…

Pfff…

'You OK, Guv?'

A one-shouldered shrug. 'Missed opportunities.' He looked off down the road.

Didn't really matter in the end, did it? Lock Gordon Taylor up for a night, or a week, and he'd still hit the bottle as soon as he got out. All it would've done was delay the inevitable. Sooner or later, he'd be in the undertaker's van on the way to the mortuary.

Logan dragged in a deep breath, then let it out. Checked his watch. Might as well head back to the office and do something productive. 'Get Wheezy to deliver the death message. He knows Gordon Taylor's dad. Might be better if he finds out from a friend.'

There was only so much you could do.

Logan spat the last cold dregs of coffee back into his mug and shuddered. Time for a fresh cup.

He'd got as far as his office door when his mobile launched into its anonymous ringtone. Please let it be anyone other than Mrs Sodding Black again.

He hit the button. 'McRae.'

'Mr McRae? It's Marjory from Willkie and Oxford, Solicitors? How are you doing? That's great. I've had Mr and Mrs Moore on the phone again and they're prepared to go as far as fifteen thousand below the valuation.'

'Then Mr and Mrs Moore can go screw themselves.'

A fake laugh came down the phone as Logan let himself out into the corridor, making for the stairwell. *'Well, I had to let you know anyway. I'll get back to their solicitor. And I wanted to know if you're available this afternoon? We've had a call from a young man interested in viewing the property.'*

'I'm on duty.' Which part of serving police officer did she not understand?

'Right. Yes. Well, not to worry, I can show him around.'

Nice to know she'd be doing something for her one-per-cent-cut of the price.

He slid his phone back in its pocket and clumped up the stairs to the canteen. Froze in the doorway.

DCI Steel sat at the table in front of the vending machine,

94

working her way through a Curly Wurly and a tin of Coke. A large parcel lay on the floor at her feet, wrapped in brown paper and about a mile of packing tape. She hadn't seen him yet – too busy chewing. All he had to do was back out of the door and—

'Hoy, Laz, I'll have a hazelnut latte if you're buying.'

Sodding hell.

Too late. He stepped into the canteen. 'Any luck tracking down John Skinner's kids?'

She took another bite of Curly Wurly, chewing with her mouth open. 'Trust me, if there was you'd have heard about it. I'd be running through the station, bare-arse naked singing "Henry the Horny Hedgehog" at the top of my lungs.'

A shudder riffled its way across Logan's shoulders. 'Gah…'

'Oh like *you're* a sodding catwalk model. Least I'm getting some, unlike you. Surprised your right arm's no' like Popeye's by now.' Her teeth ripped a chunk off the twisted chocolate. 'And while we're on the subject, where the sodding hell have you been? Got missing kids to find, remember?'

He stared at her. 'It's *your* case. You took it over, *remember*?'

'Don't be so—'

'And for your information, we've got enough on our plate as it is. Spent half the morning dealing with a sudden death.' He bared his teeth. 'So forgive me if I'm not available to run about after you all day.'

Steel leaned back in her chair and waved her Curly Wurly at him. 'Oh aye, I heard all about your "sudden death". Two missing kids trumps one dead tramp.' The Curly Wurly jabbed towards the canteen counter. 'Now backside in gear, and tell them no' to skimp on the chocolate sprinkles this time.'

Typical.

He got a coffee for himself, and Steel's hazelnut latte. Brought them both back to the table. 'I've spat in yours.'

'No you didn't.' She took a sip. Sighed. 'Got two dozen bodies manning the phones. Heidi and Toby Skinner have been spotted everywhere from Thurso to the Costa del Sol, via Peebles and Chipping Norton.' The creases between her eyebrows deepened. 'Getting a bad feeling about this one, Laz.'

'Just because we haven't found them yet, doesn't mean we won't.'

'When are we ever that lucky?' Steel sank back in her seat and scrubbed her face with her palms, pulling it about like pasty plasticene. Then let her arms drop. 'In other news: tomorrow night. You and Jasmine, daddy–daughter time, with *Despicable Me* one and two.'

'No.'

'You're no' watching a Disney film, Laz: I know you get aroused by all those princesses in their pretty dresses.'

'I'm not being your unpaid babysitter.'

'Come on: it's our *anniversary*.' Steel nudged the parcel with her toe. 'Got Susan the perfect gift. Want to know what it is?'

He glanced beneath the table. Large, rectangular, with a website address printed on the delivery label. 'Something you've ordered off the internet? Nah, I'd rather not know.' It was bound to be something filthy. Probably battery operated.

'You're no fun.' She unwrapped the last inch of twirly toffee and jammed it in her mouth. 'Tell you what: ten quid, *cash*. And a pizza. Can't say fairer than that.'

'No.'

'OK: ten quid, a pizza, and a bottle of red…' She narrowed her mouth to a little pale slit. 'Uh-ho. Crucifixes at the ready, Laz, here comes Nosferatu Junior.'

Logan turned and peered over his shoulder. Superintendent Young was marching across the green terrazzo floor towards their table. Dressed all in black, with a silver crown on each epaulette attached to his black T-shirt. The fabric stretched tight across his barrel chest.

Steel hissed. Then stared at the tabletop, keeping her voice low. '*Don't* move. Don't make eye contact. Don't even *breathe*. He'll get confused and walk away.' She took a deep breath.

Young stopped at the head of the table. 'Inspector. Chief Inspector.'

She didn't move.

Logan nodded. 'Superintendent.'

He pulled up a chair. 'Mrs Black has made another complaint.'

What a surprise. 'Let me guess – Wheezy and I are corrupt because we didn't arrest Justin Robson this morning?'

'Apparently he's bribed you with drugs and dirty magazines. He...' A frown. 'Why is Chief Inspector Steel going purple?'

'Because she's not right in the head.' Logan took a sip of coffee. 'And for the record, there was nothing we could do. Robson killed Mrs Black's parakeets – no doubt about that – but he burned all the evidence. Even his shoes.'

'I see. And is DCI Steel planning on holding her breath till she passes out?'

'Probably. Look, we can't arrest Robson, because we've got nothing on him that'll stand up in court. I've sent the dead parakeets off to the labs, but you know what the budget's like. Assuming we can even get past the backlog.'

'But you're not hopeful, are...' A sigh. Then Young leaned over and poked Steel hard in the ribs. 'Breathe, you idiot.'

Air exploded out of her, then she grabbed the table and hauled in a deep shuddering breath. 'Aaaaaa...'

'I understand you could've arrested the pair of them last night, but didn't.'

'Oooh, the world's gone all swimmy...'

Logan twisted the coffee cup in his hands. 'We felt it was more appropriate to try and defuse the situation with a warning.'

'But Mr Robson didn't take it.'

'Not so much.' A shrug. 'Mrs Black poured paint all over his car and carved "Drug Dealer" into the doors. Probably have to get it completely resprayed. Going to cost him, what – three, maybe four grand?'

Steel blinked. Shook her head. 'Wow. That's a hell of a lot cheaper than a bottle of chardonnay.'

'And in light of this morning's actions?'

Logan raised one hand and rocked it from side to side. 'The aggravated assault and vandalism got no-crimed. I doubt the PF would let us go back and do the pair of them retrospectively.'

'Going to try that again.' Steel took another huge breath and scrunched her face up.

Young frowned at her for a while. 'Has she always been this bad?'

'No, she's getting worse.'

He poked her again. 'We've got twelve different news organizations camped outside the front door, do you think you could try acting a bit more like a grown-up?'

She scowled at him. 'Doing everything we can, OK?' She held up a hand, counting the points off on her fingers. 'National appeal in the media. Whole team going through all Heidi and Toby's friends. Posters up at every train station, bus station, airport, and ferry terminal. We did *three* complete door-to-doors where they live. And...' Steel wiggled the one remaining finger. 'Erm ... This little piggy's being held in reserve in case of emergency.'

'Piggies are toes.'

'Whatever.' She put her hand away. 'If you've got any helpful suggestions, I'll take them under consideration.'

Young shifted in his seat.

'Aye, didn't think so.'

He stood, slid his chair back into place. Straightened his T-shirt. Stuck a huge, warm, scarred hand on Logan's shoulder. 'And make sure you're getting every encounter with Mrs Black on video. I've got the nasty feeling this is going to blow up in our faces.'

DS Rennie popped his coiffured head around Logan's door. His mouth stretched out and down, like someone had stolen his pony. 'Guv, you got a minute?'

Logan shoved the keyboard to one side. 'If it's more interesting than budget projections for the next quarter, I've got dozens of them.'

'Cool.' He stepped into the office and sank into a visitor's chair. Unbuttoned his suit jacket, then pulled out his notebook. 'I spoke to the janitor at Heidi and Toby Skinner's school, and—'

'Going to stop you right there.' Logan held up a hand. 'Don't tell me, tell Steel. She's running the case.'

A shrug. 'Yeah, but she's doing a press conference, and this was sitting on her desk.' He held up a sheet of A4 with, 'OFF BEING A MEDIA TART – ANYTHING COMES UP, TELL DI MCRAE.'

Typical. Couldn't have given the reins to one of her minions, could she? No, of course not. Not when she could make Logan's life more difficult.

'Anyway…' Rennie went back to his notebook. 'So I spoke to the janitor, the professor from Aberdeen Uni who runs the Saturday maths club, and a really camp Geordie who takes the ballet class. All say the same thing: John Skinner picked Heidi and Toby up at midday.'

'Damn it.' Logan frowned at the screen, ignoring the spreadsheet and its irritating little numbers. Skinner picked up the kids. Did he do it before, or after he killed their

99

mother? Did he make them watch? 'What about family and friends?'

Rennie flipped the page. 'Teams been going through them all morning, but no one's seen the kids.'

And John Skinner's car was still missing.

'OK: if you haven't already done it, get a lookout request on Skinner's BMW. Tell traffic and every patrol-car team it's category one. I want it found. Might be something in there that'll tell us what he's done with Heidi and Toby. Make sure the SEB sample any dirt in the footwells – get it off for soil analysis.' He tapped his fingertips along the edge of the desk, frowning at those horrible little numbers. 'Maybe it's parked on a side street somewhere near where he dropped the kids?' After all, that's how they'd found Emma Skinner. Not that it'd done her any good.

'Yes, Guv.' Rennie stood. 'So … you in charge till Steel gets back?'

Logan folded over and banged his head on the desk a couple of times.

'Guv?'

Of course he sodding was.

Because DCI Steel had struck again.

11

'OK, thanks Denise.' Rennie put the phone down.

Logan looked at him. 'Well?'

'Sod all.'

'Pffff…'

The Major Inquiry Team room was a *lot* grander than the manky hole CID had to work out of. New carpet tiles that were all the same colour, swanky new computers that probably didn't run on elastic bands and arthritic hamsters, electronic whiteboards, a colour printer, a fancy coffee machine that took little pods, and ceiling tiles that didn't look as if they'd spent three months on the floor of a dysentery ward.

How the other half lived.

A handful of officers were on the phones, talking in hushed voices and scribbling down notes.

Logan picked up one of the interactive markers and drew a circle on the whiteboard. There was a small lag, then a red circle appeared on the map of Aberdeen that filled the screen, taking in a chunk of the city centre around the casino. 'John Skinner didn't park in the Chapel Street multistorey and walk the length of Union Street to kill himself. He was clarted in blood – someone would've noticed.'

DS Biohazard Bob crossed his arms and poked out his top lip, as if he was trying to sniff it. It wasn't a good look: with his sticky-out ears, bald patch, and single thick hairy eyebrow, he bore more than a passing resemblance to a chimpanzee at the best of times. 'What about the NCP on Virginia Street? It's just round the corner.'

Rennie shook his head. 'The one on Shiprow's closer.'

'Pair of twits. It's the same car park.' Logan drew a red 'X' on the screen. 'Doesn't matter – logbook says it's been searched. No dark-blue BMW M5.'

Biohazard had a scratch. 'There's a council one on Mearns Street, that's pretty close too. Or Union Square?'

'Or…' Rennie pointed at the map. 'What if he had a long coat on? Like a mac, or something. Could cover up the bloodstains and no one would notice. Dump it when he gets onto the roof of the casino.'

'Nah.' Biohazard shook his head. 'We would've found it on the roof.'

'Not if the wind got hold of it. Could be in Norway by now.'

'True.'

Logan took the pen and marked on all the public car parks within a fifteen-minute walk. 'Rennie – get down to the CCTV room and tell them to go over the footage from Saturday. Any route to the casino from any of these car parks. See if they can find John Skinner.'

'Guv.'

'Biohazard – grab some bodies and work your way through the car parks, find that BMW. Start with the closest, work your way out.'

'Guv.'

The pair of them turned and marched off, leaving nothing but a cloying eggy reek behind.

Logan gagged, wafted a hand in front of his face. 'Biohazard!'

Giggling faded away down the corridor.

'That's us done Union Square. Got a dark-blue beamer, but it's not his. I'm … Hold on.' Biohazard Bob's voice went all muffled, barely audible. *'I don't care. You should've gone before we left the station.'* Then he was back. *'Sorry, Guv, logistical problems.'*

Logan drew a red cross on the whiteboard, eliminating Union Square. 'Might as well try College Street multistorey, while you're there. Then hit the Trinity Centre.'

'Guv.'

The MIT office was nearly deserted. A handful of plain-clothes officers were bent over phones, taking sightings from members of the public. A whiteboard by the fancy coffee machine bore a list of possible locations that now stretched from Lerwick to Naples. A woman with bouffant hair and pigeon toes put her phone down, shambled over, and added 'Port Isaac' to the roll.

She puffed out her cheeks, then turned to Logan. 'I know they're only trying to help, Guv, but why do they all have to be *nutters*? Oh, here we go.' Her eyebrows climbed up her forehead and she pointed over Logan's shoulder. 'Showtime.'

He turned and there was Steel on one of the large flatscreen TVs. A media liaison officer sat on one side of her, fiddling with his notes and looking uncomfortable. On the other side were an elderly couple: a grey-haired woman and a bald man, both with dark circles beneath watery eyes. The lines in their faces had probably deepened an inch since Saturday.

Officer Bouffant scuffed over to Logan, staring up at the screen. 'Both sets of grandparents wanted to do it, but the boss thought it'd be best to stick to the wife's side of the family. Might be harder to get sympathy with the murdering wee sod's mum and dad there.'

Logan grabbed the remote and turned the sound on.

'... *thank you.*' The media officer shuffled his papers again. Then held out a hand. '*Detective Chief Inspector Roberta Steel.*'

It looked as if she'd had a bash at combing her hair. And failed. '*Heidi and Toby Skinner were picked up by their father from Balmoral Primary School at twelve o'clock on Saturday afternoon. At one forty-five, John Skinner jumped from the roof of the Grosvenor G Casino on Exchequer Row. At some point between twelve o'clock and one forty-five, Emma Skinner – Heidi and Toby's mother – was subjected to a brutal and fatal attack, along with her friend, Brian Williams, at a house in Newburgh Road.*'

At that, the elderly couple sitting next to Steel quivered and wiped away tears.

Officer Bouffant tilted her head. 'We're calling Williams her "friend". Thought it'd be kinder.'

A copy of that morning's *Daily Mail* sat on the desk beside her. 'Mum And Toyboy Lover In Bloodbath Horror'.

'How did that work out for you?'

She picked up the newspaper and dumped it in the bin. Shrugged. 'Well, it was worth a go.'

'... *appealing for any information that will help us locate Heidi and Toby. Did you see John Skinner's dark-blue BMW M5...*'

Then a sigh. 'Wasting our time, aren't we? Fiver says that gets us nothing but more phone calls from nutters.'

'Yup.'

'... *extremely concerned for their wellbeing...*'

Officer Bouffant curled into herself a bit, shoulders rounding. 'You know what? Being in the police would be a great job, if we didn't have to deal with members of the sodding public.'

'*Thank you.*' The media officer had another shuffle. '*And now Mr and Mrs Prichard would like to read a brief statement.*'

The old man's voice was cracked and raw, trembling with each breath. '*We've already lost so much. Emma was the brightest, most wonderful human being you could ever meet. She lit up every room…'*

'Think they'll get custody of the kids? You know, assuming we find them.' She folded her arms. 'I mean, the court won't give Heidi and Toby to the dad's parents, will they? Not after what *he* did.'

'Haven't you got phones to answer?'

Sigh. 'Yes, Guv.'

'… bring our grandchildren home, safe and sound. Please, if you know anything, if you saw … their father…' The poor sod couldn't even bring himself to say John Skinner's name. *'… if you know where our grandchildren are…'* He crumpled, both hands covering his face. His wife put her arm around him, tears shining on her cheeks.

Mr Media did some more shuffling. *'Thank you. We will now take questions.'*

A forest of hands shot up.

'Yes?'

'Carol Smith, Aberdeen Examiner. *Why did John Skinner jump off the casino? Did he have a gambling problem?'*

Steel shook her head. *'No' that we know of. The casino has no record of him ever being in the building before. As far as we—'*

Logan killed the sound and left Steel chuntering away to herself in silence.

It was all just for show anyway. The illusion of progress. Yes, someone *might* spot John Skinner's BMW, but it wasn't likely. The only way they were going to get Heidi and Toby back was by working their way through every parking spot in the city, and hoping there was something in Skinner's car that would point the way.

And hope even more that it didn't point to a pair of tiny shallow graves.

His phone buzzed deep inside his pocket, then launched into 'If I Only Had a Brain'. That would be Rennie.

Logan hit the button. 'What have you got?'

'Guv? Think we've found him.'

'There.' The CCTV tech leaned forward and poked the screen. A figure was frozen in the lower left-hand corner, shoulders hunched, long blue raincoat on over what looked like a grey suit. John Skinner.

Logan nodded. 'It's him.'

She spooled the footage backwards, and he reversed onto Union Street, disappearing around the corner of the Athenaeum pub. 'Took a while, but we managed to—'

'Hoy!' The door thumped open and Steel stood on the threshold, with a mug in one hand and a rolled-up newspaper tucked under her arm. 'Who said you sods could start without me?'

And everything had been going so well. 'Thought you were off being a media tart.'

'Did you see me on the telly? I was spectacular. Like a young Helen Mirren.' She thumped the newspaper against his chest. 'Page four.'

Logan opened the *Scottish Sun* to a spread on 'FATHER OF TWO IN MURDER-SUICIDE SPREE' complete with photos of John Skinner, his two victims, and his missing children.

She poked the article. 'See? "The community has been stunned by Skinner's terrible crimes, and now fears for Heidi – seven – and Toby – six – are growing."' A nod. 'Told you: missing kids trumps dead tramp. Think they're going to run a two-page spread on Gordy Taylor choking on his own vomit? Course they're no'.'

He dumped the paper in the bin. 'That doesn't mean we don't—'

'Blah, blah, blah.' Steel leaned on the desk, close enough to brush the tech's hair with an errant boob. 'What are we looking at?'

'John Skinner.' She shuffled an inch sideways, getting away from Steel's chest. 'So, we track him backwards from the casino...' Her fingers clattered across the keyboard and the scene jumped to the security camera at the junction of Union Street and Market Street. John Skinner reversed across the corner of the image, clipping the edge of the box junction before disappearing again.

'Can barely see the wee sod; can you no' follow him properly?'

The CCTV tech shook her head, flinching as her ear made contact. 'If someone does something and we're there, we can follow him from camera to camera. But we can't jump back in time and tilt and pan, can we? You're lucky we got anything at all.'

Logan's phone rang, deep in his pocket. Please don't be Mrs Black, please don't be Mrs Black. But when he checked the display it was only Marjory from Willkie and Oxford, useless solicitors and rubbish estate agents to the stars. Probably calling with another derisory offer from the Moores. Well, she could go to voicemail. Let it ring.

Steel glowered at him. 'You answering that, or do I have to shove it up your bumhole. We're working here.'

Right. He pressed the button to reject the call. 'Sorry.'

'Think so too.' She eased a little closer to the CCTV tech. 'Come on then – where now?'

Another rattle of keys.

'Markies and the Saint Nicholas Centre probably got him on their cameras, but the next time he shows up is here...' A view across School Hill at the traffic lights. Three cars and a bus stopped on one side, a motorcyclist and a transit van on the other. Skinner lurched backwards across the road and into a short granite canyon blocked off by metal bollards. He reversed past the bank and in through the line of glass doors leading into the Bon Accord Centre. Or

107

more properly, out of it – given the way he'd been going in real life.

She poked the screen as the doors shut, swallowing him. 'That's it.'

'That's *it*?'

'Doesn't appear on foot on any of the other CCTV cameras in the area.' A smile put dimples in her cheeks. 'But I found this.'

The screen jumped to a view down Berry Street, where it made a T-junction with the Gallowgate. Bland granite flats on one side, and a bland granite office block on the other side. A dark-blue BMW M5 came down the Gallowgate and paused in the middle of the junction, indicating right. The opposing traffic dribbled away and it turned onto Berry Street.

She hit pause. 'Number plate matches.'

Steel pressed in even closer. 'So what are we saying?'

Logan poked her on the shoulder. 'Get your boob out of the poor woman's ear.' He pointed. 'Down there you've got John Lewis and the Loch Street Car Park. What about the CCTV camera at the corner of St Andrew Street and George Street?'

'Nope. Far as I can tell, he dumps the car in the car park and walks through the Bon Accord Centre.'

Steel smacked her hand down on the desk. 'Saddle the horses, Laz, we've got two wee kids to save!'

12

The patrol car's sirens carved a path through the Monday rush hour. It was still excruciatingly slow though, crawling along under thirty miles an hour till they got to the junction with Berry Street, where John Skinner had turned right. Then the traffic thinned out and Rennie put his foot down, gunning the engine, throwing them hard around the corner and— 'Eeek!' He locked his arms and stamped on the brakes as the back end of a Citroën Espace burst into view. Its 'BABY ON BOARD' sticker loomed huge, getting huger...

They slithered sideways in a juddering rumble of antilock brakes, coming to a halt half on the pavement.

Steel leaned over from the passenger seat and skelped him round the ear. 'What have I told you about no' getting me killed?'

'Pfffff... That was close.'

'Moron.'

The Espace pulled forward up the ramp, apparently unaware that they nearly had an extra three passengers in the back seat, complete with patrol car.

Rennie backed off the pavement and followed them under the curved blue sign and into the concrete gloom. A wee queue of traffic led up to an automatic barrier, issuing tickets slower than tectonic plates move.

Steel slumped in her seat. 'Gah. Would've been quicker sodding walking.'

Logan's mobile gave its anonymous ringtone. He pulled it out and checked the screen: Marjory from the estate agents again. He stuck the phone back in his pocket, let it go to voicemail.

Finally, Rennie grabbed a ticket from the geological machinery and pulled up onto the first level. Stopped, craning left and right. 'Which way?'

A forest of concrete pillars reached away into the distance, the space between them packed with cars, all washed in the grimy glow of striplights.

Steel jabbed a finger at the tarmac. 'Follow the arrows. Nice and slow. Anyone spots a BMW, they shout.'

'One more time?' Rennie ran his fingers across the top of the steering wheel as their car emerged from the darkness into the evening sunshine. The ramp curled around to the right, then across a short flyover – suspended three storeys above the street below – and they were back on the roof of John Lewis again.

The last gasp of overflow parking was nearly empty. Half a dozen huge, expensive-looking, shiny, four-by-fours stood sentry on the seagull-speckled tarmac, each one parked as far away from the others as possible, in case someone marred their showroom finish.

Could pretty much guarantee that none of them had seen anything more off-road than the potholes on Anderson Drive.

Steel checked her watch. 'Sodding hell.' She sighed. 'He's no' here, is he?'

Logan leaned forward and poked his head between the front seats. 'What if he looped round the back of the Bon Accord Centre and onto Harriet Street? Parked in there?'

Rennie shook his head. 'Nah: Harriet's one way.'

Ah. 'Still be a lot of wee places you could leave a car round here though. Not legally, but if you've just stabbed your wife and her lover to death, you probably aren't too bothered about that.'

Steel covered her face with her hands and swore for a bit. Then straightened up. 'One last time round the car park, then we try Crooked Lane. Then Charlotte Street. And anywhere else we can think of.' She kicked something in the footwell. 'Buggering hell!'

'… your news, travel, and weather at seven, with Jackie.'

'Thanks, Jimmy. The trial of Professor Richard Marks enters its third day today, with one prosecution witness claiming the psychiatrist sexually assaulted him on eighteen separate occasions…'

Rennie swung the car around Mounthoolie roundabout. 'Where now?'

'… at Aberdeen University since 2010…'

The massive lump of earth and grass slid by the driver's side, easily big enough to hold its own housing scheme. Surprised no one had thought of that yet. Could make a fortune.

Steel slumped against the passenger window. 'Back to the ranch.'

'… twenty-three counts. Next up: the grandparents of two missing local children issued an appeal today for information. Heidi and Toby Skinner have been missing since their father committed suicide on Saturday…'

Rennie took the next left, up the Gallowgate. Grey three-storey flats on one side, grey four-storey flats on the other. The grey monolithic lump of Seamount Court towered over the surrounding buildings with its eighteen-storeys of concrete, narrow windows glittering in the sunlight.

'… you, please: we just want our grandchildren back…'

111

The North East Scotland College building drifted past the driver's side – in yet more shades of grey.

Logan shifted in his seat. 'Maybe he had an accomplice? Maybe he got out at the Bon Accord Centre and someone drove the kids away?'

'Maybe.' Steel raised one shoulder. 'Or maybe he decided the whole family would be better off dead. You know what these scumbags are like – she's shagging around on him, so *everyone* gets to die.' She stared out of the window at the sea of grey buildings. 'You've really managed to cock this one up, haven't you?'

What?

Logan reached forward and poked her on the shoulder. 'How have *I* cocked it up?'

Rennie kept his eyes on the road, mouth shut.

'You should've had a lookout request going on the kids soon as they scraped Skinner off the cobblestones!'

'Really? Because I remember you saying it was all his own fault and Guthrie should head round and try to shag the widow.'

A sniff. A pause. Then Steel raised an eyebrow. 'To be fair, given what she'd been up to with Brian Williams, Sunshine might have been in with a chance, so—'

'And I don't see you showering yourself in glory here. If it wasn't for me, we wouldn't even *be* searching the car parks!'

Steel's eyes narrowed. 'Nobody likes a smart arse.'

Rennie knocked on Logan's door frame. 'Thought you'd have gone home by now.' His hair was back to its usual blond quiffiness, the tie loosened and top button undone. Bags under both eyes.

Logan leaned back in his office chair. 'Could say the same for you.'

112

A small smile and a shrug. 'Got everyone we can out looking for Skinner's car. Might have to organize a mass search tomorrow. Half of Aberdeen rampaging through the streets, shouting at blue BMWs. Fun. Fun. Fun.'

'The joy of working for Detective Chief Inspector Steel.'

'Tell me about it. Our Donna's less of a hassle, and she's only six months old. Still, at least we don't have to change Steel's nappies.'

'Yet.'

Rennie curled his top lip. 'Shudder.' Then he hooked a thumb over his shoulder, towards the corridor. 'Bunch of us are heading off to Blackfriars. You wanna?'

Logan shut down his computer. 'Tempting, but I've got to check on a nutjob before I go home.'

Violent pink and orange caught the underside of the grey clouds, as the sun sank towards the horizon. Logan tucked the pool car in behind a Mini on the other side of Pitmedden Court.

Across the road, lights shone from Justin Robson's windows, but Mrs Black's house was slipping into darkness. She was probably sitting in there, on her own, mourning her dead parakeets at the bottom of a vodka bottle. Wondering where her life went so badly wrong.

Maybe plotting revenge on her horrible next-door neighbour.

Not that Justin Robson didn't deserve a good stiff kicking for what he'd done. And got away with.

Still, at least they didn't seem to be at each other's throats this evening. That was something. But there was no way it would last. Sooner or later, one of them was going to open fire again.

Logan pulled away from the kerb, heading back towards Divisional Headquarters.

Should've arrested the pair of them when they had the chance.

Logan let himself into the flat. 'Cthulhu? Daddy's home.' He clunked the door shut. Hung up his jacket. Grabbed the last tin of Stella from the fridge. 'Cthulhu?'

She was through in the lounge, stretching on the window-sill – paws out front, bum in the air, tail making a fluffy question mark. A couple of *proops*, a *meep*, then she thunked down on to the laminate floor and padded over to bump her head against his shins.

The answering machine was giving its familiar baleful wink again.

Well it could sodding wait.

He squatted down and scooped Cthulhu up, turning her the wrong way up and blowing raspberries on her fuzzy tummy as she stretched and purred.

'Daddy's had a crappy day.'

More purring.

The answering machine bided its time, glowering.

Might as well get it over with.

He carried Cthulhu over and pressed the button.

'You have five new messages. Message one:' Bleeeeeep.

'Mr McRae? It's Dr Berrisford from Newtonmyre Specialist Care Centre, we've got your application in for a bed for Samantha Mackie in our neurological ward. Normally there's a waiting list of about six months, but we've had a cancellation. Can you call me back please? I'll be here till about eight. Thanks.'

He hit pause and checked his watch, making Cthulhu wriggle. Seven forty-five. Still time. Cthulhu got placed on the arm of the chair while Logan dug out the paperwork from the coffee table's drawer. Flipped through to Dr Berrisford's contact details. And punched the number into the phone.

Listened to it ring.

'Newtonmyre Specialist Care Centre. How can I help you this evening?'

'Can I speak to Dr Berrisford, please? It's Logan McRae.'

'One moment…'

He sank into the couch. Then stood again. Paced to the window and back.

A deep, posh voice purred down the line. *'Ah, Mr McRae, how are you?'*

'You've got an opening for Samantha?'

'That's right. We were holding a bed for someone, but unfortunately they've passed away.'

'That's great…' Logan cleared his throat. 'Sorry, obviously it's not great for them. I just meant—'

'It's OK. I understand. Now, there are a few things we'll need to sort out, to make sure Miss Mackie can get the best care possible. You are aware of our fee structure?'

Right to the chase.

Logan glanced down at the letter, with its columns of eye-watering figures. 'Yes.'

'Excellent. Well, if you can organize the phase-one payment we'll get the ball rolling.'

Phase one cost more than he made in a year.

He forced his voice to stay level. 'When do you need it?'

'Well, normally we'd say straight away – there is a waiting list – but if you need time to sort things out I can probably extend that to two weeks? Any more than that and I'll have to release the bed again.'

Two weeks. Could probably get a second mortgage organized on the flat by then, couldn't he?

Or he could take Wee Hamish Mowat up on his offer. Borrow enough money to pay the care centre's fees till the mortgage came through.

Sweat prickled the back of Logan's neck. Cross that line and there was no going back. No 'plausible deniability'. He'd be in Wee Hamish's pocket, and that would be that.

115

Logan's eyes widened. Oh crap…

Wee Hamish.

He'd taken an interest in Samantha's care. Said he'd put in a word. What if he'd done more than that? What if he'd *made* the opportunity.

'Mr McRae? Hello?'

'Sorry.' Logan licked his lips. 'Dr Berrisford, the person who died, how did… Was it…?'

'Pneumonia. She was due to come up from Ninewells Hospital three weeks ago, but there were complications.' A sigh. *'It's often the case with people in long-term unresponsive states. Chest infections are very difficult for them to deal with and, sadly, she was simply too weak to fight this one off.'*

The breath whoomphed out of Logan, leaving him with eyes closed, one hand clasped to his forehead. Thank God for that. At least Wee Hamish didn't have her killed.

'I see. Right. Two weeks.'

'Let me know if that's not going to be possible, though, OK?'

'No, yes. Right. Thanks.'

He listened till the line went dead, then clicked the phone back in its charger.

Two weeks.

Another deep breath. First thing tomorrow – get an appointment with the bank. See what they could do.

Two weeks.

It was as if something huge and heavy was sitting on his chest.

Logan pressed play on the answering machine again.

'Message two:' Bleeeeeep.

'Logan? What exactly *is wrong with you? I'm your mother and I deserve—'*

'You can sod off too.' Poke.

'Message deleted. Message three:' Bleeeeeep.

'Guv? It's Rennie. We're in Archie's, where are you?' The sound

116

of singing and cheering drowned him out for a moment. '...
*buck naked. Anyway, we're having another couple here, then maybe
grabbing a curry. Give us a call, OK?'*

'*Message deleted. Message four:*' Bleeeeeep.

'*Aye, DI McRae? It's Alfie here from Control. Yon horrible wifie
Mrs Black's bin on the phone aboot a dozen times, moaning aboot
her neighbour. Are you—*'

'*Message deleted. Message five:*' Bleeeeeep.

'*Mr McRae, it's Marjory from Willkie and Oxford, Solicitors
again. Hello. I've been trying to get in touch about the young man
who came round to view the property this afternoon. He loves the
flat and he's made an offer...*' She left a dramatic pause.

That was the trouble with people these days – too much
time spent watching *Who Wants To Be A Millionaire*, and
Celebrity MasterChef, and *Strictly Come Sodding Dancing*. They
couldn't just come out and say something, they had to build
it into a big production number.

'*Mr Urquhart wants to know if you'll take the property off the
market for twenty thousand pounds over the valuation.*'

Logan stared at the machine. '*How* much?'

'*Anyway, it's nearly five o'clock, so if you want to give me a call
back tomorrow morning, we can see how you'd like to proceed. OK.
Thanks. Bye.*'

Bleeeeeep.

'How much?' He pressed the button to play the message
again.

'*Mr Urquhart wants to know if you'll take the property off the
market for twenty thousand pounds over the valuation.*'

Damn right he would.

He played the message three more times. Then kissed
Cthulhu on the head, popped her down on the couch, and
toasted her with the tin of Stella. 'Daddy's sold the flat!'

God knew it was about time *something* went right.

— every silver lining —

13

'OK, any questions?' Standing at the front of the MIT office, Steel clicked the remote and the screen behind her filled with the photos of Heidi and Toby Skinner.

A hand went up at the back. 'We still looking for live kids, or is it kids' bodies now?'

Steel scowled through the gathered ranks of uniform and plain-clothes officers. 'You looking for a shoe-leather suppository, McHardy? Cos I don't use lubricant.'

He lowered his hand. 'Only asking.'

'Well don't.' She turned to the crowd again. 'Heidi is seven. Toby is six. They're only wee, and we are damn well going to find them while they're still alive. Am I clear?'

A muffled chorus rippled around the room.

'I said: am I sodding clear?'

This time the answer rattled the ceiling tiles. 'Guv, yes, Guv!'

'Better.' She straightened the hem of her shirt, pulling it down and increasing the amount of wrinkly cleavage on view by about an inch. 'Now our beloved Divisional Commander is going to say a few inspirational words.' She jerked her head towards a big man with a baldy head and hands like a gorilla. 'Come on, Tony, fill your boots.'

While Big Tony Campbell was banging on about civic responsibility and the weight of the public's expectations, Logan flicked through the short stack of Post-it notes that had been stuck to his monitor when he got in. All pretty much the same: 'MRS BLACK CALLED AT 21:05 COMPLAINING ABOUT THE NOISE FROM NEXT DOOR (RAP MUSIC).', 'MRS BLACK CALLED AT 21:30 STILL COMPLAINING ABOUT THE NOISE.', 'MRS BLACK CALLED AT 22:05 COMPLAINING ABOUT RAP MUSIC AND SWEARING FROM NEXT DOOR (AGAIN). SOUNDED DRUNK.' The next six were the same – every fifteen to twenty minutes she'd call up to moan about Justin Robson, apparently sounding more and more blootered each time.

Suppose they'd have to go around there again and read them both the riot act.

So much for the ceasefire.

Big Tony Campbell still hadn't finished being motivational: the power to make a difference, serving the community, proving our detractors wrong. Blah, Blah, Blah.

Steel sidled her way around the outside of the room, till she was standing next to Logan.

Keeping most of her mouth clamped shut, she hissed at him out of one side. 'Don't forget – you're on babysitting duty tonight.'

He kept his face front, expressionless.

She sighed. 'OK: a tenner, a pizza, a bottle of red, and a tub of Mackie's.'

Logan didn't move his mouth. 'What kind of pizza?'

'Microwave.'

'Get stuffed.'

Up at the front, Big Tony Campbell came to the end of his speech and held up his hands in blessing. 'Now get out there and find those children. I know you can do it.'

The younger members of the audience launched into a round of applause. That petered out under the withering stares of the older hands. Some embarrassed clearing of throats and shuffling of feet. Then they started drifting out of the MIT office, heading off on their allotted tasks.

Rennie appeared at Steel's shoulder, stifling a yawn. 'All set, Guv. Both lots of grandparents are on their way for the press conference at eight.'

She didn't look at him. 'I *know* when the press conference is.'

'You knew when the last one was, and you were still fifteen minutes late.'

Her lips pursed, wrinkles deepening at the corners as her eyes narrowed. 'Coffee. Milk and two sugars. And a bacon buttie. *Now*, Sergeant.' Soon as he was gone, she tugged at her shirt again. Any further and there'd be bra on show. 'Cheeky wee sod that he is.'

Logan stuck his hands in his pockets. 'Thought you weren't using John Skinner's parents.'

'United front, Laz. We want them kids back. Our beloved Divisional Commander thinks if we stick both sets up there, the public's more likely to help hunt down John Skinner's beamer.'

'OK, well, have you got a team going door-to-door on Newburgh Road, where we found the wife's car?'

She closed one eye and squinted at him. 'Do I look like a complete and utter numpty to you? Course I have.'

'If someone saw John Skinner turn up to murder his wife, maybe they saw someone else in the car? An accomplice.'

'Yeah, I did *actually* think of that. It's no' my first murder, thank you very much.' A sniff, then another shirt tug, revealing a line of black lace. 'Tell you, Laz, that nasty feeling of mine's getting worse.'

'You're not the only one. I— Sodding hell.' His phone was going again, playing that same irritating anonymous

123

ringtone. 'Sorry.' He pulled it out and pressed the button. 'Hello?'

Nothing.

'Hello?'

A woman's voice, thin and trembling. *'Is this ... Are you Sergeant McRae?'*

'Can I help you?'

'It's over.'

OK. He took a couple of steps away and stuck a finger in his other ear. 'Who am I talking to?'

'It's over. It's finally over. I'm free.'

'That's great. Now, who am I speaking to?' The voice was kind of familiar, but not enough to put a name to it. Distorted and distant, as if whoever it was wasn't really there. 'Hello?'

'I'm free.' Then nothing but silence. She'd hung up.

Nutters. The world was full of nutters.

He checked his call history: 01224 area code – didn't help much, that covered nearly everything from Kingswells to Portlethen and all points in between. Including the whole of Aberdeen. He dialled the number back. Listened to it ring. And ring. And ring. And ring. More soup. And ring...

'Hi, this is Justin's answering machine. I'm afraid he's too busy to come to the phone right now, but you know what to do when you hear the...' Followed by a long *bleeeeeep.*

'Hello? Anyone there? Hello?' Nothing. 'Hello?' Silence. Logan hung up. Frowned down at his phone: Justin.

But it had been a *woman's* voice he'd heard: *It's over. It's finally over. I'm* free.

Logan's eyes widened: *Justin.*

Sodding hell.

He ran for the door.

* * *

124

Grey houses streaked by the pool car's windows. The siren wailed, lights flashing, parting the early morning traffic as Logan tore up Union Street doing fifty. 'Call Control – whoever's closest, I want a safe-and-well check on Justin Robson. Grade one!'

Sitting in the passenger seat, Wheezy Doug dug out his mobile and dialled. Braced himself with his other hand as the pool car jinked around a bendy bus. 'Control from Sierra Charlie Six, I need a safe-and-well check…'

The Music Hall flashed by on the right, pedestrians stopping on the pavement to gawp as the car screamed past.

'… Justin Robson. … No, Robson: Romeo – Oscar – Bravo – Sierra – Oscar – November. … Yes, *Robson*.'

Shops and traffic blurred past. Across the box junction by the old Capitol Cinema.

'Don't care, Control, as long as they get there *now*. We're en route.'

A hard left onto Holburn Street. A van driver's eyes bulged as he wrenched his Transit up onto the kerb. Silly sod should've been on his own side of the road in the first place. The needle crept up to sixty.

'OK.' Wheezy pinned the mobile to his chest, covering the mouthpiece. 'Control want to know what are they sending a car into?'

'Something horrible: Now tell them to get their backsides in gear!'

'Guv.' And he was back on the phone again.

The needle hit sixty-five.

Logan abandoned the Vauxhall sideways across the road, behind a patrol car, and bolted for Justin Robson's house. The front door was wide open, raised voices coming from inside: *'I don't care what they're doing, tell the Scenes Examination Branch to get their backsides over here.'*

He battered into the hall. 'Hello?'

A uniformed officer appeared in the kitchen doorway, hair scraped back, tattoos poking out from the sleeves of her police-issue T-shirt. She had her Airwave up to her ear. 'OK, make sure they do.' Then she twisted it back onto one of the clips on her stabproof vest and nodded at him. 'Sir.' Her mouth turned down at the edges. 'Sorry.'

Logan jogged to a halt. 'Is he…?'

She jerked her head back and to the side. 'Through there.' Then stood back to let Logan in.

Justin Robson's immaculate kitchen wasn't immaculate any more. Bright scarlet smeared the granite worktops. More on the big American fridge freezer. More on the walls. A few drops on the ceiling.

Robson sat on the tiled floor, with his back against one of the units. Legs at twenty-five to four. One arm curled in his lap, palm up, fingers out, the other loose and twisted at his side. Head back, mouth open, eyes staring at the rack lighting. Skin pale as skimmed milk.

He was dressed for work: brand-new trainers, blue jeans, shirt, and tie. Everything between his neck and his knees was stained dark, dark crimson. One of his own huge, and probably very expensive, kitchen knives stuck out of his chest, buried at least halfway in. It wasn't the only wound – his torso was covered with them.

The PC eased into the room and stood well back from the spatter marks with her arms folded. Staring down at the body. 'He's still warm. I've called an ambulance, but *look* at him. Has to be stabbed at least thirty, forty times? No pulse.'

Logan cleared his throat. 'Where's Marion Black?'

She was in the living room, sitting on Justin Robson's couch. Red and brown streaks covered both arms, the black leather

126

seat beside her clarty with more blood. Her tartan jimjams were frayed at the cuffs, the front spattered and smeared.

Logan beckoned the PC over. 'Your body-worn video working?'

She tapped the credit-card-style cover. 'Already running.'

'Good. Stay there.' He stepped in front of Mrs Black – where the BWV would catch them both. 'You phoned me.'

She looked up and smiled. Slow and happy. Peaceful. Like her voice. 'Isn't it lovely and *quiet*?' Her pupils were huge and dark, shiny as buttons.

'Mrs Black, Justin Robson's dead.'

'I know, isn't it wonderful? He's dead and gone and it's all lovely and quiet.' Her fingers made tacky sticky noises on the leather couch. 'He killed my babies and then...' A frown. 'That horrible music at all hours. Pounding away through the walls. Boom, boom, boom...'

'Mrs Black, what—'

'I asked him to turn it down, and he laughed in my face. He killed my babies, and laughed at me. Played that horrible music till I couldn't...' She looked down at her blood-smeared fingers. The nails were almost black. 'And now he's dead and it's lovely and quiet again. We can all live happily ever after.'

'I'm going to need you to come with me.'

She waved a hand at the huge flatscreen TV and the games consoles. 'Why would a grown man need all this stuff?'

'Marion Black, I am detaining you under Section Fourteen of the Criminal Procedure – Scotland – Act 1995, because I suspect you of having committed an offence punishable by imprisonment: namely the murder by stabbing of Justin Robson.'

'It's pathetic, isn't it? All this stuff. All that money. And what good did it do him?'

'You are not obliged to say anything, but anything you

do say will be noted down and may be used in evidence. Stand up, please.'

She unfolded herself from the couch. Rubbed each thumb along the tips of her filthy fingers. Caught, literally, red-handed. A frown. 'I'm glad he's dead.' Then the smile was back. 'Now I can sleep.'

14

Steel stood on her tiptoes and peered over Logan's shoulder into the interview room. 'She cop to it?'

'Yes and no.' He eased the door closed, leaving Mrs Black alone with DS Baird and the PC from the house. 'We've got her on BWV admitting she killed him, but in there? She "can't remember". She's "confused". And now she's decided she *does* want a lawyer after all.'

'Gah...' Steel's face soured. 'Want to bet whatever slimy git she gets will tell her to no comment all day, then aim for a diminished responsibility in court tomorrow morning?' Steel went in for a dig at an underwire. 'No' saying I wouldn't buy it, mind. She's off her sodding rocker.'

'She's off her face too. Had pupils the size of doorknobs when we picked her up.' Which was kind of ironic, given her obsession with Robson being a drug dealer. 'Odds on it's antidepressants.'

'Five quid says she cops a plea, gets three or four years in a secure psychiatric facility. Out in two.'

'Ever wonder why we bother?' He tucked the manila folder under his arm and started down the corridor. 'What's the news with Heidi and Toby Skinner? Search turn up anything?'

'Maybe we could get someone to section her? Indefinitely detained in a nice squishy room with a cardie that buckles up the back.'

'He must've parked that damn car somewhere.'

Steel gave up on the underwire and had a dig at the bit in the middle instead. 'Can't be hard getting a shrink to say she's a danger to herself and others, can it? No' with three pints of Justin Robson's blood caked under her fingernails.'

'I was thinking – the big car parks have ANPR systems, don't they? In case you do a runner without paying, they can track you through your number plate.'

'We could get your mate Goulding to section her, assuming he's finished stuffing Professor Marks like a sock puppet. Pervy wee sod that he is.'

Logan frowned. 'Goulding or Marks?'

'Bit of both.' She blew out a breath and sagged against the corridor wall. 'You want to know what we've got on the hunt for Skinner's kids? Sod all, *that's* what. Even with a massive search, there's no sign of the car anywhere. No one's seen it or the kids.' She covered her face with her hands, fingertips rubbing away at her temples. 'McHardy was right – they're dead, aren't they? Don't get them in the first twenty-four hours: they're dead. And it's been three days.'

'We'll find them. And we'll find them *alive*. All we need's one—'

A clipped voice cut through the corridor: 'Ah, *there* you are.' A cold smile followed the words, attached to an utter bastard in Police ninja black. Chief Superintendent Napier. His brogues were polished to dark mirrors, one pip and a crown glowing on his epaulettes. His hair glowed too, a fiery ginger that caught the overhead lighting like a Tesla coil. Napier spread his hands. 'And if it isn't Acting Detective Inspector McRae as well. Just the officers I need to talk to.'

Oh great.

Steel took a deep breath and held it.

Logan poked her. 'If it didn't work on the apprentice, it's not going to work on the Sith Lord, is it?'

A frown creased Napier's forehead. 'Sith…?'

She puffed out the air. 'This about Justin Robson?'

The smile widened and chilled. 'Indeed it is, Chief Inspector. Tell you what, why don't we start with you, and then move on to Acting Detective Inspector McRae? Call it privilege of rank.'

Some privilege. But Logan wasn't about to volunteer to go first.

He backed away down the corridor. 'Right. I'd … better get on with that investigation, then.'

Nice and slow to the corner, then run for it.

Logan wandered up the pavement, away from the knot of smokers kippering each other outside the Bon Accord Centre's George Street entrance. The ribbed, concrete, Seventies lump of John Lewis squatted in the sunlight like a big grey wart, facing off against a row of charity shops, a supermarket, and a pawnbroker's with ideas above its station.

He stuck a finger in his other ear, to shut out the wails of a passing toddler. 'You're sure? *Twenty* grand?'

'*I know, it's marvellous, isn't it? He's starting a property portfolio and thinks your flat's an excellent rental prospect. And the offer's unconditional. He's paying cash: we don't even need to do another Home Report!*' Marjory sounded as if she was about to pop the champagne. Eighteen months on the market, and it was going for twenty thousand over the asking price. Willkie and Oxford would probably give her a badge. And a hat. '*So, shall I tell him…?*'

'It's a deal.' An extra twenty grand would make a *huge* amount of difference.

'Wonderful. I'll get the paperwork drawn up and pop it in the post—'

'Actually, I can probably nip by and sign it. Get the ball rolling.' Before Mr Property Portfolio changed his mind. Or sobered up.

'Even better. Should be ready for you by lunchtime. We can—'

Logan walked away a couple of paces and lowered his voice. 'What about the moving date?'

'Well, standard terms are four weeks, but we can probably stretch that to a month and a half if you need time to—'

'No, I mean does it have to be that long? Can we make it a week, or ten days, or something?' Ten days – it'd be cutting it close, but at least he'd be able to afford the phase-one payment for Samantha's place at the care centre.

'Well, it's unusual, but I can try.'

'Please.' Logan waited till she'd hung up, then had a quick look around to make sure no one was watching before doing a little happy dance. Straightened his tie. Wandered back to the entrance and nodded at DS Baird. 'We good?'

She had one last sook on her cigarette, then nipped the end out and dumped it in the bin. 'Ahhh … I needed that.'

Logan pointed over her shoulder. 'Let me guess, Wheezy?'

Wheezy Doug paced the pavement in front of John Lewis, on his phone, head down, brow furrowed.

'Not this time.' She shook her head, then dug in a pocket for a packet of mints. 'Police Constable Allan "Sunshine" Guthrie. Got stuck with him for three hours this morning. I swear to God, Guv, if I hear the story of how he had a threesome with the cast of *Snow White* one more time, I'm going to kill him.'

'Understandable.'

Baird shuddered. 'I mean, can you imagine it?'

'Rather not.'

Wheezy Doug got to the end of the kerb and stopped,

head bowed over his phone, eyes screwed up. Then there was swearing and coughing. A gobbet of phlegm hit the gutter.

Baird shook her head. 'It's a miracle he's not been invalided out yet.'

Logan stuck his hands in his pockets. 'Steel thinks the kids are dead. We're looking for bodies.'

'Probably. You know what these selfish wee gits are like. Kills the wife, kills the kids, kills himself. If he's going to die, the rest of them have to too.' Her top lip curled. 'How could they *possibly* live without him?'

Wheezy stuffed his phone back in his pocket and lurched over, wiping his mouth with the back of his hand. Eyebrows down. Shoulders hunched. Hands curled into fists. 'Sodding goat-buggering hell.'

Baird grinned at him. 'Good news?'

'Postmortem result on Gordy Taylor. Pathologist says he'd scoofed down about a litre of rough whisky before he died: stomach was sloshing with it. Official cause of death is asphyxia caused by aspiration of regurgitated particulates.'

'Choked on his own vomit.'

'We knew that yesterday.' Logan folded his arms. 'So why all the swearing?'

'Lab's got a new piece of kit in, so they rushed through the tox report as an excuse to play with it. Gordy's blood was full of sleeping pills, painkillers, and ...' he checked his notebook then took his time pronouncing the word in little chunks, 'bro-ma-dio-lone.'

'What's that when it's at home?'

'It's a fancy way of saying "rat poison".'

The smile died on Baird's face. 'Poor Gordy.'

'According to the labs, it was probably soaked into whole grain wheat: you know the stuff they sell in tubs coloured bright blue? You use it to bait traps. Only Gordy didn't have

133

any wheat in his stomach, or in the puddle of vomit he was lying in.'

'That's all we need.' Logan let his head fall back and stared at the sky for a beat. A breath hissed out of him. The other stuff – the drugs – that was easy enough to explain. Gordy breaks into someone's house, raids their medicine cupboard, decides he fancies getting high on whatever he finds, it doesn't react well with the booze, he throws up and dies. But rat poison?

And what had Logan done when the poor sod had been hit by a car and assaulted? Blamed him for being a drunken idiot. Told him it was basically his own fault.

Wonderful: more guilt.

Logan squeezed it down with all the rest. 'Any ideas?'

Wheezy spluttered a bit. Then spat. 'Lab says if you dumped the rat bait in milk, water, or alcohol, you could leach the bromadiolone *out* of the poisoned wheat. And as his stomach was full of whisky...'

'So he drinks a bottle of supermarket McTurpentine laced with rat poison and dies.'

'Nope. Apparently, it takes a day, day and a half for bromadiolone to kick in. It thins the blood and causes internal bleeding – he'd have popped like a water balloon during the postmortem.'

Baird nodded. 'So whoever did it didn't know it'd take thirty-six hours. I mean, it's not suicide, is it? You don't kill yourself with rat poison, you kill other people.'

'Doesn't matter if he choked on his own vomit or not, he would've been dead by Wednesday anyway.' Wheezy's shoulders slumped an inch. 'Suppose it's not my problem any more then. Have to hand it over to the Major Investigation Team.'

Logan patted him on the shoulder. 'Welcome to Police Scotland.'

'Sod Police Scotland. I miss Grampian Police.'

'Better head back to the ranch and get the paperwork started.'

A sigh. 'Guv.' Then Wheezy slouched off.

Baird screwed up one side of her face. 'Rat poison.'

'Not our problem any more.' Logan pushed through into the shopping centre.

'Yeah, but still… It's a CID case, *we* should be the ones chasing it down.'

They marched past the juice bar and into one of the atrium spaces, queuing for the escalator behind a group of schoolkids in squint uniforms.

'That's the way things work now. Fighting it will get you nothing but ulcers. And possibly a reprimand, so—' Logan's phone launched into 'The Imperial March' as they glided slowly upwards. That would be Steel, calling up to whinge about Napier.

Baird raised an eyebrow and tilted her head at his pocket. 'You going to answer that?'

'Nope.'

'What if it's important? Maybe they've found Skinner's kids?'

As if they could be that lucky. But maybe Baird was right.

He pulled the phone out and hit the button as they hit the top of the escalator. 'What?'

Steel's voice was low and whispery. *'I need you to set off the fire alarm.'*

Typical.

'I'm not setting off the fire alarm.' Logan followed Baird past a couple of shops, then through a bland grey door marked 'STAFF ONLY'.

'Don't be a dick! Had to fake a dose of the squits so I could get away and phone you. Napier's lurking outside the ladies', making sure I don't do a runner. How untrusting is that?'

'I'm in the Bon Accord Centre.' His voice echoed back from the corridor walls. 'Doubt that setting off the fire alarm here's going to help you any.'

'You rotten sod! This is no time to do your shopping, get your puckered rectum back here and rescue me!'

A handful of doors sat at the end of the corridor. Baird knocked on the one with 'Security' on it.

'I can't come back, I'm *busy*.'

'Busy my sharny arse. If you don't get back here right now, I'm—'

Logan made a grating hissing noise. '... lo? Hello? Whhhhh...' More hissing. '... an you hear me? Hello?'

'How thick do you think I am?'

Ah well, it'd been worth a try. 'Look: I can't come back and rescue you, because I'm trying to find your missing kids. We're...'

There was a clunk, the security door opened an inch, and a little old lady in a brown peaked cap peered out. 'Can I help you?'

'Got to go.' Logan hung up and produced his warrant card. 'Police Scotland. We need to see Saturday's ANPR data for the Loch Street car park.'

'Oh.' She squinted at Logan's ID, then nodded. 'Better come in then.' She opened the door wide, revealing a turd-brown uniform with sweetcorn-coloured buttons and piping. 'You looking for anything specific?'

The room was small, lined with television monitors showing multiple views of the shopping centre. People going about their shoppy business, dragging stroppy toddlers and stroppier boyfriends behind them.

Baird took out her notebook. 'Dark-blue BMW M5, parked here sometime before two.' She rattled off the registration number as the old lady sank into a swivel chair and pulled a keyboard over.

Grey fingers flew across the keys. 'Of course, I should really be asking to see a warrant – data protection and all that – but it's my last day on Friday, so sod it.' A line of letters popped up on the screen. 'Here you go. Got it coming in at twelve oh three.'

Logan leaned on the desk. 'When did it leave?'

More lightning keystrokes. 'That's odd...' A frown, then she leaned forward and peered at the screen. Another frown. Then she put her glasses on. 'Oh, no – here we go. Left at three twenty-two.'

Over an hour and a half after John Skinner did his Olympic diving routine onto the cobblestones.

Baird wrote the details down in her notebook. 'We were right – he had an accomplice.'

Logan hooked a thumb at the bank of screens. 'Can you bring up the car park CCTV footage for then?'

The old lady's fingers clattered across the keys again, and half of the monitors filled with concrete, pillars, and cars. 'There you go.'

He flicked from screen to screen. 'Anyone see Skinner's car?'

'Guv?' Baird tapped one in the top left corner of the display. 'That not it there?'

A dark-blue BMW was heading down the ramp to the exit, only it wasn't doing it under its own steam, it was being towed by a truck with 'Abertow Vehicle Services – Parking Enforcement' stencilled along the side.

You wee beauty.

'Baird?'

'I'm on it.' She pulled out her phone, poked at the screen then held it to her ear as she pushed out of the room. 'Control? I need the number for a local company...'

The door swung shut, leaving Logan alone with the security guard.

She spooled the footage backwards, following the tow truck from camera to camera. 'So, what's this bloke supposed to have done?'

'Killed himself.'

'Poor wee soul.'

'But he killed his wife and kids first.'

The old lady pouted for a moment, then nodded. 'Well, in that case, however he committed suicide, I hope it bloody well hurt.'

15

Logan marched across the tarmac, mobile to his ear. 'I don't care if she's got an audience with the Queen's proctologist, get her on the phone. Now.'

'Oh dear...' A deep breath from PC Guthrie, then there was a thunk. A scuffing noise. And the crackle of feet hurrying down stairs.

Abertow's vehicle impound yard sat on the edge of the industrial estate in Altens. Rows of confiscated vehicles sat behind high chainlink fencing. Razorwire curled in glinting coils along the top. Big yellow warning signs hung every dozen feet or so, boasting about dirty big dogs patrolling the place. Should have been one about the seagulls too. They screeched and crawed in wheeling hordes, a couple of them squabbling across the top of a Nissan Micra that had been liberally spattered a stinking grey.

'Yeah, some people just couldn't give a toss.' The large man in the orange overalls tucked his hands into his pockets, the added strain threatening to burst the outfit apart at the groin. He pulled his huge round shoulders up towards his ears. Sunlight sparkled off his shaved head. 'It wasn't really parked, more like abandoned. Right in front of the emergency exit too. What if there'd been a fire?' A sniff. 'Doesn't bear thinking about, does it?'

Another thunk from the phone, then three knocks. Guthrie was barely audible. *'He's going to kill me…'*

What sounded like a door opening. Then a cold voice, slightly muffled by distance. *'This better be important, Constable.'* Napier.

Baird snapped on a pair of blue nitrile gloves, then ripped open the evidence bag with John Skinner's keys in it. The plastic fob for the BMW was cracked and stained with blobs of cherry red.

Guthrie cleared his throat. *'Sorry, sir. But I need to get a message to the Chief Inspector. Ma'am? It's DI McRae, says it's urgent.'*

Baird pointed the fob at the car and pressed the button. Nothing happened.

Napier didn't sound impressed. *'Constable, I think you'll find—'*

'Sunshine!' Steel's smoky growl got louder. *'I take back nearly everything I said about that lumpy misshapen head of yours. That for me? Come on then, give.'* A crackle as the phone was handed over.

Baird shook the keys and tried again. Still nothing.

'Detective Chief Inspector I must insist—'

'Don't think I'm no' enjoying our wee chat, sir, but operational priorities and all that.'

Baird gave up on the fob and stuck the key in the lock instead. *Clunk.* The central locking kicked in.

And Steel was full volume. *'Who dares interrupt my meeting with the glorious head of Professional Standards?'*

'It's—'

'What's that? It's an emergency? Dear God… No, don't worry: I'll be right there.' A sigh. Then the sound became muffled, as if she was holding the phone against her chest. *'Sorry, sir,*

much though I'd love to stay and chat, I gotta go. But we'll always have Paris!' The sound of Steel's boots clacking up the corridor, reverberated out of the phone. Making good her escape. *'Laz, what the hell took you so long?'*

'We've found John Skinner's car. He dumped it in the Loch Street car park and it got towed Saturday afternoon.'

'It got towed?' Some swearing rattled down the line. *'You tell those Automatic Number Plate Recognition idiots I'm going to bury my boot in their bumholes right up to the laces. They were supposed to check!'*

Baird ducked into the car and had a rummage in the BMW's footwells.

'Not their fault. The ANPR camera on George Street only gets traffic coming toward it. The tow truck was in the way.'

'Sod… Any clue where he dumped the kids?'

'Searching the car now. We need to get the SEB up here. See if they can pull fingerprints, or fibres, or something. Maybe get some soil off the floormats and wheech it off to Dr Frampton for analysis? See if she can ID where it came from.'

'Gah.' A click, then a sooking sound. *'Going to cost a fortune, but it's two wee kids we're talking about. If the boss wants to moan about budgets he can pucker up and smooch my bumhole.'*

Baird stood upright. Shook her head. 'Sorry, Guv. Loads of bloodstains and empty sweetie wrappers in there, but nothing obvious.'

Back to the phone. 'You hear that?'

'I'll scramble the Smurfs. And—'

'Guv?' A crease appeared between Baird's eyebrows. She pointed at the boot.

'—you to make sure everyone keeps schtum. I don't want—'

Logan squatted down and peered at the boot lid. A scattering of dark-red fingerprints marked the paintwork beneath the dust. A palm print in the middle, where you'd lean on it to slam it shut. He held his hand out. 'Give me the keys.'

141

'Keys? What keys? What are you talking about?'

Baird pulled off one of her gloves and turned it inside out over the BMW's fob, sealing it away. Then handed it over.

'Laz? What's going on?'

'Shut up a minute.' He placed his phone on the ground and put the key into the boot lock. Or tried to. There was something in the slot already – a wedge of metal, the end matt and ragged, as if someone had snapped a key off in there.

Making sure it couldn't be opened.

Oh sodding hell...

He looked up at Baird and tried to keep his voice level. 'There'll be a boot release in the car. Hit it.'

She stared at the boot. Then at him. Then the boot again. 'You don't think...' Baird grimaced. Then scrambled around to the driver's side and ducked in. A dull clunk came from the mechanism, but the boot remained firmly shut. 'Anything?'

'Try again.'

'Come on you little...'

Clunk. Clunk. Clunk.

Still nothing.

The big guy in the too tight overalls sniffed. 'Got a crowbar if you need it?'

'Thanks.' Logan picked up the phone as the yard supervisor lumbered off towards a bright-yellow Portakabin festooned with the Abertow logo. 'There's something in the boot.'

'What?'

'If I knew that I would have said.'

'Don't you get snippy with me, you wee—'

'Here.' Mr Overalls was back, carrying a long black crowbar covered in scars. He offered it to Baird, then hesitated, hand still wrapped around it. 'Here, do I need to see a warrant or something? You know, if you damage the guy's car—'

142

'He can sue me.' Baird pulled the crowbar out of Mr Overalls's hand. 'Might want to stand back, Guv.'

On the other end of the phone, Steel was shouting at someone to get the Scenes Examination Branch up to Altens ASAP, followed by various invasive rectal threats involving her boot, fist, and a filing cabinet.

Baird wedged the curved end of the crowbar in under the lip of the boot. 'One, two, three.' She humphed her weight down on the end. *Creak. Groan.* A squeal of buckling metal. Then *pop* and the boot lid sprang open.

The crowbar clattered to the tarmac.

Everyone stepped forward and stared down into the boot.

Then the smell hit. Rancid, cloying, sharp. It dug its hooks into the back of Logan's throat, clenched his stomach, curdled in his lungs.

'Oh God.' Mr Overalls slapped a hand over his nose and mouth, staggered off a dozen paces and threw up all over a Peugeot's bonnet.

Two small bodies lay curled on their sides in the BMW's boot. A little boy and a little girl. Heidi and Toby Skinner, barely recognizable. Sunken cheeks, cracked lips, electric cable wrapped around their wrists and ankles. Faces smeared with blood. Still and pale.

Baird chewed on her bottom lip. Looked away. 'You shouldn't have let him jump, Guv. You should've dragged that bastard down from the ledge so we could all kick the living *shite* out of him.'

Poor little sods.

Baird was right.

Logan let out a long shuddering breath. Stood upright. Squared his shoulders. Snapped on a pair of blue nitrile gloves. Cleared his throat. 'Denise, I need you to get on to the Procurator Fiscal. And we'll need the Pathologist. Better get the Duty Doctor out too.'

A nod. But she didn't turn around. 'Guv.'

Two little kids. How could *any* father do that?

Logan reached into the boot. Brushed the hair from little Heidi Skinner's face. Seven years old.

'Guv? You shouldn't touch them. The SEB need to take photos.'

A flicker. There. That was *definitely* a flicker.

You wee beauty!

Logan scooped Heidi out of the boot.

'Guv!' Baird grabbed his sleeve, voice low and hard. 'Have you lost your bloody marbles? The PF—'

'Get the car! Get the sodding car, now!'

16

Logan pulled on his jacket, then poked his head into the CID office. Wheezy Doug was hunched over the photocopier, jabbing at the buttons as if the machine had suggested his mother was romantically intimate with donkeys on a regular basis.

No sign of Stoney. But DS Baird was on the phone, elbows on the desk, one hand pressed to her forehead.

'Uh-huh. … Yeah. … OK, well, let me know.' She put the phone back in its cradle and looked up. 'Hospital says Heidi Skinner's responding well to the IV fluids. Just woke up.'

'What about Toby?'

'Heidi's freaking out. Three days, locked in a boot with your brother. In a car parked in the sunshine … I'd be freaking out too.'

'Denise: what about Toby?'

She puffed out her cheeks. Stared down at the phone. 'He was only six, Guv.'

'Sodding hell.' Something heavy grabbed hold of Logan's ribcage and tried to drag him down to the grubby carpet tiles. A deep breath. Then another one. 'I should've checked

145

the car park's ANPR sooner. I should've done it soon as we found out the car was missing. I should've…' He mashed his teeth together. Clenched his fists. Glowered at the filing cabinet. Then took two quick steps towards it and slammed his boot into the bottom drawer, hard enough to rattle the mugs and kettle balanced on top. Hard enough to dent the metal. Hard enough to really regret it five seconds later as burning glass rippled through his foot. 'Ow…'

'Three days.' Baird slumped further down in her seat. 'It's a miracle she's alive at all. Doctor said any longer and her internal organs would've started shutting down.'

Wheezy jabbed away at the photocopier again. 'Don't know about anyone else, but I'm going to the pub tonight and getting sodding wasted.'

Baird nodded. 'I'm in. Guv?'

Logan turned and limped back towards the door. 'I'll see you there. Got something to sort out first.'

Marjory stood up and held a hand across her desk for shaking. Her smile looked about as real as the potted plant in the corner. 'Mr McRae, I was beginning to think you'd changed your mind.'

Three walls of the office were covered with racks of schedules, complete with photographs of various bungalows, flats, and semidetatched rabbit-hutches in Danestone and Kincorth.

Logan settled into the chair on the other side of the desk. 'Been a rough day.'

'Well, not to worry, there's still time.' She dug into a tray on her desk and came out with a chunk of paperwork. Passed it across to him. 'As you'll see, there are no demands or conditions. They asked for a four-week entry date, but I went back to them with your proposal for ten days and they accepted.' The fake smile intensified. 'Now, if you need help finding a new property in a hurry, we'd be delighted to help you with that. We've got a lot of excellent homes on—'

'I've got something sorted, thanks.' Even if it was a static caravan, equidistant from Aberdeen's worst roundabout, a sewage treatment plant, and a cemetery. At least the chicken factory had moved somewhere else. That was something.

And ten days from now, Samantha would be getting the specialized care she needed. Everything else was just noise.

'Oh. Well, I'm sure you know best.' Marjory handed him a pen. 'If you sign where I've put the stickers, we'll get everything faxed over to Mr Urquhart's solicitors and that's that.'

Logan skimmed the contract, then scrawled his signature where the big pink stickers indicated.

'Excellent.' She took the paperwork back. 'Congratulations, Mr McRae, you've sold your flat.'

It should have been a moment of joy. An excuse to celebrate for a change. But after what happened to poor wee Toby Skinner?

Logan scraped back his chair and stood.

Time to go to the pub. Meet up with the team. And try to drink away the horror of two little bodies, locked in a car boot.

The celebration could wait.

— boxes, bins —
— and dead little bodies —

17

'Gah...' Steel pulled the e-cigarette from her mouth and made a face like a ruptured frog. 'Look at it. Could you no' have picked a better day to move?'

Rain rattled against the kitchen window. Wind howled across the extractor fan outlet – mourning the end of an era.

Logan wrapped a strip of brown parcel tape around the last box. 'Don't know what you're moaning about.' He printed 'BOOKS' across the top in big black-marker-pen letters, then put it with the other two by the front door. 'Not as if you've *actually* been helping.'

'Supervising's helping.'

'Not the way you do it.' Logan stuck the marker back in the pocket of his jeans.

His footsteps echoed from the laminate floor to the bare walls and back again as he checked the bedroom for the final time. Empty. Then the living room. Empty. Then the kitchen. Empty. And the bathroom. Every trace of him was gone – packed away over the last ten days and carted out to the removal van. Nothing but echoes and three packing boxes left to show he was ever there at all.

Steel slouched along behind him. 'You've got OCD, you know that, don't you? Place is cleared out.'

The front door clunked open and Duncan was back. Rain had darkened the shoulders of his brown boilersuit, plastered his curly fringe to his forehead. A smile. 'Nearly done.' He stacked two of the last boxes, hefted them up with a grunt, then headed back down the stairs again.

Logan turned on the spot. One last slow three-sixty.

No point being sentimental about it. It was only a flat. A container to live in. Somewhere to sleep and brood and occasionally drink too much.

Still...

Steel sniffed. Dug her hands into her pockets. Stared off down the corridor. 'Susan says you can always come stay with us for a bit, if you like. Don't have to be trailer trash, down by the jobbie farm.'

Logan grabbed the final box. 'It's a lovely offer. But can you imagine *you* and *me* living together? In the same house? Really?'

'No' without killing each other.'

He pulled a thin smile. 'Thanks though. Means a lot.'

She thumped him on the arm. 'Soppy git.' Then sniffed. 'Well, suppose I better get back to it. Got a rapist to catch.'

Logan followed her out onto the landing, then pulled the door shut with his foot. The Yale lock clunked. And that was it. No more flat.

Steel thumped down the stairs.

Look on the bright side: at least now he could pay for Samantha's care.

Deep breath.

He nodded, then followed her. 'Any closer to catching the scumbag who killed Gordy Taylor?'

'Pfff ... I wish. No' exactly doing my crime figures any good. Nearly a fortnight, and sod all progress.' They got to

152

the bottom and she held the building's front door open. Then screwed up one side of her face. 'Sodding hell. Going to get soaked.'

Rain bounced back from the grey pavement, darkened the granite tenement walls of Marischal Street. Ran in a river down the steep hill, fed by the overflowing gutters.

The removal van was parked right outside, the back door open as Duncan strapped the fridge-freezer to the wall.

Steel stayed where she was, on the threshold just out of the rain. Pulled a face, then dug into her coat and pulled out a copy of that morning's *Aberdeen Examiner*. A picture took up half of the front page – a smart young man, standing to attention, with medals on his chest and a beret on his head. 'War Hero "Let Down By Police" Say Grieving Parents'

She gave it a wee shake as rain drops sank into the newsprint. 'Apparently it's *our* fault he ended up dead behind the bins. Well, us and those shiftless sods in Social Services. Oh, and the NHS. Don't want to be greedy and claim *all* the guilt for ourselves.'

'What were we supposed to do?'

'Every morning it's like waking up and going for a sodding smear test.' She produced her phone and poked at the screen with a thumb. 'I've had two reviews, three "consultancy" sessions with a smug git from Tulliallan, supervisory oversight from Finnie *and* Big Tony Campbell, and we're no closer than we were when Gordy turned up dead behind the bins. Rennie's latest theory is we've got a serial killer stalking the streets, knocking off tramps.'

'Well...' A frown. 'He *could* be right, I suppose. Maybe?'

'After a heavy night on the Guinness – with a dodgy kebab, a box of Liquorice Allsorts, and a bag of dried prunes – I'd still trust a fart before I'd trust one of Rennie's theories. My bet? Gordy fell out with one of his mates and they poisoned him.' She hoiked up her trousers. 'That, or the silly

153

sod thought rat poison would be a great way to get high...'
Steel frowned at her phone. 'Buggering hell.' She held it
out. 'Speaking of DS Useless, look at that.'

        Guv. We got anuthr vctim 4U @ Cults.

        U cming Ovr??

        Wnt me 2 snd U a car??!?

'I swear, his spelling's getting worse.' She thumbed out a
reply. 'You sure you don't want me to transfer him back to
CID? Be a valuable addition to your team.'

'Bye.' Logan squeezed past her into the rain. Hurried
around to the back of the removal van and handed the box
of books up to Duncan. 'That's the lot, we're done.'

'Good stuff.' He put it with the others, strapped it into
place, then hopped down to the ground and hauled the
rolling door shut. 'Right. See you over there.'

Logan stepped back onto the pavement. Gave the van a
quick wave as it pulled away from the kerb and grumbled
its way up the hill.

Rain seeped into the shoulders of his sweatshirt.

Well, that was that then. Fourteen years in the same flat.
A stone's throw from Divisional Headquarters, two bakers,
three chip shops, and loads of good pubs. And now he'd
have to fight his way around the sodding Haudagain
Roundabout at *least* twice a day. Oh joy of joys. It was—

'Mr McRae?'

He turned, and there was Marjory from the solicitors,
sheltering beneath a golf umbrella with the firm's name
plastered around the outside.

Logan dug into his pocket and came out with the flat's
keys. 'Was on my way up to see you.'

154

She smiled her fake smile. 'That's very kind, but at Willkie and Oxford we want to make everything as easy as possible for you.' She held out her hand, palm up.

Fourteen years.

He passed her the keys.

'Excellent. Thank you.' She turned and waved at an Audi TT, parked a little bit up the hill. 'I'll give these to Mr Urquhart, and we're all done. Congratulations, Mr McRae, I hope you'll be very happy in your new home. And if you ever decide to sell it, I *do* hope you'll think of Willkie and Oxford.' One last go on the smile, then she marched up to the Audi.

The driver buzzed open the window and she bent down, had a brief chat, handed over the keys, shook his hand, then marched off towards Union Street.

Ah well, might as well head over to the caravan and get unpacking.

He unlocked his manky old Renault Clio. Pot plants and picture frames filled the back, but a large cat-carrier sat on the passenger seat – the seatbelt threaded through the handle on the top, bungee cords securing the whole thing into place.

Cthulhu pressed up against the carrier's door and yowled, a pitiful wailing noise that sank its claws in his chest. Her fur poked out through the bars in grey and brown tufts, one paw scratching at the hinge.

'I know, shhh … We'll be in our new home soon, I promise.' He slipped a finger between the bars and stroked her on the head. 'Shhh … it's OK. Daddy's here.'

There was a brief honk, and Logan peered out through the rain-rippled windscreen. The Audi had pulled into the space where the removal van used to be. Its driver grinned and waved at him.

The guy looked familiar. No idea why, though.

Logan gave Cthulhu another stroke. 'Wait here, Daddy will only be a minute.'

He climbed back out into the rain and closed the door on her tortured wails.

Mr Audi stepped out and popped a collapsible brolly up above his head. Expensive-looking black suit, lemon shirt open at the neck, neat brown hair, flashy stainless-steel watch. Couldn't have been much more than twenty, twenty-five tops. Little pockmarks covered both cheeks, the ghosts of acne past. He stuck out his hand. 'Mr McRae, no' seen you for ages, yeah?'

OK...

Logan took the proffered hand and shook it. Tilted his head to one side. Nope, still no idea. 'Mr Urquhart?'

He grinned again, showing off small white teeth separated by little gaps. 'It's the hair, isn't it? Finally grew out of dying it green. You like the suit?' He did a little catwalk two-step. 'Got it made special like.'

Green hair?

No. Couldn't be.

Logan squinted at him. 'Wait a minute. Urquhart. *Jonny* Urquhart?'

'Bingo!' He stuck a thumb up.

Oh sodding hell. No, no, no, no, no...

'You bought my *flat*?'

'Yeah.' He glanced up at the building. 'Cool, isn't it? Starting my own property empire. Mr Mowat says a man's got to put down proper business roots in the community.'

Christ. What if Professional Standards found out?

What if Napier found out he'd sold his flat to someone who worked for Wee Hamish Mowat, Aberdeen's biggest bloody crime lord? And if that wasn't bad enough, that they'd paid twenty thousand pounds over the asking price. *Twenty thousand* sodding pounds.

Logan took a couple steps away, then back again. 'You *can't* buy my flat! What the hell were you thinking?'

Jonny Urquhart's eyebrows went up. 'Eh? Steady on, it's win-win, right?'

'Win-win? WIN-WIN?' He threw his arms out. 'DO YOU HAVE ANY IDEA HOW THIS *LOOKS*?'

'Don't worry: the money's clean. Laundered to a crisp and shiny white.' He placed a hand against his chest, fingers spread, as if he was about to pledge allegiance to something. 'Mr Mowat gives me a bonus for my loyal service. You get your flat sold. And your girlfriend gets to go to a nice private hospital with excellent facilities. Win-win-win.'

'Oh God...'

He was screwed. Completely and utterly *screwed*.

18

First would come the investigation. Then the accusations. Then the recriminations. Prosecution. And eight to twelve years in Glenochil Prison with all the other bribe-taking dodgy police officers.

Oh God.

Logan closed his eyes and let his head fall back against the wall. 'Brilliant.' He gave it a little thump. Then a harder one. 'Sodding – bloody – brilliant.' Banging his head with every word.

Samantha's static caravan had developed its familiar peppery soil-and-dust scent again. The smell of mildew and neglect. Served him right for not coming down here and airing it out more often. Boxes filled the living room and the bedroom. More piled up in the tiny galley kitchen, with the mouse droppings. Green-brown slime growing in the shower cabinet and across the bathroom tiles. A lovely view across the river to the sewage treatment plant.

Welcome home.

But it was better than a cell.

Cthulhu clearly didn't agree. Her cat carrier sat on the

couch, amongst the pot plants, and she glowered out from its depths. Refusing to come out.

Logan let out a long, rattling breath.

Might be a good idea to head over to the B&Q in Bridge of Don and see if they had any anti-mildew paint, maybe a dehumidifier. And something to take away the *smell*.

And maybe just enough rope to hang himself.

'… *because we've got hundreds of bargains, bargains, bargains!*' Whoever was on the store's PA system, they needed battering over the head with a lump-hammer. Then stuffed in a sack with a couple of breezeblocks and dumped in the River Don. '*There's* massive *savings on tiles and laminate in our flooring department, right now!*'

Logan drifted along the aisle, hunched over his trolley. Phone to his ear, staring down at the three pots of paint, set of brushes, roller, and paint tray in there. 'There's no way? You're sure? I mean, a hundred percent positive?'

On the other end, Marjory sighed again. '*Mr McRae, we've been over this. Missives have been exchanged, money's changed hands. You signed the contract. You've handed over the keys. That's it done.*'

'But … there has to be a loophole, or something. People wriggle out of contracts all the time.' He turned the corner, slouching his trolley past burglar alarms and home CCTV systems. 'I checked with my bank, the cash hasn't come through yet, so he hasn't—'

'*Mr Urquhart paid cash: it's in our account. And as we're your legal representatives, the minute that money hit our bank account it's deemed to be paid to you. There's nothing you can do.*' A sigh. '*Now, I'm really going to have to go. The money will be in your account, less our fee, as soon as your bank clears our cheque. Goodbye, Mr McRae.*'

And she hung up on him. Unbelievable.

The CCTV systems gave way to locks and bolts. Then padlocks. Then chains and ropes. For all your wholesale bondage-dungeon needs.

Napier was bound to find out.

Then Logan would be screwed.

And probably in for a spanking.

He stopped. Stared at the paint. *Swore*.

It'd take at least three days for the solicitor's cheque to clear. Plus the ten days they'd already taken...

Oh sodding hell. And it was Friday. So the useless greedy sods at the bank wouldn't do anything about it till Monday.

Which would be fifteen days, in total, since Dr Berrisford at Newtonmyre Specialist Care Centre said he'd keep Samantha's bed open for two weeks.

Sodding, buggering, bloody hell.

He pulled out his phone and called Directory Enquiries. Got them to put him through to the centre. Maybe Dr Berrisford would give him a little leeway? He only needed a day. Twenty-four hours. *Surely* they could do that.

The phone rang.

Logan pushed his trolley around the corner, into an aisle lined on either side with hardware. Hammers. Pliers. Screwdrivers.

Still ringing.

A chirpy voice: '*Newtonmyre Specialist Care Centre, how can I help you today?*'

'I need to speak to Dr Berrisford. It's Logan McRae.'

'*Oh, I'm sorry, but Dr Berrisford has gone home for the weekend. Would you like to leave a message?*'

'Yes. Tell him...' Logan stared at the claw-hammers. 'Tell him I'll put the cheque for phase one in the post tomorrow. You should get it on Monday.' After all, it would take *their* bank three days to clear it as well, wouldn't it?

'*That's lovely. You have a good weekend, Mr McRae.*'

'You too.' He hung up.

Oh – thank – God. They'd take the cheque, Samantha could go into the care centre, everything would be fine.

All that panic, and there was nothing to worry about.

Clunk.

Logan's trolley jerked in his hand as someone collided into it. He looked up to apologize, even though he'd been standing perfectly still, and froze.

The man was huge, tall and wide, hands like bear-paws wrapped around his trolley's handle. Face a mixture of scar tissue and fat, stitched together by a patchy beard. A nose that was little more than a gristly stump. He pulled on a piranha smile. 'Well, well, well. Look who the cat coughed up.'

Logan swallowed. Stood up straight, shoulders back. 'Reuben.'

He'd lost a bit of weight since last time – but not enough to shrink that massive frame – and ditched his usual grubby overalls for a dark-grey suit. Blood-red shirt. No tie. 'Fancy running into you here. What are the chances, eh?'

Logan didn't move.

'Aye, well, maybe no' such a coincidence after all.' He reached out and plucked a crowbar from the rack beside him. Shifted his grip, then smacked the chunk of metal down into the palm of his other hand. 'What with me following you and everything.'

'Why?'

'See, I don't need to worry about you, do I?' *Smack.* 'Don't need to worry about you at all.' *Smack.*

Don't back off. Don't stare at the crowbar. 'Really.'

Reuben's trolley was stacked with rubble sacks. Duct tape. A bow saw. A hand axe. A box of compost accelerant. And a shovel. The smile graduated from piranha to great white. 'See, if you try to move against me –' *smack,* '– try to take

161

what's *mine* –' *smack*, '– I'm no' gonnae bother ripping your arms and legs off.' *Smack*. 'No' gonnae haul out your teeth and cut off your tongue.' *Smack*. 'Gouge out your eyes. Nah. Don't have to do any of that.'

There was something worse?

Reuben winked. 'All I've got to do, is clype.'

Something dark spread its claws through Logan's chest. 'Clype?'

'Oh aye.' He placed the crowbar in his trolley. 'What, you think Jonny came up with the idea to buy your flat all on his *own*?' A laugh barked out of that scar-ringed mouth. 'Nah. See, some people think I'm thick. Think I'm all about the violence and no' so much the brainpower. The planning. Nah.'

Oh sodding hell. Sodding, *buggering* hell.

The claws dug in deeper.

'See, McRae, I own you. Get in my way and I'll squash you like a baby's skull. When Mr Mowat passes, I'm stepping up. And then we can talk about what kinda favours you're gonnae do me to stay out of jail.' One last wink, then Reuben walked his trolley past. Whistling *The Dam Busters* theme tune.

Something happened to Logan's knees. They didn't want to hold him upright any more.

Reuben knew. *Reuben*.

No, no, no…

Oh God.

He rested his chest against the trolley's handlebar. Let it take the weight for a bit. Closed his eyes.

Agh…

Think.

There had to be a way out of this.

OK, so he couldn't break the contract. At least there was a chance of proving that he'd *tried* to. Get Marjory from

Willkie and Oxford up on the stand and question her under oath. *'Yes, Mr McRae tried to weasel his way out of the contract.'* That would help, wouldn't it?

Might cut a year or two off his sentence...

Oh God.

Why did it have to be *Reuben*?

He was completely and utterly screwed.

A woman's voice: 'Are you OK?'

Deep breath.

Logan blinked a couple of times. Straightened up. 'Sorry. Having a bit of a day.'

She was tiny, with long red hair and round freckled cheeks. According to the name badge pinned to her bright-orange apron, this was Stacey. Stacey smiled at him. 'Anything I can help you with?'

He sighed. Pulled out the envelope he'd jotted everything down on and frowned at it. 'Mildew, damp stuff, paint, mice, and something to clean grout with.' He held the list out.

'Right, OK. Well, we can cross out "paint". Is your damp coming through a wall, or is it condensation?'

'Condensation. Probably. Maybe.'

'Right, follow me then!' She led the way, down to the end of the aisles, then over another two.

Maybe he *should* take Wee Hamish up on his offer after all? If Reuben was face down in a shallow grave, he couldn't tell anyone, could he? Or better yet – fed to the pigs. They wouldn't care how ugly he was, they'd chomp through flesh and bone, leaving nothing but Reuben's teeth behind.

Stacey came to a halt, and swept a hand up. 'Here we go.' The shelves were filled with bottles, jars, sprays, and tubs, beneath a sign marked 'DAMP, MOULD, AND MILDEW CONTROL'.

She scanned the rows of products. 'You're going to need some of this...' She hefted a ten-litre pot of anti-mould paint into the trolley. Added a second one. 'Just in case. Nothing worse than getting halfway through a job and having to come back.'

Mind you, might be a better idea to go DIY with Reuben too. The more people who knew, the more chance of getting caught. Wee Hamish wasn't going to kill his right-hand man himself, was he? In the old days, maybe. But now? Lying on his back, wired up to drips and monitors, being devoured by cancer? He'd have to farm it out.

Stacey grabbed half a dozen plastic tubs containing silica gel that promised to suck moisture out of the atmosphere. 'You want to keep these in the cupboards where the mildew is.' She checked the list again. 'Right: grout cleaner.'

Maybe he should head back and pick up a crowbar of his own? Or a lump hammer. Something to crack Reuben's head open with. Too risky trying to get his hands on a gun…

Who was he trying to kid?

He couldn't kill Reuben. Couldn't.

That hollowed him out, left him standing there in the middle of B&Q, with a hole in his chest the size of a watermelon.

He was going to prison…

Oh God.

Stacey teetered down the aisle a bit and plucked a spray bottle from a shelf. 'That should help. So I think that leaves "mice", right? You want to keep them as pets, or get rid of them?'

'Rid.' Then again, why bother? Why do up a manky static caravan, when he was going to spend the next eight years in a cell anyway?

'Follow me.'

Two aisles along she stopped and pointed. 'We've got humane traps, normal traps, and *in*humane traps.' She picked up a couple of plastic things that looked as if they could take a finger off. 'These are pretty much instant death, so the mouse won't suffer much.'

Lucky mice. A quick and painless death…

Might not be a bad idea. He could jump off something tall, like John Skinner. Ten storeys, straight down. Goodbye cruel world. Splat.

'These are the humane ones.' She held up what looked like a small, bent, rectangular telescope. 'They get stuck inside, and can't get out. Then you drive at least four miles away and release them into the wild.' Her mouth turned down at the ends. 'Or you could go inhumane and poison them.' She poked a box marked 'Bait Station Bravo!' with a finger.

Sitting next to it was a tub with a red lid and a warning sticker across the top and 'BROMADIOLONE-TREATED WHOLE WHEAT' down the side.

Rat poison.

Logan picked it off the shelf. Turned it over in his hands. The contents hissed against the plastic innards.

'My bet? Gordy fell out with one of his mates and they poisoned him.'

No chance. What, someone living on the streets marched into B&Q, bought themselves a thirty-quid tub of this stuff, then a litre of whisky, mixed them together and let them sit till the poison was all leached out, put it back in the bottle, and gave it to Gordy Taylor as a gift? Why not drink the whisky yourself and batter his head in with the empty bottle? Why go to all that trouble?

'Rennie's latest theory is we've got a serial killer stalking the streets, knocking off tramps.'

Yeah, but Rennie was an idiot.

But there *was* something a lot more likely. What if—

'Hello? Excuse me?' Stacey was tugging at his sleeve.

Logan blinked at her. 'Sorry, miles away.'

She shook her head. 'You've got a cat, haven't you? I can tell by the hairs all over your jeans.' Stacey looked up at him, still holding on to his arm. 'If it was me, if I had a cat, I wouldn't want poisoned mice staggering around the house looking to get caught and eaten. Would you?'

'Ah...' He slid the tub back onto the shelf. 'No.'

Then stopped, fingertips just touching the label.

Poisoned mice staggering around.

All you have to do is put the stuff where they can find it. They eat it, because it's in their nature to eat whatever they can get their paws on. It's what mice do. Make the poison tasty enough and they'll do all the hard work for you...

Stacey tugged at his sleeve again. 'Are you sure you're OK?'

Logan grabbed four of the finger-snappers. 'Thanks for your help: gotta go.' Then marched the trolley away to the tills.

'Guv?' Wheezy paused for a cough. *'Thought you were having a day off.'*

The Clio crawled along the Parkway, around the back of Danestone in the rain. Fields on one side, identikit houses on the other, with a long slow-moving clot of rush-hour traffic in-between.

It was only four thirty-five. All these sods should still have been at work instead of clogging up the bloody roads.

Logan switched the phone to his other ear and put the car in gear again. Easing forward another six feet as the windscreen wipers groaned across the glass. 'When we did the door-to-doors on Harlaw Road, did you check everyone's alibis?'

'Guv?'

'When Gordy Taylor died. We questioned all the residents

166

– did someone chase up the alibis? Was everyone where they said they were?' A gap had opened up in front of the Nissan he was grinding along behind – had to be at least three car-lengths and the silly sod in front still hadn't moved. Logan leaned on the horn. 'COME ON, GRANDAD!'

'But…'

'Not you, Wheezy, this pillock in front.'

'It wasn't a murder when we were in charge, it was a sudden death. There wasn't any reason to check. Then the MIT took it over.'

The Nissan finally got its bum in gear and they all inched forward a bit.

'What about Steel's team then, did they check alibis?'

'Er, hold on.' There was some clunking and rattling. The cars drifted forward another two lengths. Rustling. A thump. Then the sound of fingers punishing a keyboard, and Wheezy was back. *'Right. According to the system, pretty much everyone was home that night. A couple families were at the cinema, two went to the theatre, and one guy was on a works night out. Looks like the MIT followed up and everything checked out. Why?'*

'Thinking.' Logan tapped the fingers of his free hand along the top of the steering wheel. 'What if DCI Steel's right, and Gordy *did* poison himself? Just not on purpose. He thinks his ship's come in – a whole litre of whisky, all to himself. So he crawls off behind the bins and swigs it down. But he doesn't know it's laced with bromadiolone.'

Someone behind leaned on their horn, and Logan looked up to see a four car-length gap between himself and the Nissan in front. Another *bleeeeeeeeeep*.

Impatient git.

Logan eased forward into the space. 'Did you get any prints off the bottle?'

'What bottle?'

'The bottle of whisky Gordy drank: did you get finger-prints?'

167

'*There wasn't one. Don't think so, anyway.*' The rattle of fingers on a keyboard sounded in the background. '*Nothing got signed into evidence.*'

They'd finally reached the corner where the Parkway turned downhill towards the Persley roundabout. The traffic snaked away in a solid ribbon ahead, trapped single-file by the double white lines protecting the overtaking lane on the other side of the road. And once he'd managed to fight his way through all this, there would be the Haudagain. And then Anderson Drive to traverse. At rush hour. It would take hours.

Maybe not though.

A patrol car was coming the other way, up the hill. He flashed his lights at it, leaned on his horn ... but they drove right past. Didn't even clock him on his mobile phone. Lazy sods.

'Wheezy, I need you to get onto Control, tell them...'

Blue lights flickered in his rearview mirror. The patrol car was doing a three-point turn.

'*Guv?*'

'Never mind. Meet me where they found the body, and make sure you bring some photos of Gordy Taylor with you.'

The patrol car pulled up alongside, lights flickering. The officer in the passenger seat wound down his window. 'Sir, do you know it's an offence to use your mobile phone while—'

'Murder enquiry.' Logan flashed his warrant card. 'Get the blues-and-twos on. You're escorting me to Harlaw Road.' Nothing happened. '*Now*, Constable.'

The officer blinked a couple of times. 'Yes, Guv.'

And they were off: siren roaring, lights blazing, carving a path through the oncoming traffic with Logan's manky old Clio puttering along behind.

19

'And they searched all round here?' Logan pointed at the bushes behind and on either side of the council's communal bins.

Wheezy nodded, rain drumming on the skin of his black umbrella. 'Far as I know. Got a couple of condoms and some litter, but that was it.'

No empty whisky bottle.

Harlaw Road huddled beneath the slate-grey sky, all the colours muted by the downpour. The patrol car sat at the kerb, blue-and-whites spinning. A few of the residents stood in their front rooms, ogling out at the spectacle. But none felt the need to step out into the wet to satisfy their curiosity.

Logan brushed his hands on his jeans. 'You've got the photos?'

Wheezy held them up. 'We already did this, Guv.'

'Then we're doing it again, aren't we?' He led the way up the path to the house directly opposite where they'd found Gordy Taylor's body. Leaned on the bell.

A tall woman, stooped forward by a rounding between her shoulder blades, peered out at them with sharp features. 'Yes?'

Wheezy showed her two photos. One from way back, when Gordy was still in the army. A confident young man with a broad smile and shiny eyes, sitting on the bonnet of a military Land Rover. The other photo was from the ID database, the one they used to make books to show witnesses with a height chart in the background – long greasy hair and an unkempt beard, the shiny eyes turned narrow and suspicious, sunken into dark bags. 'You seen this man?'

She barely glanced at the pictures – stared at the patrol car instead. 'Do you have any idea what this is doing to property prices round here? Dead bodies, policemen, *journalists*.' The last word was pronounced as if it smelled of raw sewage.

Wheezy tried again. 'Have you seen him?'

'*Yes*, I *recognize* him. He was the dead tramp they found over there. His face was in the papers. Now if there's nothing else, I've got to get the dinner on.'

Logan stepped a bit closer. The porch was tiny, but it kept some of rain off his head. 'Take another look.'

She shook her head, setting a severe brown bob wobbling. 'Don't need to. It was horrible. I mean the smell, and the shouting, and *oh, my God*, the singing. Well, if you could call that singing, I certainly couldn't. It was like someone drowning parrots in the bath, it really was, and the *language*! Don't speak to me about the language he used.' She sniffed. Snuck a glance at the patrol car. Lowered her voice. 'I know we're not supposed to speak ill of the dead, but he made life unbearable for everyone. I mean, there are people here with small children! Well, it's not wholesome, is it?'

The man in the suit frowned at the photos in Wheezy's hand for a bit, then nodded. 'It's that poor sod, isn't it? The one who drank himself to death behind the bins.' A tut.

170

A wee voice sounded in the hallway behind him. 'Daddy, you're missing *Peppa Pig*!'

He turned. 'I'll be there in a minute, darling. Daddy's speaking to the nice policemen right now.' And back to Logan. 'It's a terrible thing, isn't it? Of course, I blame society. These people don't need Care in the Community, they need proper medical help...'

The woman blinked a couple of times, brushed a strand of grey hair away from her face. Then pulled on her glasses and had a good squint at the photographs, deepening the lines around her eyes. 'Oh dear. He was such a wholesome looking young man.' She took off her glasses and let them dangle on the chain around her neck. Then stared back at Logan. 'I'm so sorry. I really am.'

She didn't glance over his shoulder at the patrol car with its spinning lights. Kept her eyes on Logan instead.

He tilted his head to one side. Why did she look familiar?

Right – she was the nosy old bat pretending to prune her rosebush the first time he was there. The one with the double-glazing van parked outside. The one who'd called the police to complain about Gordy Taylor three times in one week.

'You weren't very happy about him being here, were you, Mrs...?'

'Please, call me Olivia.' A blink. 'And no, I wasn't really. Would you be?'

Logan pulled on his brightest smile. 'Sorry to bother you, Olivia, but is there any chance my Detective Constable could use your toilet? Standing out in the rain, you know how it is.'

She moved to block the door. Then pursed her lips. And pulled on a smile of her own. 'No, of course. Do come in.' She backed away, top lip curling slightly as Logan and

Wheezy Doug stepped over the threshold and dripped on the polished floorboards. 'First on the right.'

The hallway was beige, with a smattering of photographs and a framed poster advertising a railway journey from the fifties. Panel doors. A dado rail.

Wheezy excused himself and squeezed past, into the downstairs loo.

Logan gave it a pause, then clapped his hands together. 'Don't suppose there's any chance of a cup of tea as well?'

The smile brittled. 'Of course. Where are my manners.'

She led him through to an immaculate kitchen. More beige. A large, stripy, ginger cat lay full length along the radiator, tail twitching. The cat turned and peered at him with emerald eyes.

Logan closed the kitchen door. 'Lovely home you have here.'

'Thank you.' The kettle went on, and three china mugs appeared from a cupboard. 'My Ronald was in the building trade for years, so we were able to get a lot of things done.'

A creak from outside, in the corridor. That would be Wheezy going for a poke about.

Logan raised his voice a bit to cover the noise. 'I like the patio doors. Very stylish.'

The white PVC monstrosities overlooked a perfect lawn, lined with perfect bushes, and perfect apple trees groaning with fruit. A nice little seating area, with a wrought-iron table, four chairs, and a barbecue.

'They're French doors, not patio.' She dumped teabags in the mugs. 'Patio doors slide, French doors are hinged.'

'My mistake.' He tried the handle. They weren't locked, so he pulled the door open, letting in the hiss of rain through the leaves. 'Very swish. Look brand new.'

'Yes, well.' She curled her lip again. 'We had to get them replaced.'

'Ah, right.' The only thing *not* perfect about the lawn was the pigeon staggering along the fenceline. One wing flapping, head lolling. 'I saw the glazier's van. Was it an accident?'

The kettle's rumble hit its crescendo, then *click*, it fell silent.

Olivia brought her chin up. 'Someone tried to break in.'

'I see.' He stepped over to the ginger cat and ran a hand along its back. The tail went straight up, then the cat hopped down from its radiator and sauntered towards the open French doors. Paused to stretch with its bum in the air. 'Did you report anything? Any stolen property? Ooh, I don't know … Sleeping pills, painkillers, big bottle of whisky – that kind of thing?'

Her back stiffened. 'I don't think I like your tone.'

Logan nodded toward the mugs. 'Just milk for me, thank you. Detective Constable Andrews is milk and three: he's got a sweet tooth.'

She put the kettle back on its base unit. 'I think I'd like you to go now.'

'What did you do with the empty whisky bottle?' He narrowed his eyes. 'No, let me guess: it went out with the recycling.'

The ginger cat slipped out into the rain and padded across the lawn, making straight for the struggling pigeon.

Colour rushed up Olivia's cheeks. 'Now look what you've done!' She pushed past him, through the patio doors, sandals slapping on the wet paving slabs. 'Paddington! You come back here this instant, young man!'

The cat didn't seem to care. It hunkered down on its front legs, bum wiggling in the air, then pounced.

'NO!' Olivia lunged, but she was too slow to grab Paddington before he crashed his orange-stripy weight down on top of the pigeon. 'Don't you dare eat that!'

Logan stepped out into the garden as she wrestled the pigeon away from her cat.

'Dirty! Bad Paddington!'

An outraged meow, then Paddington turned and stalked off to lurk under the bench by the back wall.

The pigeon may have been half-dead to begin with, but it was all-the-way dead now. It dangled in Olivia's hands, head swaying on the end of its neck like a soggy pendulum.

'Honestly.' She glowered after the cat. 'You *know* these make you sick.' Then Olivia yanked the lid off the dustbin and dumped the dead little body inside. Clanged the lid shut again.

Logan stared at the bin.

Stacey looked up at him, still holding on to his arm. 'If it was me, if I had a cat, I wouldn't want poisoned mice staggering around the house looking to get caught and eaten. Would you?'

'The pigeons make him sick?'

Olivia pulled her shoulders back. 'That's why I don't let Paddington eat them. They're foul little things; who knows where they've been?' She sniffed. 'Why those idiots next door insist on feeding them, is beyond me. They don't even *like* pigeons.'

The idiots next door – Mr Sensitive, with his Peppa Pig obsessed little girl.

Logan crossed to the fence and peered into the adjoining garden.

A bird table poked out of the lawn. Not your standard wee house on a stick, this was a fancy wrought-iron thing with different levels, all suspended around a central pole. One layer had a wide, round base and a pitched roof over it to keep the bird feed dry. Whole wheat birdseed, from the look of it. Whole wheat and bright blue.

He turned and hurried back into the house. Banged his hand on the kitchen door as he barrelled through it. 'WHEEZY! WE'VE GOT THE WRONG HOUSE!'

20

Logan leaned on the bell again while Wheezy dragged the two officers from the patrol car. One blinking and scrubbing at her face as if she'd been catching a nap in the passenger seat.

The door popped open, as they started up the path.

Mr Sensitive pulled on his smile. 'Can I help you?'

Logan wedged his foot in the open door, stopping it from closing. Stared back. 'We know.'

The smile slipped. Then fell. Mr Sensitive licked his lips. 'Really? That's…' He cleared his throat. 'I have no idea what you're talking about.'

'Rat poison and whisky.'

A breath huffed out of him. Then he clicked his mouth shut. Blinked at the police officers looming in front of his house. Swallowed.

The same little voice sounded in the hall behind him. 'Daddy, you're *missing* it!'

Fingers trembled across his lips. 'Oh God…'

'Daddy!'

'I think you'd better come with us, don't you, sir?'

He closed his eyes and swore.

*　*　*

Mark Cameron stared down at his hands – coiled into claws on the interview room table. The skin nearly as pale as the white Formica top. 'Does my daughter have to know?'

Logan shrugged. 'Probably. It's going to be in the papers. On the news. Someone will say something.'

A shudder. 'I don't want her to know.'

The camera lens stared down at them, the red light glaring in judgement.

'Are you sure you don't want a lawyer, Mark?'

A nod.

'For the record, Mr Cameron is nodding his head.'

A deep breath, then he spread his claws. 'That … *man* was hanging out on the street for days. Going through the bins. Shouting. Swearing. Singing. Then one day he pushed Jenny off her bike. Probably didn't do it on purpose, probably too drunk to know *what* he was doing, but he did it.'

Logan folded his arms. 'Is that why you killed him, Mark? Because he hurt Jenny?'

Cameron shook his head. 'I was…' He blinked. Wiped the back of one hand across his eyes. 'We were asleep. Must've been about two in the morning, when there's this crashing noise. And Angie's convinced someone's in the house.'

The digital recorder whirred away to itself.

Outside in the corridor, someone laughed.

A car drove by.

Then Mark Cameron licked his lips. 'So I got up. And it was *him*. Broke one of the conservatory windows and got into our house.' Mark looked away. 'He was outside Jenny's room when I found him and I lost it. I punched him and kicked him and kicked him and stamped on his filthy head…' A shuddering breath. 'I wanted to *kill* him. But I couldn't. Not like that. Not like an animal.'

What was probably meant to be a smile twisted Cameron's face. 'So I apologized. I *begged* him not to report me to the police. And I gave him something for the pain – stuff Angie gets for her migraines.'

This time the pause didn't last for nearly as long. 'Only that wasn't enough, was it? Next day he came back demanding more painkillers. And booze. The day after that too. And the next. Every evening, there he'd be with his hand out.' Mark Cameron closed his eyes. 'I couldn't kill him like an animal, because he wasn't an animal – he was *vermin*. And we all know what you use to kill vermin.'

'Well?' DCI Steel was waiting outside Interview Room Number Three, one hand jammed into her armpit, an e-cigarette poking out the corner of her mouth.

Logan closed the interview room door, shutting out the sobbing. Then started down the corridor. 'Didn't have to burst him, he burst himself.'

'He *definitely* killed Gordy Taylor?'

'Got it all on tape.'

'Ya beauty.' She slammed a hand into Logan's back. 'Well done, that man! I'm impressed.'

'I'm going home. Get some unpacking done.'

'Don't be daft.' Steel linked her arm through his, gave it a little squeeze. 'You've got to celebrate! Big win like this calls for something special. Like a bit of quality daddy–daughter time.' A wink. 'Susan's taking me out to see a film. Don't know when we'll be back, but don't wait up, eh? Might get lucky in the back seat of the cinema.'

Logan stopped in the middle of the corridor, stared up at the ceiling and swore. 'I just moved house; I *need* to unpack.' And to sit in the dark for a bit, drinking whisky and trying to figure out what the hell he was going to do about Reuben.

'Nah, what you need's a pizza, a tenner, a bottle of red wine, and to babysit your daughter.' She gave his arm another squeeze. 'You ever watched *Peppa Pig*?'

'Oh God...'

DI Steel's Bad Heir Day

December 23rd

'Sod...' DI Steel stood on one leg in the doorway, nose wrinkled up on one side. 'Thought I smelt something.' She ground her left foot into the blue-grey carpet, then dragged it along the floor behind her as she lurched into the briefing room: a hunchless wrinkly Igor in a stain-speckled grey trouser suit. Today, her hair looked like she'd borrowed it from an angry hedgehog.

DC Allan Guthrie chucked another spoon of coffee in a mug and drowned it with almost boiled water. Topped it up with milk, and bunged in a couple of sugars. No point asking if she wanted one. 'Guv?'

She stopped, mid-scrape. Standing completely still. Not looking at him.

Half past four and the CID room was quiet, everyone off dealing with Christmas shoplifters and snow-related car crashes, leaving the little maze of chest-high cubicles and beech-Formica desks almost deserted. The whole place smelled of feet and cinnamon.

Allan dumped the teaspoon on the draining board. DI Steel just stood there, like one of those idiots who appeared every summer outside the St. Nicholas Centre, spray-painting themselves silver and pretending to be statues.

He cleared his throat. 'Guv, is everything OK?'

Someone's phone rang.

Allan cleared his throat.

She still hadn't moved.

'Guv?'

Not so much as a twitch.

'Guv, you all right?'

'If I stay really still you can't see me.'

Mad as a fish.

'OK...' He held out the mug. 'Two and a coo.'

She sighed, shoulders drooping, arms dangling at her sides. 'See, this is what I get for no' bunking off home after the Christmas shopping – accosted by chunky wee police constables.'

'I'm *not* chunky. It's a medical condition.'

'It's pies.' She took the coffee, sniffed it, then scowled up at him. 'I just stood in something that smells better than this.'

He pulled the envelope from his pocket – a thick, ivory, self-sealing job with the DI's name in spidery script on the front. 'Courier dropped it off about ten.'

'Don't care.' She snatched a roll of sticky-tape from the nearest desk, turned on her heel, jammed her shoe down again, and lurched back towards the door. 'Two hours of fighting grumpy auld wifies for the last pair of kinky knickers in Markies has left me all tired and emotional. Soon as I've finished pinching everyone's Sellotape, I'm offski. Taking the wee one to the panto tonight and there's no way in hell I'm going sober.'

Allan waggled the envelope at her. 'Looks kinda important.'

She stuck her fingers in her ears, singing as she scraped her shoe across the carpet tiles. 'Jingle Bells, Finnie Smells, Rennie's hair is gay...'

Detective Constable Rennie stuck his head up above his

purple-walled cubicle, blond mop jelled into spikes, eyebrows pinched together in a frown. 'Hey, I heard that!'

Steel disappeared down the corridor, still doing her Quasimodo impersonation. Then came the slam of an office door. Then silence.

Woman was an absolute nightmare.

Allan slipped the envelope back in his pocket. Just have to try again tomorrow when she was in a better mood. That was the thing about detective inspectors, you had to manage them like little children, or they stormed off in a huff and spent the rest of the day thinking up ways to make your life miserable.

A thump echoed out from the other side of the CID door, then an angry voice: 'Aw, for... Who made sharny skidmarks all over the carpet?'

December 24th – Christmas Eve

DI Steel's office looked like Santa's grotto... Assuming Santa worked in a manky wee room with greying ceiling tiles, a carpet covered in little round burn marks, and a desk festooned with teetering stacks of forms and folders. The three filing cabinets lined up along one wall were topped with stacks of presents, all wrapped in brightly coloured paper by someone who obviously favoured enthusiasm and sticky tape over skill.

The inspector was behind her desk, fighting with a roll of dancing-penguin paper and a big cardboard box.

Allan knocked on the doorframe. 'Guv?'

She peeled an inch-long strip of Sellotape from the corner of her desk, and forced down a flap of wrinkly penguins. 'I'm no' in.'

'Got a memo from the boss.' He pulled it out of the folder and held it up.

Another strip of tape. 'Well? Don't just stand there looking like a baked tattie: read it.'

Allan did.

She scowled at him. 'Out loud, you idiot.'

'Oh, right. "To all members of staff – the cleaners have lodged a complaint about the state of the carpets in the CID wing. If I catch whoever it was that wiped dog—"'

'Blah, blah, blah. Anything else? Only I'm up to my ears in urgent police work here.' She tore off another length of tape.

'Yeah, you've got a missing person.' Allan dumped the mis-per form on the inspector's desk, next to a bright-yellow Tonka tipper truck. 'Mrs Griffith says her husband—'

'Give it to Biohazard or Laz.' She gave the box another lashing of sticky tape. 'Better yet, palm it off on those shiftless layabouts in GED. No' like they've got anything better to do, is it?' She stuck out a hand. 'Pass us the scissors.'

Allan did. 'DS McRae and DS Marshall aren't in today – firearms refresher – and General Enquiry Division's already passed: they say it's a CID case.'

'Typical.' Steel's tongue poked out of the corner of her mouth as she snipped a raggedy line through the wrapping paper, disembowelling half a dozen penguins in the process. 'How come I'm the only one round here who ever does any work?'

Allan just stared at her.

She narrowed her eyes. 'Cheeky sod.' The parcel went on the floor, then Steel dug into a green-and-white plastic bag and produced a set of something lacy and skimpy. More paper. More sticky tape.

He pulled out the thick ivory envelope with its spidery script. 'There's this too.'

Steel held out her hand. 'Give.' She grabbed it off him, ripped it open, and squinted at the contents, moving the letter back and forward, as if that was going to help.

'You want to borrow my glasses?'

'I don't *need* glasses. How come no one can write properly anymore? It's like a spider got blootered on tequila, then threw up green ink everywhere.'

'So what do you want to do about this missing person?'

'You know what kind of person uses green ink? Nutters, that's who. Nutters, freaks and weirdos.' She chucked the letter across the desk at him. 'Read.'

'Erm...' The whole thing was packed with almost impenetrable legalese, but it was just about understandable. 'It's from a law firm on Carden Place. Says you've been left a chunk of cash in someone's will.'

The inspector sat upright, a smile rearranging the wrinkles on her face. 'How much?'

'Doesn't say. They want you to go into the office and discuss it.'

'Well, whoever's snuffed it, they better be rich.' She picked up her phone. 'Give us the number.'

Allan read it out and she dialled, swivelling back and forth in her seat, singing 'I'm in the Money' while it rang. Then stopped. Licked her lips. 'Aye, hello, this is Detective Inspector Roberta Steel, you sent me a... Uh-huh... Uh-huh... Yeah, terrible tragedy. How much?' Silence. Her eyes widened. '*Really*?' The smile turned into a grin. 'Oh, yes, aye, couldn't agree more... Uh-huh... Yeah, one thing though: who is it? Who died?' And the grin turned into a scowl. 'I see. Excuse me a moment.' Then she slammed the phone down and embarked on a marathon swearing session. Threw her Sellotape across the room. Banged her fist on the desk. Swore and swore and swore.

Allan fiddled with the folder and waited for her to finish. 'Good news?'

'Don't you start.' She snatched the letter back, crumpled it up into a ball, and hurled it into the bin. Then spat on it.

'So … missing person?'

'All right, all right – missing person. Honestly, you're worse than Susan. Nag, nag, nag. Go get a car, we'll pay Mrs … Gifford? Guildford?'

'Griffith.'

'Right. Get a car and we'll pay Mrs *Griffith* a visit.' Steel thumped back in her chair, face all pinched, jaw moving like she was chewing on something bitter. 'Maybe stop off for a few messages on the way.'

Allan sat in the driver's seat, hands wrapped around the steering wheel, gritting his teeth every time someone blared their horn at him. They'd made it as far as the Trinity Centre before Steel had slammed her hand on the dashboard and told him to pull in for a minute. That was half an hour ago.

The car's hazard lights blinked and clicked, digging orange knives into his forehead.

A loud BREEEEEEEEEP! sounded behind him, then again. And again. Then a bus grumbled past, sending up a spray of grey-brown slush to spatter against the pool car's windows. A couple of the passengers gave him the two-finger-salute on the way past.

Like traffic on Union Street wasn't bad enough at the best of times. A thick rind of dirty white was piled up at the edge of the kerb, the road covered in a mix of compacted snow, ice and filthy water. Pedestrians slithered by on the pavement, bundled up in thick coats, scarves, and woolly hats, fresh snow coating their shoulders like frozen dandruff. Every now and then someone would stop and stare into the car, as if it was *his* fault he was stuck here, holding up the rotten traffic.

Soon as Steel got back he was going to give her a piece of his mind. Put her in her place. Let her know this wasn't acceptable. He hadn't joined the force just so she could go on shopping expeditions.

Clunk. The passenger door swung open and an avalanche of plastic bags clattered into his lap.

Steel clambered in, pulled the door shut, and shuddered. 'Oooh, bleeding heck: brass monkeys out there.' She frowned. 'How come you've no' got the heating on?'

Allan glowered at her. 'With all due respect, *Inspector*, you—'

'Don't be a prawn, or you'll no' get your present.'

'Present?' That was more like it. He turned the key in the ignition and cranked up the heater. 'Is it good?'

'Course it's good. Has your aunty Roberta ever let you down?' She dug into one of the plastic bags and came out with something bright red with white furry bits. 'Here.'

He turned it over in his hands, the smile dying on his lips. 'Oh...' It was one of those cheap Santa hats they flogged in the Christmas market on Belmont Street.

'Well, put it on then.'

'It's ... not ... with the uniform and everything...'

Steel poked his black stab-proof vest with a red-painted fingernail. 'Put – it – on.'

Brilliant. Allan hauled the hat on over his head, the bobble on the end dangling against his cheek. Soft and fuzzy. Like he was being tea-bagged by a Muppet.

She peered at him for a bit. 'It's missing something.' Then she leaned over and grabbed him by the lapel, hauling him towards her.

Oh God, she wasn't going to kiss him, was she? But there wasn't so much as a sprig of mistletoe in the car. It wasn't fair! You couldn't just go about kissing people – you had to give them fair warning about stuff like that. It was sexual harassment!

Run. Get out of the car and run. RUN!

She grabbed the bobble on the end of his Santa hat and something inside went 'click'. Little coloured lights winked

187

on and off inside the fur. Like it wasn't undignified enough in the first place.

Then again, given the alternative...

Steel nodded. 'Much better.'

A deafening HONNNNNNNNNNK! belted through the air behind them and a massive eighteen-wheeler loomed in the rear-view mirror, lights flashing.

She peered over her shoulder. 'Well, don't just sit there: you're holding up traffic.'

Mrs Griffith scrubbed a soggy hanky under her plump red nose, getting rid of the twin lines of silver. She sat on the couch in an over-warm living room, her pale-pink twinset and pearls looking all rumpled and out of kilter: as if she'd got dressed in the dark then fallen down the stairs a couple of times. Her chocolate-brown hair was greying at the roots, watery eyes blinking behind Dame Edna glasses. A big woman who wobbled when she sniffed.

A Christmas tree sat in the corner of the room, decorated with scarlet bows, gold dangly things, and white lights. Very tasteful. A mound of presents sat on the floor, beneath a thin layer of fallen pine needles, much more professionally wrapped than the Frankenstein's monsters in DI Steel's office. The mantelpiece was covered in cards, and so were the sideboard and the display cabinet by the large bay windows. Popular couple.

Allan underlined the words 'MISSING SINCE LAST NIGHT' in his notebook. 'And your husband's never gone off like this before?'

She blinked and shook her head. Not looking at him.

Couldn't really blame her. When you call the police to help find your missing husband, you probably don't expect a uniformed PC to turn up wearing a flashing Santa bobble hat.

'And he didn't mention anything that was bothering him?'

Mrs Griffith sniffed again, blinked, then stared up at the ceiling as the sound of a toilet flushing came from the floor above. Nice house. Fancy. Three bathrooms; four bedrooms, one en-suite; dining room; living room; drawing room; kitchen bigger than Allan's whole flat; conservatory; dirty big garden hidden under a thick blanket of pristine white. Had to be at least knee deep out there.

'Well, it's early days yet. Might just have got stuck in the snow, or something. Did you try his work?'

Mrs Griffith stared down at the crumpled hankie in her thick fingers. 'I... I phoned the hospital all night, just in case he'd ... you know, with the icy roads... An accident.' A single drip swelled on the tip of her nose, clear and glistening in the lights from the tree. 'Then I tried his work first thing this morning...'

It was the most she'd said in one go since they'd got there.

'I see.' Allan made a note in his book. 'And where does your husband work?'

She tortured her hanky for a bit. 'He doesn't.' The drip dropped, splashing down on the sleeve of her cardigan. 'The man I spoke to, Brian, he was Charles's boss. He said... He said Charles was made redundant three months ago. Said they couldn't keep everyone on with the economic down-turn.' She gave a little moan in the back of her throat. 'Why didn't Charles *tell* me?'

Clump, clump, clump, on the stairs, then the living room door opened and DI Steel shambled into the room, hauling up her trousers with one hand. 'Sorry, went to the panto last night. Too much fizzy juice and sweeties always goes right through me. You know what they say: you don't buy chocolate buttons, you just rent them.' She collapsed down on the other end of the sofa, then patted Mrs Griffith on a chunky knee. 'Went for a rummage through your bedroom while I was upstairs, knew you'd no' mind.'

Mrs Griffith opened her mouth, as if she was about to disagree, then closed it again. 'What am I going to tell the children?'

Steel wrinkled her lips and raised one shoulder in a lopsided-shrug. 'You sure there's nothing missing? Clothes, toothbrush, razor, stuff like that.'

'He wouldn't just run out on Jeremy and Cameron and me. He dotes on those boys, nothing's too good for them.' Her eyes flicked towards the pile of presents under the tree. 'Something must have happened. Something *terrible*...'

'Found this stuffed under the mattress.' The inspector produced a big clear plastic envelope thing, with 'Ho-Ho-Ho! HAPPY SANTA SUIT!' printed in red and white on a bit of card. The hanger was stuffed inside, but there was no sign of the costume. 'Your Charlie like to dress up for a bit of kinky fun?'

Mrs Griffith sank back in her seat, eyes wide, one chubby hand pressing that soggy hanky to her trembling lips. 'No! Charles would *never* do anything like that.'

'Shame. Partial to a bit of the old "naughty nun" myself.' Steel patted her on the knee again. 'Any chance of a cuppa? Digging through other people's drawers always gives me a terrible drooth.'

A bit of flustering, then Mrs Griffith hauled herself up from the couch and lumbered off to the kitchen, sniffing and wobbling.

Allan waited till the kitchen door clunked shut, before leaning forward. 'You'll never guess – the husband was made redundant—'

'Three months ago, aye, I know.'

'How did—'

'Found a P45 in his bedside cabinet, along with two *Playboys*, one *Big-'N-Juicy*, and a stack of receipts.'

'Oh.' Allan stuck his notepad back in his pocket.

'Something a wee bittie more interesting too...' She produced a slip of yellow paper and waggled it at him. 'It's—'

The door thumped open again and Mrs Griffith backed in, carrying a tray loaded down with china cups, saucers, and an ornately painted teapot.

Steel smiled. 'That was quick. Don't suppose there's any chance of...' She peered into the tray as Mrs Griffith lowered it onto the coffee table. 'Chocolate biscuits. Perfect.'

'I didn't know if you'd want. What with...' Pink rushed up Griffith's cheeks, clashing with her twinset. 'Your digestive problems.'

The inspector helped herself, talking with her mouth full. 'I'll risk it.' Chomp, chomp, chomp. 'Your husband ever mention someone called Matthew McFarlane?' Crumbs going everywhere.

'Em...' She fussed with the teapot, eyes down, the pink in her cheeks getting darker. 'I don't think so...'

Steel nodded. 'Well, probably not important anyway.'

Allan eased the car out onto the main road, the front wheels *vwirrrring* and slithering through the thick white snow, blowers going full pelt. 'So who's this Matthew McFarlane?'

'You've no' heard of Matt McFarlane? Matt "the Hat" McFarlane?' Steel slouched in the passenger seat, fiddling with her bra strap. 'Pin back your lugs and learn something for a change. Matthew McFarlane's what you might call an unregulated personal finance facilitator.'

Ah. 'Loanshark?'

'I remember there was this one woman, single mother, got into a bit of trouble with her council tax. Borrowed three hundred quid from Matt the Hat; couldn't pay it back. The interest was crippling, *literally*. He broke both her legs, then did the same to her wee boy. Gave her two weeks to come up with the cash, or he's coming back to do their arms.'

Steel breathed on the passenger window, making it all misty, then drew an unhappy face with her fingertip. 'Poor cow was too scared to press charges, so soon as she gets out of the hospital: that's it.'

Allan slowed down to let a bus out. 'Did a runner?'

'Locked herself and the kid in a car. Hosepipe from the exhaust.' Steel gave her left breast one last hoik, then pointed at the windshield. 'Crown Street. I fancy spreading some Christmas cheer.'

Matthew 'the Hat' McFarlane stood in the doorway, arms folded. He wasn't a tall man, but he was wide, like he'd been squashed. Cold little eyes, a squint nose, and a ridiculous Magnum-PI-moustache. He was wearing an ugly jumper with a couple of deformed reindeer knitted into the pattern and a flat cap with holly embroidered all over it. 'No, you can't come in.'

Steel stomped her feet, hands jammed deep into her armpits, voice streaming out on a cloud of white as thick flakes of snow spiralled down from the pale grey sky. 'Charles Griffith.'

'Never heard of him. Now, if you don't mind…' McFarlane tried to close the door, but the inspector jammed her foot into the gap. He looked down. 'You're dripping in my hall.'

Inside, the house must have been huge – a big chunk of grey granite, halfway down Crown Street. Iron railings stood to attention out front, guarding a little sunken courtyard with patio furniture just visible under a thick crust of snow. Allan stood on his tiptoes and peered over McFarlane's head into the hallway: antique furniture, hunting prints on the wall. Looked nice and warm in there too…

Steel pulled out the slip of yellow paper again. 'That's funny, cos right here it says Charles Griffith owes you four grand.'

192

A shrug. 'Overcommitted himself for Christmas, didn't he? I offered to help him out, seeing how it's the season of good will and that. Didn't want to see his kiddies going without.'

'Four grand down. What's he owe now, after you've stuck your usual extortionate interest rate on it?'

McFarlane folded his arms. 'Extortionate interest rate? Nah, that'd be illegal. Was just Christian charity, wasn't it? Charley can pay me back when he's on his feet again.' He smiled. It was all little pointy teeth, small yellow pegs set in pale-pink gums. 'No problems.'

Steel leaned forward. 'Listen up, sunshine, Charles Griffith has gone missing. And I don't mean he's done a bunk, I mean he's disappeared. See if he turns up dead in a ditch, I'm coming right back here, hauling your hairy backside down the station, and pinning everything I can on you. We clear?'

'You're letting all the heat out.'

She stepped back onto the pavement and McFarlane slammed the door.

Allan cupped his hands and blew into them, making a little personal fog bank. Didn't make his fingers any warmer though. 'Back to the ranch? Or we could go and see those solicitors, if you like? About your inheritance?'

She just scowled at him.

'Well, it's obvious, isn't it?' Allan dropped a gear, the engine growling and complaining as it struggled to haul the pool car around the Denburn Roundabout, wheels shimmying through the slush. 'You see that pile of stuff under their Christmas tree? Griffith probably spent a fortune kidding on he's not been fired. Borrows four grand to keep up appearances, can't pay it back.'

'Mmm...' Steel just scowled out of the passenger window.

'Then last night, McFarlane turns up on Griffith's doorstep, roughs him up a bit, Griffith drops everything and limps off into the sunset before McFarlane comes back with a pair of pliers. He'll be halfway to Barbados by now.'

'Mmm…'

'Well, not if he's flying out of Heathrow, but you know what I mean.'

Silence.

They were only doing fifteen miles an hour, but the car still fishtailed its way onto the Gallowgate.

Steel thunked her head sideways against the passenger window. Sighed.

Allan feathered the clutch, finally getting the thing under control. 'How come you're so bent out of shape about someone leaving you loads of cash?'

'None of your business.'

'I mean, if someone wanted to give me a dirty big handout, you wouldn't catch me complaining. Bet Charles Griffith wouldn't say no either.'

Steel hauled out a packet of Benson & Hedges and a lighter, the wheel making scratching noises against the flint as she quested for fire. Lit up. Puffed out a lungful of smoke. Then the grumble of traffic oozed into the car, riding a breath of frigid air as she buzzed the window down. 'Get a photo and description out to all the hospitals in Scotland. If Charlie-boy *has* done a bunk after a visit from Matt the Hat, he's going to need a doctor. If he's no' already in the mortuary.'

'I mean, who couldn't do with some more cash?'

A cloud of smoke broke against Allan's cheek.

'I'm only—'

'I'm not taking money from that…' She puckered her lips. 'Just shut up and drive.'

The solicitor's receptionist was making eyes at him. Or maybe she was making eyes at the pot plant in the corner? It was kind of hard to tell, the way that they both pointed off in different directions like that. Long curly blonde hair, little chin, heart-shaped face, scarlet lips. Cute, in a sort of Marty Feldman meets Christina Aguilera kind of way. She pulled off her glasses and polished them on the hem of her skirt, flashing an inch of milk-bottle-white thigh and the top of a hold-up stocking. A smile, squint like her eyes. 'I'm sure they won't be long. Would you like another cup of tea?'

It was an old-fashioned kind of room, with wooden panelling and dark red carpets, the walls covered in framed watercolours and certificates.

Allan shifted in his green leather armchair. 'No, thanks. I'm good.' Tea and coffee were just wheeching right through him today. Must be the cold. 'So … have you worked for Emmerson and Macphail long?' OK, not the smoothest of lines, but slightly better than, 'Do you come here often.'

'Two months. Mostly it's just answering the phones and making tea.' She bit her bottom lip, one eye lingering its way up his body – while the other went off for a wander on its own – coming to rest on the flashing Santa bobble hat at the very top. 'We don't usually get anyone as exciting as the *police* in here. Are you working on a case?'

'Actually,' he scooted forward, lowering his voice, 'we're—'

The office door banged open and the inspector stormed out, arms going in all directions. 'Don't you sodding tell me to calm down, you patronising, sanctimonious, hairy-eared, old—'

'But Mrs Steel,' a baldy-headed man shuffled out after her, the front of his white shirt soaked through with what looked like tea, 'you have to understand, we're talking about a considerable sum of money here. At least *think* about it.'

She marched straight through the reception area and out the main door, slamming it hard enough to make all of the certificates on the wall shudder.

'Oh dear.' He ran a hand across his forehead, then stood there, dripping on the carpet. 'She really is quite excitable.'

Allan stood. Pointed at the door. 'I'd probably better—'

'Constable, can you do your inspector a favour?' The solicitor pulled a handkerchief from his pocket and dabbed at his damp face. 'Tell her the time limit contained in the behest is very precise. Mr MacDuff will be cremated at three o'clock on the twenty-seventh, whether she's there to deliver the eulogy or not. And considering how much is at stake... Well, it would certainly be in her best interests.'

'Er, exactly how much are we talking about?'

'I really don't think it would be appropriate for me to discuss that.' He turned to the receptionist. 'Daphne, can you be a dear and fetch me a towel? I appear to have had an accident.'

December 27th

Half past nine and Allan was in the canteen, piling foil-wrapped bacon butties onto a brown plastic tray. Good job he wasn't one of those *evangelical* vegetarians, or he'd be spitting in every one. CID were just a bunch of lazy sods. Should be getting their own damn butties. Whatever happened to good will to all men?

He squeezed in half a dozen assorted coffees at the other end of the tray and carried the lot down to the CID wing. Really it was just of a handful of rooms lurking at the end of a smelly corridor marked with brown streaks, but that didn't sound quite as impressive.

DI Steel was lurking in her office, scowling at the phone and drumming her nails on the desktop. 'Took your time.'

Allan dumped a buttie and a big wax-paper cup beside her in-tray. 'You're welcome.'

'Don't start.' She unwrapped the floury roll and sank her teeth into it. 'Mmmph, mnnnnphmmm?'

'Today's the twenty-seventh.'

'Stunning powers of observation there, Constable Guthrie. You'll go far.'

'What I mean is, it's the funeral today. Of your mate, MacDuff.'

'Desperate Doug MacDuff's no sodding mate of mine.' Another mouthful, washed down with a scoof of coffee. 'Get a car.'

'*How* much?' Allan turned to stare at her.

'Watch the road!'

He snapped back just in time to see the back end of a bus. 'Argh!' The brake pedal juddered under his foot, the ABS twitching as the car slid into the kerb. So much for the weather getting better after Christmas. The roads were like glass, and everyone drove like an idiot. 'Stupid bus driver...' Allan wrangled the car back out onto the road. 'Fifty-four thousand quid, and all you have to do is deliver the guy's eulogy?'

'It's no' as simple as that. I'd have to be nice about him. And if his greasy lawyer thought I'd no' been enthusiastic enough, I'd get sod all. Enthusiastic, about Desperate Doug MacDuff?' She stared out of the window, mouth a narrow, pinched line. 'Man worked as an enforcer for the McLeods, Wee Hamish Mowat, *and* Malk the Knife. Killed at least six people we know of, probably a hell of a lot more. Then there's the beatings, abductions. Rape...'

'So lie. Fifty-four grand! Say he was a great guy, a credit to his family, loved by women, admired by men. Take the money and run; who cares if he was a complete scumbag?'

'*I* care.'

*   *   *

197

'No answer.' Allan stuffed his hands back in his pockets.

'Try it again.'

The Griffiths' street was like Dr Zhivagoland – everything covered in rounded mounds of white. Cars, hedges, trees, the lot. Icicles made glass fangs from the guttering, twinkling in the morning light. Sky so blue it was almost painful to look at.

He leant on the doorbell again and a deep *brrrrrrrrrrrrrring* sounded somewhere inside. 'Maybe she's gone out?'

Steel shook her head. 'Look at the drive.'

Someone had dug it clear, all the way down to the slippery road; a snow-blanketed Range Rover was parked in front of the garage, one of those big ugly Porsche Cayennes blocking it in. The paintwork frost-free and glistening. Allan nodded. 'She's got visitors.'

'Once more with feeling.'

He ground his thumb into the brass bell, keeping the noise going. 'You know, there's still plenty time to head out to the Crem.'

'I'm no' telling you again.'

'Just saying: fifty-four grand goes a long way when you've got a wee kid to bring up. Good nursery, maybe a private school, couple of nice holidays. Otherwise, what, it all goes straight in the Taxman's pocket?'

'Where the hairy hell is...' Steel screwed her eyes up, peering through the glass panel beside the door. 'Here we go.'

A muffled voice. 'Who is it?'

The inspector stepped forward and slammed her palm into the wood. 'Police. Open up.'

'Oh... But, I—'

'*Now.*'

A clunk and rattle, then the door creaked open a crack and a big pink face stared out at them. 'Have you found

Charles? Is he all right?' Her cheeks were all flushed, a pale fringe of hair sticking to her glistening forehead.

Steel smiled. 'Can we come in?'

'Ah… Well, I'm… It's not really convenient, right—'

The inspector placed a hand against the door and pushed, forcing her back into the hall. 'Won't take long.'

Allan followed Steel inside, clunking the door closed behind him, shutting out the cold.

Mrs Griffith stood in the hallway, one hand clutching the front of her silk kimono, keeping everything hidden. Thank God. 'Look, can't this wait till—'

'Where is he?'

The pink on her cheeks darkened. 'I… Don't know. That's why I called you. He's missing and I'm very upset.'

'Oh aye. But no' upset enough to put you off a wee bit of the old mid-morning delight, eh?' Steel wandered over to the foot of the stairs, leaning on the polished wooden banister.

Mrs Griffith stuck her nose in the air, stretching out the folds in her neck. 'I think you should go.'

'Come out, come out wherever you are! Game's a bogey, the man's in the lobby!'

'I must protest, you shouldn't—'

Steel cupped her hands into a makeshift megaphone. 'Come on McFarlane, I know you're in here, I recognised your car! Lets be havin' you!'

Silence. Then a voice echoed down from upstairs. 'Erm… I'm a little tied up at the moment. Well, handcuffed, technically…'

The inspector grinned. 'Bingo.' She bounded up the stairs two at a time, Mrs Griffith lumbering after her, making little groaning noises.

'It's not what you think, really!'

Allan followed them up to a plush bedroom that could

have come straight from the pages of a swanky magazine. Oatmeal carpet, red velvet curtains, polished oak units, and a big four-poster bed with a naked man manacled to it. Matt 'the Hat' McFarlane, wearing nothing but a smile and a couple of crocodile clips in a very sensitive location. OK, so the magazine would have to be *Better Homes and Perverts*, but it was the thought that counted.

McFarlane tried a shrug. 'I'd get up, but … you know.'

Allan winced. 'Does that not *hurt*?'

Steel plonked herself down on the edge of the bed. 'No' interrupting anything, am I?'

'What do you think?'

Mrs Griffith grabbed the duvet and hauled it up, covering McFarlane's wee hairy body. 'I really don't see how this is any of your business.'

'What's the deal, she paying off her husband's debt in naughty favours? That it?'

'Actually—'

Mrs Griffith put a hand on his chest. 'Matthew and I are deeply in love. We have been for nearly a year. When Charles gets back, I'm going to ask him for a divorce.'

'Divorce?' The inspector bounced up and down a couple of times, making the springs creak. 'Tell you what I think: I think the pair of you decided you couldn't be bothered with a long, drawn out legal battle, so you killed him, dumped the body somewhere, and reported him missing. Cooked up the receipt for four grand so we'd think he'd done a bunk to get out of paying his debt.' She smiled. 'How am I doing so far?'

McFarlane looked at her for a minute, then burst out laughing. 'We're gonna get married. You any idea how hard it'd be for Mags to get a divorce if Charles is missing? Couldn't even have him declared dead for what, seven, eight years? No way we're waiting that long. Nice quickie divorce, and we can all get on with our lives.' He winked. 'Might even send you an invitation.'

'Pull over.' Steel scowled out of the windscreen, arms folded across her chest, jaw jutting.

'You sure? It's half two, you don't want to be late for—'

'I swear to God, Constable, if you don't pull over right now I'm going to take my boot and I'm going to jam it right up your—'

'OK, OK, pulling over.' Talk about a bear with a sore bum.

The car crunched and bumped over a moonscape of compacted snow, coming to a halt outside a wee corner shop on Queens Road. A little billboard thing was screwed to the wall: 'ABERDEEN EXAMINER – END IN SIGHT FOR WINTER CHAOS!' Aye, right.

Steel unclipped her seatbelt and clambered out onto the crusty pavement, slipped, grabbed the door, wobbled for a bit, then straightened up. 'No' a word.'

'I didn't say anything!'

She slammed the door and picked her way into the shop.

How could someone be *that* miserable about inheriting fifty-four grand?

Steel was back five minutes later with a white carrier-bag clutched to her chest. Buckled herself in, then pulled out a half bottle of Famous Grouse. The top came off with a single twist, then she stared at the whisky for a moment, before knocking back a mouthful. Closed her eyes and shuddered. Took another glug. 'What you looking at?'

'Just thought it was kind of … you know … on duty and…' He swallowed. She was glowering at him.

'Drive.'

She was about a third of the way down the bottle by the time they reached the rutted driveway to the crematorium. The memorial gardens were covered in a thick layer of white,

201

stealing the sharp edges from everything. According to the car's temperature display, it was minus one out there.

Allan crept along the road, making for the bulky building at the end. The place was a collection of grey and brown rectangles, bolted together into a single unappealing ugly lump. As if just being a crematorium wasn't depressing enough.

There was only one other vehicle in the car park, a frost-rimed 4x4. Allan parked a couple of spaces along and checked the clock: two fifty-eight. 'Doesn't look like he was all that popular.'

Steel took another slug of Grouse. 'I was nineteen, only been on the beat for a couple of weeks... Was doing door-to-doors for this abduction case – woman, mother of two, snatched outside the bookies she worked at.' Steel screwed the top back on the bottle, one eye half-shut, like it wouldn't stay in focus. 'And then I chapped on Desperate Doug MacDuff's door...'

Silence.

'Guv? You want me to come in with you?'

'Going to go in there and tell the truth. Let everyone know what he was *really* like. Give that manky old git a piece of my mind. Who needs his filthy money?' She climbed out into the snow, breath streaming around her head. Slipped the half bottle of whisky into her pocket. 'You wait here. Might need to make a quick getaway.'

December 31st – Hogmanay

'Guv?' Allan peered around the edge of the door into DI Steel's office.

She was slouched in her seat, feet up on the desk, cigarette dangling from the corner of her mouth. The smoke curled out through the open window, letting in the constant drip-drip-drip of melting snow. A cup of coffee was growing a wrinkly skin, sitting next to a cardboard box with 'FRAGILE – THIS WAY UP' stencilled on the side.

'Guv?'

Steel blinked, then swung around. 'What?'

'Just got a call from Mrs Griffith's next-door neighbour. Think we've found the missing husband.'

Steel turned and stared back towards the road. 'You sure you locked the car?'

'*Yes*, I locked the car.' Snow crunched and squelched under Allan's boots as he picked his way along the edge of the next-door neighbour's garden. It was horrible out here, cold and wet and soggy as the thaw ate its way through the drifts.

The neighbour was standing by a six-foot wooden fence, clutching an umbrella – melt-water from the roof drummed on the black and white fabric. She bounced a little on her feet as they got nearer, green eyes shining, big smile on her face, Irn-Bru hair curling out from the fringes of a woolly hat. 'He's over there.' She pointed through a gap in the fence. 'Saw him when I was trying to defrost the garden hose, and I was certain it was a body, and then I thought I can't leave it, what if it disappears like in *North by Northwest* and nobody believes me? Or was that *Ten Little Indians*? I don't suppose it matters really, but it was something like that, so I ran inside and grabbed my mobile and came back out and it was still there, which is great.' All delivered machine gun style in one big breath.

Allan peered between two of the boards that made up the fence. There was a pair of legs sticking out of a drift of glistening snow: black boots; red trousers trimmed with white fur. An electrical cable was wrapped around one leg, studded with large multicoloured light bulbs. 'Ouch. You think he's...?'

203

Steel hit him. 'Course he's dead. Been lying upside down in a snowdrift for a week. It's no' like he's hibernating in there, is it?'

The end of a ladder was just visible on the other side of the mound. 'On the bright side, at least he's not missing any more.'

Steel sat in the passenger seat, clutching that fragile cardboard box to her chest. Allan turned up the heater, then peered through the windscreen up at the house. Mrs Griffith was standing in the bay window of the lounge, staring as the duty undertakers wrestled her husband's remains into the back of their unmarked grey van. It wasn't easy: he'd frozen in a pretty awkward shape, like a Santa-Claus-themed swastika... Matt 'the Hat' McFarlane had his arms wrapped nearly all the way around her shoulders – as far as his wee arms would reach – holding her tight while she sobbed.

Allan sniffed. 'Still think they did it?'

'The lovebirds? Nah. Silly sod was clambering about on the roof practicing his Father Christmas in the snow. Deserved all he got.'

The funeral directors finally managed to force the last bit of Charles Griffith into the van, then slammed the doors shut and slithered off into the defrosting afternoon.

Allan put the pool car in gear. 'Back to the ranch?'

'Nope. You can drop me off at home, I'm copping a sicky.' Steel opened the top of the cardboard box and hauled out a brass urn that looked like a cross between a cocktail shaker and a thermos flask. A plaque was stuck to the dark wooden base: 'DOUGLAS KENNEDY MACDUFF – IN LOVING MEMORY'. She opened the top and peered inside. 'Hello again, Doug, you rancid wee scumbag. Your mate the solicitor says I've got to give you a dignified farewell. Something befitting your standing in the community.'

'Fifty-four grand... Knew you'd see sense.' Allan eased the car out onto the road. 'So where you going to scatter him: Pittodrie? North Sea? Maybe out Tyrebagger or something?'

'Litter tray.' Steel grinned and screwed the top back on. 'If we just use a little bit at a time, he should last for *months*.'

Stramash

stramash /strəˈmaʃ/ *noun*
an uproar; a disturbance; a row; a brawl: *Strong drink having been taken, the police were called to break up the stramash outside the pub.*

'Sodding hell.' *Logan peered out through the rain-slicked glass of*
what passed for a passenger lounge – a bus-stop-style shelter squeezed
in at the side of the car deck. Just big enough for Logan, his wheelie
case, and a stack of vegetables in wooden boxes – their paper labels
bloated and peeling off in the downpour.

The dock looked as if it'd been hacked out of a quarry: a bowl
of slate-grey rock with a couple of dented pick-up trucks huddling
together for warmth. No sign of an MX-5.

Typical.

The tiny ferry shook and rattled, lurched ... then clanged
against the concrete slipway. Another gust of frigid water rattled
the glass.

She was late.

'You bloody promised.'

The ramp groaned down and a dripping wee man in a
high-viz jacket waved at the rust-flecked blue Transit van
taking up most of the car deck. It spluttered into life and
inched forwards.

Logan stuck out his thumb and smiled at the driver... He
looked familiar. That was good right? Made him more likely
to give Logan a lift? But the rotten sod didn't even glance

at him, just drove off the Port Askaig ferry and away onto Jura.

Logan yanked out the wheelie case's handle. 'Thanks, mate. Thanks a bloody heap!' And stomped off into the rain.

The minibus bounced through yet another minefield of potholes, then purred to a halt on the grass at the side of the track.

'Here we go: Inverlussa.' The driver coughed, peering out through the windscreen as the wipers squealed across the glass. 'Are you sure?'

No. Not even vaguely.

The sea was a heaving mass of granite-coloured water, white spray sparking like fireworks in the wind. A thin curve of yellow-brown sand separated the crashing waves from the land. A wee house squatted on the other side of a bridge over a river, the hills rising behind it, dark and glistening.

The minibus rocked and whistled with each gale-force blast.

A small table sat on the sliver of grass overhanging the beach, with a couple of chairs facing out to sea. Someone was sitting in one of them, bundled up in a heavy red padded jacket, a blue bobble hat pulled down low over their ears, a yellow Rupert-the-Bear scarf whipping out behind them.

Logan hauled his case out into the storm, dragging the thing through the wet grass towards the table. The rain had faded to a stinging drizzle and the air had that salt-and-iron smell of the sea, the dirty-iodine whiff of churned seaweed.

Christ it was cold, leaching through his damp trousers, making his legs ache.

He stopped at the table. Loomed over the sod responsible.

DI Steel sniffed. 'About time you got here.' She was only visible from the nose up – the bottom half of her face wrapped in the scarf, wrinkles making eagle's feet around her narrow eyes, grey hair poking out from beneath her woolly hat. 'Park your arse.'

Logan stared down at her, put on a throaty cigarette-growl. '"Don't worry Laz, I'll pick you up at the ferry terminal."'

She shrugged. 'Someone got out the bed on the wrong side.'

'Wrong side of the...? I had to sleep in the bloody *car* last night!'

A figure in bright-orange waterproofs lurched along the path towards them, carrying a tray of tea things, struggling to keep it level in the wind.

Logan dumped his case under the table. 'Took me six bastarding hours to drive to Tarbert yesterday: all the hotels and B&Bs were full. You got any idea what it's like sleeping in a car in the middle of a bloody hurricane? Bloody *freezing*, that's what it's like.'

'Oh don't be so wet.'

The figure in the waterproofs leaned into a gust of wind, took two steps to the side, then made a final dash for the table. She smiled at them from beneath the dripping brim of her sou-wester. She couldn't have been much over eighteen. 'Right, that's a pot of tea for two, one lemon drizzle cake...' She placed them on the tabletop. 'And a toffee brownie. If you want a refill,' she pointed at a little walkie-talkie in a clear Tupperware box, 'just give me a buzz.'

'Ta.' Steel poured herself a china mug of tea from the stainless steel teapot as the girl headed back towards the house and sanity.

Logan looked out at the bay – the howling wind, the breakers, the heaving dark sea, the heavy clouds. 'You've gone mental, that's it, isn't it? You've finally gone stark—'

'Just park your arse and have some cake.'

He lowered himself into the folding wooden chair.

Clenched his knees together. Hunched his shoulders up around his ears, stuck his dead-fish hands into his armpits. 'Bloody freezing...'

Steel clunked a mug down in front of him, steam whipping off the beige surface. 'You bring that fancy fingerprint stuff?'

'Catch my death. And *then* what? Sitting out here in the wind and the rain like a pair of idiots.'

'Moan, moan, bloody moan.' She sipped her tea; had a bite of cake, crumbs going the same way as the steam. 'Now: where's my fingerprint stuff?'

'Not till you tell me why I drove all the way across the bloody country, slept in a car, took two ferries, tromped half a mile in the hammering rain, then sat in a bus for half an hour to watch you stuff your face with tea and cake.' He grabbed the brownie and ripped a bite out of it, chewing and scowling. 'I'm cold, I'm wet, and I'm *pissed* off.'

'Jasmine doesn't moan this much, and she's no' even two yet.' Another bite of lemon drizzle. 'We're sitting here in a howling gale, because we're watching someone.' She pointed out into the storm, where a small white fishing boat with a red wheelhouse roller-coastered up-and-down and side-to-side on the angry water.

'Wouldn't have been so bad if I could've got the car on the Islay ferry, but every idiot in the whole—'

'Can you no' give it a rest for five minutes? *Look.*'

Logan wrapped his hands around the mug, leaching the heat. 'At what?'

Sigh. Her voice took on the kind of high-pitched sing-song tone usually reserved for small children. 'At the wee fishing boat, bobbity-bobbing on the ocean blue.'

'I was right: you *are* mental. It's a fishing boat, that's what they do. Can we go inside now before I catch bloody pneumonia?'

She hit him on the arm. 'Don't be a dick.' Then passed

him a pair of heavy black binoculars. 'Less whinging, more looking.'

The eyepieces were cold against his skin, the focussing knob rough beneath his fingertips as he unblurred the little boat. The wheelhouse was just big enough for a grown man to stand up in, but whoever was in charge of the boat was hunched over, wearing one of those waistcoat-style life jackets, holding a Spar carrier-bag to their mouth, shoulders heaving in time with the sea.

Finally the man straightened and wiped a hand across his purple slash of a mouth. His skin was pale, tinged with yellow and green. Sticky-out ears, woolly hat, pug nose, puffed out cheeks... And he was vomiting again.

'Not exactly the best sailor in the world.'

'If you spent more time reading our beloved leader's inter-force memos and less time moaning about everything, you'd know that was Jimmy Weasdale.'

Logan squinted through the binoculars again. 'Jimmy the Weasel? Thought he retired to the Costa Del Sol. Did a runner when Strathclyde CID fingered him for cutting Barney McGlashin into bite-sized chunks...' More squinting. 'You sure it's him?'

'What do you think the fingerprint stuff's for? Saw him in the hotel bar last night drinking with this hairy wee bastard wearing a number seven Dundee United football shirt...'

Logan lowered the binoculars, leaving Jimmy to puke in peace. 'Not Badger McLean?'

'The very man. Jimmy the Weasel and Badger the Tadger: together again. No' exactly Mother Nature's finest hour.'

'So where's Badger?'

'Squeezed himself into a rubber drysuit half an hour ago. Thought he was going to get his kinky on, but nope – scuba gear. He's down there now.'

Logan went back to the binoculars. 'What are they after?'

A gust of wind rattled the stainless steel teapot on the little table.

Steel made slurping noises. 'Tell you what, I'll activate my X-ray vision and take a peek below the waves, shall I? Then we can all sod off down the pub for a game of Twister and some chocolate cake.' She hit him again. 'How the hell am I supposed to know? That's why we're here – *watching*.'

Fifteen minutes later an ungainly deformed seal surfaced next to the fishing boat. It thrashed its arms for a moment, before a hump of charcoal-coloured water slammed it into the hull. More thrashing.

Logan shifted his grip on the binoculars. 'Silly sod's going to get himself killed.'

Jimmy the Weasel lurched out of the wheelhouse and threw a line to the diver. More thrashing. Then some hauling – and what looked through the binoculars like swearing – and finally the seal was dragged over the boat's railing, bum in the air, little legs kicking out. Then gone: hidden from sight by the bulwark.

Steel poked Logan in the shoulder. 'What's happening? He drowned?'

'Almost.'

A couple of minutes passed, then a cloud of exhaust fumes burst from the back end of the boat before being torn away by the wind. The tiny vessel swung around and puttered away into the heaving sea, leaving behind a bright-orange buoy bobbing in the angry water.

Logan passed the binoculars back to Steel. 'Before you ask: no. I am *not* going to swim out there and find out what they've been up to.'

She puffed out her cheeks, then tipped the dregs of tea from her mug. 'Fancy a wee walk down by the beach?'

'No.'

'That's the spirit.' Steel stood, stuck her hands in her pockets and lurch-staggered through the storm along the edge of the grass verge.

A quick shove and she probably wouldn't wash ashore till she reached Ireland... Logan sighed, swallowed the last of his tea, and hurried after her, shivering as the gale snatched away the little body heat he had left. Hypothermia was bloody overrated.

By the time he'd caught up she was standing beside a large rock, frowning down at a knot of liquorish-coloured seaweed – the kind that looked as if it had boils. Steel nudged it with her toe. 'What's that look like to you?'

'Seaweed. Can we just...' Something was tangled up in the glistening coils, something rectangular – about the size of a house brick, only wrapped in clear plastic and brown parcel tape. He squatted down, damp trousers clinging to his legs, and levered the package out of the seaweed. 'About a kilo.' There was another one, three or four feet further down the thin strip of sand, and another just past it. 'Bloody hell.'

She patted him on the shoulder. 'Don't know about you, but I'm gasping for a pint.'

DI Steel froze in the doorway. Her eyes bugged, mouth pinched into a chicken's-bum-pout as she stomped towards Logan. 'I told you to wait outside!'

The Jura Hotel's bar was a sort of elongated bay-window-shape. A handful of people sat around small circular tables, eating crisps and drinking beer, while an old woman in a grey twinset hustled her grandson at pool.

Logan paid for his pint of Eighty Shilling. 'It's raining.'

'Go!' She grabbed him by the arm and pulled him towards the exit. 'Out: before Susan sees you.'

'I've ordered food!'

'I don't care if you've ordered three strippers and a tub of cottage cheese – if Susan sees you she'll chew me a new hole. Aye, and no' in a good way. Supposed to be here on a jolly, no' police business.' She gave him a shove. 'Out, out. Go sit in the car.'

'I'm bloody freezing, and there's—'

'Laz: it's her work's team-building, OK? She thinks I'm off reading books and scratching my bumhole in quiet contemplation of nature's island splendour. You want to upset her? That what you want? You want to ruin the only time we've had off together since Jasmine was born?'

'You dragged me all the way across the bloody country! I'm cold, I'm wet, I'm hungry, and I'm having my bloody lunch inside in the *warm*, whether you like it or not.'

DI Steel knocked on the steamed-up car window.

Logan scowled at her from the passenger seat, then took a mouthful of Eighty from his half-empty glass. The MX-5's cloth roof buckled and groaned, rain bouncing off the bonnet, making a noise like a thousand angry ants playing a thousand angry drums, fighting against the background drone of the engine and the roar of the blow heaters.

Craighouse was a tiny village, strung out along a single-track road. A mini stone-walled harbour, a community hall, a restaurant, a wee Spar shop, and an old-fashioned red telephone box. A collection of whitewashed buildings loomed in the rain – opposite the hotel – 'ISLE OF JURA' painted in big black letters on the distillery wall. Steel's MX-5 sat in a roped off car park marked 'STAFF ONLY'.

She clambered in behind the wheel and handed Logan a plate piled high with langoustines, some salad, and little curled red things that looked worryingly like oversized boiled woodlice.

He poked one of them. 'I ordered the steak pie.'

'Seafood platter. Good for the brain. And don't get fishy fingerprints all over my car.' She turned off the engine and the heaters went quiet.

'Hey!'

'I'm no' made of bloody petrol.'

Logan twisted the tail off a langoustine and clicked it out of its pale pink carapace. Dipped it in the mayonnaise. 'Did you get me a room?'

'Course I did. Got you one right next door to Susan and me, that way you can bump into her and let her know I'm hunting down villains when I'm supposed to be on holiday.' Steel pulled out a glass tumbler wrapped in a paper napkin. The smoky scent of malt whisky curled through the car. 'Badger and Weasel are in there playing pool like good little woodland animals, so I nabbed the bugger's glass. Where's the fingerprint thing?'

'Don't you think Susan *might* just notice something's up when she tries to get her bags back in the car and finds the boot full of drugs?'

'Oh...' Steel's eyebrows drooped, taking the corners of her mouth with them. 'Sod. Well ... er... Fine: we solve everything today, you bugger off back to Aberdeen with our druggie friends, and Susan never needs to know.' A nod. 'Right – that's officially the plan.' Steel pointed at the tumbler. 'So come on, fingerprints.'

The beer slipped down, cool and dark. 'Don't nag.'

'You know, if it really is Jimmy Weasdale then we've just caught Scotland's eighth most wanted man, *and* turned up a massive stash of drugs. They'll probably want to give me an OBE.'

Logan sooked his fingers clean, dug the plastic case from his pocket, and dumped it in her lap. The iPrint kit was about the same size as a paperback book. Steel cracked it open as Logan broke his way into one of the woodlice.

217

She sniffed. 'You got any idea how to work it?'

'Instructions are inside.' He held up a little curl of white meat. 'What is this, exactly?'

'God's sake... Who wrote these instructions? Sodding handwriting's appalling.'

'Put your glasses on.'

'I don't *need* glasses. And it's a squat lobster. Eat it, it's good for you.' She laid the contents of the kit out along the dashboard: a scratched iPhone; a length of curly black cable; a plastic thing – like a matchbox with a metal strip down the middle; a soft-bristled blusher brush; a little plastic tub of Aluminium powder, and one of Amido Black.

Steel squinted at the sheet of paper for a while. 'Nah, it's no good – you'll have to do it.'

'I'm *eating*.'

'Aye, and while you're out here stuffing your face, there's a murderer in there playing pool and...' She stared out of the driver's window, then scrubbed at it with her sleeve, clearing away the fog. 'Him! There – look, look, look!'

'I can't even have lunch, can I? OK, OK: I'll do your bloody fingerprints.' Logan wiped his hands on a napkin, then reached into his jacket for a pair of nitrile gloves.

'No, you divvy – look!' She tapped at the window. 'Big bloke, tartan bunnet, parking the van.'

Couldn't keep her mind on one thing for more than two minutes...

Logan leaned across the car and peered through the clean patch. It was the rusty Transit van from the ferry this morning, driven by the same rotten sod who wouldn't give him a lift.

The man clambered out into the rain. He was wearing orange overalls, stained brown and black around the cuffs and knees. Clunky work boots. Big. Broad. Hands like dinner-plates. He pulled the tartan cap firmly down over his ears

218

as another gust of wind shook the van, driving him back a step.

Steel whistled. 'Kevin McGregor. Thought he was dead...' A frown. 'I'm *sure* he's dead.'

'Doesn't look dead.'

McGregor grabbed a holdall from the passenger seat, and lumbered off into the bar.

'Oh, he's dead all right: burned to a crisp in a house fire five years ago. Post mortem said he'd been shot twice in the back of the head, execution-style. Had to ID him from dental records.' She shrugged. 'I crashed the funeral and the wake. Tried to cop off with his sister, but she was having none of it.'

The legendary Kevin McGregor – no wonder he looked familiar.

And was that...? Logan pointed through the clear bit at two hard-looking women with ginger crewcuts and black-rimmed glasses, struggling to origami an OS map back into shape. 'Camper van, four o'clock. That's the Riley Sisters: Brigid and Niamh. Belfast drug dealers. You name it, they'll blow it up; knees capped while you wait.'

Steel sat back in her seat. 'What is this, a sodding conference for toerags and gangsters? Scumfest?'

'Wait a minute...' Logan stuck his plate on the dashboard. 'Did Kevin McGregor not beat old Liam Riley to death six years ago because he tried to move in on his turf? Think they're here to kiss and make up with the bloke who murdered their dad?'

Steel closed her eyes, pursed her lips, then banged her forehead off the steering wheel. 'Susan's going to kill me.'

'You got any of that sticky toffee pudding left?' DI Steel clambered back into the little MX-5.

'Bugger off – first hot thing I've had today.'

'Ungrateful sod.' She fidgeted with her left boob, hauling at the underwire. 'That's another four turned up. So far we've got three scheemie toe-rags from Glasgow, Badger and Weasel, a pair of scary bitches kicked out of the provisional IRA for being too violent, two Scouse wideboys, a dead gangster, four of Malk the Knife's goons, and the spotty ginger kid that works for Wee Hamish Mowat. Sodding hotel bar's like the United Nations for drug-dealers.' She reached over and poked a finger into Logan's toffee sauce.

'Hey!'

Steel sooked her finger. 'And you want to know the weirdest thing? They're all playing nice. Even Kevin McGregor and the Riley Sisters: in there, quietly sipping their pints. You'd think they'd at least chib each other for old time's sake.' Pause. 'Give us a go of your spoon.'

Logan turned away, shielding the pudding with his arm. 'Get your own.'

She stared back towards the bar. 'Never mind a paddle: if this kicks off, we're up shite creek without a *canoe*. According to the guidebook, Jura's got two special constables and that's it. No firearms team, no black maria, nothing.'

'So call Strathclyde – get them to send a helicopter.'

'And let those Weegie soap-dodgers take all the credit? No thanks.'

'No, of course not – silly me. It's *much* better if this lot tear the hotel apart and murder each other in the lounge bar. What was I thinking?'

She stared at him. 'No one likes a smart arse, you know that, don't you?'

Logan finished his sticky toffee pudding. Licked the bowl clean so there'd be nothing left for Steel. 'Only one thing for it then: we pick them off one-by-one like Rambo.'

*   *   *

220

Mid-afternoon and the sky was like boiling tar, rain battering down – bouncing off the road and a handful of parked cars. DI Steel curled her lip, buzzed down the window and spat out into the storm. '"We'll pick them off one-by-one like Rambo," he says.'

'Not my fault they all go to the toilet in pairs, is it? Who knew drug dealers were like girlies on a hen night?'

'Prat. They go to the bogs in pairs so the opposition doesn't chib them in the ribs while they're having a slash. Puts them off their aim – blood and pee everywhere.'

Badger McLean shuffled out through the bar's main door onto a raised stone patio with a handrail around it to keep anyone from falling into the bustling rush-hour traffic. Which probably consisted of a Post Office van and a sheep. If it was a really busy day.

'Did you tell the hotel owners that their bar was full of drug dealers?'

'Course I sodding didn't. What they don't know won't kneecap them.'

The wee hairy man huddled in the hotel doorway and winkled a hand-rolled cigarette out of a tin of tobacco. He lit up, shifting from foot to foot, puffing away in the torrential rain. Shivering.

Steel sighed. 'I miss fags.' She pulled out a silver hip flask, twisted the top off, took a swig, then waggled it at Logan. 'Snifter?'

'You really think that's a good idea?'

'It's no' drink driving, it's drink parking.'

Over in front of the hotel, Badger fought with his lighter again. Then looked over his shoulder back into the bar, before limping down the steps and across to an ancient maroon Peugeot with a deep gouge all the way down the passenger side. He hauled open the back door and lowered himself inside with slow stiff movements, as if his spine was

221

made of broken glass. The hot blue-and-yellow flare of a lighter. The dull orange glow of a cigarette. The pale-grey smoke drifting against the glass.

Logan stuck his pudding bowl on the dashboard next to the iPrint kit. 'One-by-one, just like Rambo.'

Badger McLean squealed as Logan wrenched open the Peugeot's door and jumped into the back seat beside him.

'I didn't—'

Then another squeal as Steel slid in on the other side, trapping him in the middle.

Silence.

Outside, the wind howled.

Steel stretched her arm along the back of the seat, behind Badger's shoulders, as if she was about to put the first-date moves on him in a darkened cinema. 'Aye, aye Badger. Badge. Badge the Tadge. Long time eh?'

He licked his lips, eyes flicking from the car door to the hotel and back again.

She pouted. 'Badger, I'm hurt – you don't remember me?'

Still nothing.

'Aberdeen, 2003: I did you for flogging aspirin round that nightclub down the beach, telling boozed-up teenagers it was E. Got you eighteen months, didn't it?'

His mouth fell open an inch. Then everything came out in a machine-gunned Fife accent, the words going up and down like the boats in the harbour. 'Oh thank God, I thought for a minute you were— ayabugger!' He dropped the cigarette, shaking and blowing on his fingers, sending ash spiralling through the car. 'Ow...'

'Here's the deal, Badge my boy: you tell me what I want to know, and my associate here won't frogmarch you back in there and let everyone know how you've been cooperating with the police like a good little boy.'

222

He sneaked a glance at Logan.

Logan grinned back at him.

Badger slouched, then ran a hand across his face. 'Aw ... shite.'

'*How* much?' Steel stared, mouth hanging open like an empty pink sock.

Badger shrugged, then winced, clutching his chest on the left-hand-side – where the wave slammed him into the boat. 'No one knows for sure, but that's what they're saying: nearly a ton of Afghanistan's finest. Grade-A. Uncut. In four submersible pods.'

'Bloody hell... A *ton*.'

'Silly bastards' yacht got caught in that big storm, had to cut the pods loose or get dragged down with them. Managed to limp into Oban three days ago. All the pods've got GPS, but one of them cracked open and it's kinda ... well, you know? Like driftwood, only kilo blocks of heroin.'

Steel pointed back at the bar. 'And young Jimmy the Weasel?'

'Turns out his son-in-law was one of the aforementioned silly bastards. The idiot got pished in Oban – you know, celebrating not being dead – and kinda let it slip... So now every dealer from Aberdeen to Belfast's turning up to do a bit of fishing.' Badger cleared his throat. 'Now that I've cooperated, there's no real *need* to tell anyone, is there? Why don't I just get out of your hair and head back to the mainland? It's not like you can actually do me for anything, is it? I'm not even in possession or anything.'

'Funny you should say that...' Logan dipped into his pocket, pulled out a block of heroin and tossed it at him. 'Catch.'

'Aagh...' Badger caught the thing before it hit him in the face.

'Your fingerprints are all over it now. That's eight years for possession with intent.'

'That's not fair!'

'Our word against yours.'

Steel licked her teeth, mouth open, making sticky noises with a pale-yellow tongue. 'Nearly a ton of uncut grade-A drugs washing up on the shores of a wee Scottish Hebridean island. It's sodding *Heroin Galore*.'

'Jimmy's going to kill me. He's going to hack me up into little pieces like poor old Barney McGlashin. He's going to—'

'If you don't shut up, *I'll* hack you into little bits.' Logan shifted in his seat. They'd parked Badger's dented Peugeot down the main road, in front of the Antlers restaurant, tucked in behind a soft-top Land Rover with an expired tax disk. The hotel bar was just visible through a knot of bushes.

Two minutes later Jimmy the Weasel stormed out of the bar into the rain, head going left and right like a pasty-faced searchlight, scanning the car park.

Logan adjusted the binoculars, focussing through the hotel windows to where DI Steel was leaning back against the pool table, grinning.

The Weasel shook his fists at the sky. 'THIEVING LITTLE BASTARD!' It echoed back from the distillery buildings, before being swallowed by the downpour.

'Oh, God.' Badger buried his face in his hands. 'That's it: I'm dead.'

And then the Weasel was off, running down the road towards them. But before he got there he took a sharp right, around the back of the village shop. Making for the tiny stone pier that curled around a miniature harbour.

'Keep your head down.' Logan turned the key in the ignition and the Peugeot made a high-pitched retching noise.

Then clunked. He tried again. Got the same result. 'Come on, come on, come on...' More retching. 'COME ON!'

Clunk.

'Bloody thing.' Logan undid his seatbelt and jumped out into the rain, running after Jimmy the Weasel: between the shop and the village hall.

The little white fishing boat with the tiny red wheelhouse rocked against the harbour wall. Light bloomed through the wheelhouse windows, then a cloud of pale-grey exhaust sputtered out around the stern. The boat backed out, turned, and lurched away into the waves.

Run. Run fast. Leap. Sail through the air between the end of the pier and the fishing boat. Crash into the deck and wrestle Jimmy the Weasel into submission. Handcuff him. Say something pithy about boats and fish. Just like in the movies.

Three, two, one...

Bugger that. Knowing Logan's luck he'd probably drown.

He scrabbled to a halt at the end of the pier, sending a pair of lobster creels splashing into the iron-coloured waves.

The wee boat puttered away, bow dipping and rearing more and more violently the further it got from shore.

The sound of another engine roared from somewhere off to the right. Logan turned. A little concrete slipway reached down from the road – between the distillery car park and the hotel beer garden – to the rolling sea. A man in dirty orange overalls was wrestling a rigid inflatable dingy out into the swell.

Kevin McGregor.

So much for Plan A.

DI Steel stared at him, rain dripping from her flattened grey fringe. 'What do you mean, "He got away"? How could he get away? You were right sodding there!'

'The car wouldn't start.'

'Well, that's not—'

'It's not even my car!' Logan pointed at the terminally ill Peugot, with Badger sitting in the back. 'It's this moron's.'

The wee man waved.

Steel stuck up two fingers at him. 'Sodding cheese-flavoured arse-monkeys... And Kevin McGregor went after him?'

'It's not my fault the plan was rubbish.'

'Hey, *my* bit of the plan went perfect, OK? I go in; I make a song and dance about some idiot in a dented Peugeot nearly running me off the road, grabbing a fishing boat and sodding off into the storm; and pop goes the Weasel – right out the front door. It's *your* bit that went bum-shaped.'

'The bloody – car – wouldn't – start!'

'Shiteholes...' She chewed at her finger for a moment. 'We need a boat, or something.'

Screw that.

'Could we not just drive back up the road to where we had tea? That's where the—'

'And *then* what? You want to swim out to the boat and arrest them? Cos I'm no' bloody doing it. We need a boat.'

'Will you hurry up?' Steel marched up and down the pontoon attached to the tiny harbour's wall. 'They'll be miles away by now!'

Badger sat up and scowled at her from the wheelhouse of a small rust-streaked fishing boat with 'CATRIONA'S HARVEST' painted along the side. Creels made a smelly pyramid in the back, coils of dirty rope and scuffed pink buoys piled alongside them. 'I've never hotwired one of these things before. A Ford Cortina I could do you in three minutes flat, this...' He waved a hand. 'This is a pain in the backside.'

'My *boot*'ll be a pain in your backside if you don't—'

The engine growled and puttered into life. Badger gave himself a round of applause. 'Ha!'

'About bloody time.' Steel scrambled aboard, then turned and waved at Logan. 'Get a move on!'

'Can't get through.' Logan slipped the phone back in his pocket. 'Mobile signal keeps cutting out.'

Badger pointed through the wheelhouse window. 'Untie the rope thing at the pointy end and chuck it in the boat. Do the one at the back too.'

Logan stared at him. '"Pointy end"? Thought you said you knew what you're doing.'

Steel wrapped her scarf around her head, until only her eyes and nose were visible. 'Laz, get your arse on this boat right now, or I swear to God...'

He untied the 'pointy end' then did the same with the line at the stern, before half jumping, half falling into the back of the boat. Up close the creels stank of stale fish and rotting onion.

Badger fiddled with the controls. Nothing happened. A bit more fiddling, and the boat thumped backwards into the pontoon with a loud crunch.

Steel grabbed the wheelhouse wall. 'Other way, you daft sod!'

'Right...' The boat surged forwards this time, then around to the left as he twirled the wheel, heading out into the bay. 'Like riding a bike.'

The sea churned like a hangover – up and down, left and right, the boat making a wobbly corkscrew path through the concrete-coloured waves. Logan tightened the padded orange lifejacket he'd found in a little locker. The deck was cold and damp beneath his bum as he sat with his back to the railing, holding on with both hands as the tiny *Catriona's Harvest* juddered through the storm.

Steel sat opposite, eyes closed, legs splayed, teeth gritted. 'Urgh...'

He narrowed his eyes at her, having to shout over the roar of the engine. 'You and your bloody Plan B!'

Standing in the wheelhouse, Badger turned and grinned at them. 'Course, you've got to watch these waters like a hawk. Reefs and rocks everywhere. Normal charts cover about a hundred miles – here you're lucky if you get twenty. No wonder Jimmy's son-in-law got into trouble. Got to keep your—' The whole boat juddered, as if a big underwater fist had slammed into it. 'Oops.' And then they were going straight again.

Steel kept her face screwed tight shut. 'If we sink I'll sodding kill you.'

'Not much further.'

'You said that twenty minutes ago!'

And the sea raged on.

'There! Told you we'd make it.' Badger clung onto the wheel with one hand, pointing with the other. To the left, Jura rose in hilly bumps of green and brown; to the right the Sound of Jura was a heaving mass of grey water; and straight ahead was the little fishing boat with the red wheelhouse, moored just off Inverlussa beach. Kevin McGregor's rigid inflatable was tied up alongside, bobbing and dipping.

Jimmy the Weasel cowered in the back of the fishing boat, arms over his head, staggering as the vessel lurched from one trough to the other. Kevin McGregor clambered over the side, back into the inflatable. Raised his arm, as if he was about to give the Weasel a telling off.

A hard *pop* broke across the waves.

The back of Jimmy's head puffed out in a cloud of bright red, shining against the dark afternoon, before the wind whipped it away.

228

Badger squealed, then ducked down behind the wheel.

Jimmy's body rocked with the next wave, then crashed forward onto the deck.

'Oh shit, oh shit, oh shit...'

Logan hauled out the binoculars and focussed on the bobbing fishing boat. 'Think he's dead?'

'Well...' Steel made a little humming noise. 'If no' he'll save a fortune on hats.'

Kevin McGregor leaned over the side of his inflatable and did something with the bright-orange buoy.

Logan cleared his throat. 'We should board him. Ram the inflatable.'

Badger peered out from the wheelhouse. 'He's got a gun!'

'Don't be such a Jessie.' Steel fiddled with her lifejacket. 'Long as we stay down, we'll be OK, right?'

Logan rapped his knuckles against the *Catriona's Harvest*'s hull. Might be thick enough to stop a bullet. Probably. Maybe. 'Erm...'

The outboard roar of Kevin McGregor's engine cut through the storm, and the rigid inflatable eased away from Lussa Bay. Going a lot slower than it had leaving Craighouse harbour.

Badger knelt in the wheelhouse, peeking over the bulwark. 'Boat's weighted down... He's got the two full pods. That's why he was following Jimmy – the thieving git's nabbed our drugs!'

Even towing two-thirds of a ton of underwater heroin, Kevin McGregor's inflatable was still faster than *Catriona's Harvest*. When they finally puttered back into Craighouse harbour, the inflatable was abandoned on the slipway. The rust-flecked blue Transit sat in front of it, the back doors open as Kevin McDonald winched the second pod inside.

He creaked the doors shut, dragging his left leg. The orange overalls were stained scarlet from knee to ankle.

Logan scrambled onto the jetty, not bothering to tie the boat up.

Steel clambered out after him, turned and pointed back into the wheelhouse. 'You, Badger Boy: *stay*. If I have to come looking for you, you'll bloody well know about it.'

The wind whipped spray off the curling waves, throwing it in Logan's face as he hurried ashore.

Streetlights made golden spheres in the driving rain. The road was deserted, except for a couple of parked cars and a mob of grumpy seagulls – hunkered down on the guttering of the distillery buildings, watching the world with glittering eyes.

Logan turned the corner of the village shop and skidded to a halt. Staring. Someone was lying face down on the road between the hotel and the distillery. Arms and legs splayed out in a broken starfish. A pair of thick-rimmed glasses lying just out of reach. Face pale and slack. A slick of dark red oozing downhill towards the sea.

The other Riley sister was crumpled in front of the distillery shop, the back of her head gone the same way as Jimmy the Weasel's.

Maybe that's why all the gulls were there – waiting for an early dinner?

No wonder the bloody street was deserted.

Steel puffed to a halt beside Logan. 'What? Why have we stopped?'

He pointed.

'Oh ... *arse*. Do you think anyone noticed?'

Logan stared at her. 'Yes, I think someone might *just* have noticed a bloody gunfight in the middle of the street, right outside the hotel bar.'

'Susan's going to kill me...'

Kevin McGregor hobbled around to the side of the Transit van.

Logan took a deep breath and stepped onto the road. Pulled out his warrant card and walked towards the van. 'Police! Put your weapon down and keep your hands where I can see them.'

McGregor froze, halfway through hauling the driver's door open. Then turned. 'Sling your hook, before you get hurt.'

'Come on Kevin, it's over. You know it's over.'

McGregor slammed his hand on the side of the van. Logan flinched. The seagulls stirred. Probably wondering if they'd get police officer for starters.

'I came back from the dead for this. It's not over till I say so.' He pointed at DI Steel's little MX-5. 'That's your car, right? Saw you sitting in it, watching the hotel.'

'Kevin McGregor, I'm arresting you on suspicion of the murders of James Weasdale, Brigid Riley, and Niamh Riley, you— Oh God!'

McGregor's gun barked twice and the MX-5's front tyres exploded in shreds of black rubber. Then he turned and blew out the tyres of the Rileys' camper van, and the Toyota pick-up parked opposite. The noise was deafening, the smell of fireworks seeping away into the rain.

'Like I said: it's not over till I say it is.' He dragged himself up into the Transit van, heaving his leg over the seat, teeth gritted. Then slammed the door.

Steel appeared at Logan's shoulder. 'My car... The... He shot my sodding car!'

Kevin McGregor grinned, gave them a wave, then put the van in gear.

A moment of utter silence. Then it was as if the whole world bellowed. The Transit van bucked, riding a mushroom of boiling orange flame, the cab expanding – a balloon of rusty blue metal and safety glass. And then the *noise*: it was like being smacked in the chest with a sledgehammer, followed by a blast of hot air that tore the ground from under Logan's feet and sent him crashing sideways against DI Steel.

The van clattered back to the blackened tarmac, bounced, fell onto its side, the rear doors twenty yards away.

A pall of white dust filled the air above it, drifting in the wind as the seagulls leapt shrieking from the distillery roof. The cloud caught them above the shop. They lurched, swooped, bumped into each other, and the walls, and the slates, then tumbled to the road. Lying on their backs, legs and wings twitching as the Transit van burned. Doped out of their tiny little minds.

Logan rolled onto his front and levered himself to his knees, ears ringing.

Steel coughed, spluttered, groaned. 'SODDING HELL...'

'WHAT?'

'THINK I BROKE MY ARSE...' She dug a finger into her ear and jiggled it about. 'CAN YOU HEAR THAT?'

The Transit van's front bumper clanged back down against the road, lying amongst the stoned seagulls.

Logan clutched at the ancient red telephone box, pulling himself up on wobbly feet. 'That's what happens when you mess with a pair of paramilitary nut-jobs who've got a thing for explosives.'

'HELP ME UP.'

He hauled her to her feet. 'Stop yelling at me.'

'WHAT?'

Christ. 'Never mind.'

'I CAN'T HEAR YOU.'

The door to the hotel bar swung open and a figure in jeans and a hooded top stepped out onto the stone balcony, her caramel-coloured hair pulled back in a ponytail: Susan. She stared at the burning wreckage in the middle of the road, then at the MX-5 with its two blown-out front tyres.

Then at DI Steel: standing next to Logan with her legs planted wide apart, one hand holding onto his arm, as if the tarmac was bobbing about on rough seas.

Susan's eyes narrowed. She stuck her fists on her hips. 'Roberta Steel, what the *bloody* hell have you been up to?'

The 45% Hangover

Friday 19th September

(The Day After)

0

'GAAAAAAAAAAAAAAAAAAAAAAAAAAAAAGH!' The scream cut through the world like a rusty chainsaw.

It reverberated back from the walls, jerking Logan fully awake. Then made him wish he wasn't. Something large and spiky was loose inside his head, scrabbling at the back of his eyes with long dirty claws. He screwed his eyes shut and lay there, till the echoes faded.

The chainsaw roared again: 'WHAT THE HELL DID YOU DO?'

He gritted his teeth and opened one eye. Then the other one. Wide. Then his mouth.

Oh dear Jesus, no...

They were lying in bed. No idea *whose* bed, but it was definitely a bed – metal framed, with a brass headboard. Floral-print duvet.

Him and Detective Chief Inspector Steel. In bed. Together.

Her hair was flat on one side, poking out in all directions on the other, her lined face pulled into a shape of utter disgust. Worse yet, it didn't look as if she was wearing a top.

No, no, no, no...

One arm wouldn't move, but he used the other one to

grab the duvet and pull it up to his chin. 'Why are we—'

'IF YOU SO MUCH AS—'

'STOP BLOODY SHOUTING!' He clenched his eyes shut again, teeth gritted. Every heartbeat made the spiky thing in his skull throb. *'Please.'*

'I'll shout if I want to! You try waking up naked, in bed, with a sodding *man* and see how you like it.'

'Naked?' Oh no, not this… He raised the edge of the duvet an inch.

'If you so much as peek, I swear to God, Laz, I'll rip your bits off and give them back to you as a suppository!' She hit him. 'Get out.'

'Arm's gone to sleep.'

She kicked him under the duvet.

'Ow!'

'Get out!'

'I can't.' His right leg wouldn't move either. He jerked it to the side, but it barely shifted, something was keeping it where it was. Something solid. 'Oh *no.*'

She glared at him. 'You bloody men are all the same aren't you? Sex, sex, sex. Well let me tell you something, you randy wee shite, if you ever breathe a *word* of this to anyone, I'm going to…' The glare turned into a frown. 'Why can't I move my arm?'

Then her head turned. She reached up with her other hand and pulled the pillow to one side.

Logan's left hand, and her right, poked between the bars of the headboard, fixed there by a set of police-issue handcuffs.

When he shifted his other foot, the duvet rode up just enough to show the handcuff holding his right ankle to the bars at the other end.

Steel slumped back against her pillow. 'Oh God… Because

naked wasn't bad enough, it had to be *kinky*!' She covered her mouth with a hand. 'I'm going to be sick.'

'Thank you very much. How do you think *I* feel?' He ran a hand across his forehead, then squeezed at the temples. Maybe, if he squeezed hard enough, the headache would vanish? Or his head would explode. Right now either was preferable to this.

'How much did I *drink* last night?'

Good question.

Thursday 18th September

(Referendum Day)

1

The rumpled lump in the wrinkled suit raised an eyebrow, then pulled the fake cigarette from her mouth. 'What time do you call this?'

Logan hung his jacket on the hook behind the door, then checked his watch – nine thirty. 'Half an hour before my shift starts.' He crossed to the window and lowered the blind, shutting out the darkness. 'Now get out of my seat.'

'You see the latest polls? We're going to do it, can feel it in my water.' Steel wriggled her bum further into his office chair, both feet up on his desk. 'Tell you, it's a momentous day, Laz. Mo-sodding-mentous.' From the look of her hair, she'd celebrated by dragging herself through a hedge, sideways.

'Seat.' He hoiked a thumb at the door. 'Some of us have work to do.'

'Course I gave my team a rousing speech when they came on, this afternoon. "Ask not what your country can do for you..."'

'You're not allowed to campaign on Police Scotland property.'

A frown. 'Since when?'

'There's been like, a dozen memos.' Logan unlocked the

245

filing cabinet and hauled out the thick manila folder sitting at the front of the top drawer. 'Now, would you *please* sod off and let me get on with it?'

Steel raised her feet from the desk and pushed off, setting the chair spinning with her still in it. Lowered her feet down onto the windowsill instead. 'This time tomorrow we'll have risen up to be the nation again…' Then she launched into a gravelly version of 'Flower of Scotland', getting all wobbly on the long notes, and battering out the optional Tourette's bits.

No point fighting with her – it'd only make it worse.

Logan dumped the folder on the desk and sank into one of his visitors' chairs. Pulled the desk phone over and punched in DC Stone's number. Listened to it ring.

A knock on the office door, and Detective Sergeant Rennie poked his head into the room. 'Sorry, Guv, but any chance you can keep the singing down a bit? Only people are complaining.'

Steel paused, mid-warble. 'Unpatriotic sods.' Then started up again.

Rennie nodded, setting his floppy blond quiff wobbling. 'Yeah, but the mortuary says the dead are crawling out the fridge drawers and hacking off their own ears.' A grin. Then he ducked out again just before the stapler battered against the door where he'd been.

If anything, Steel had got louder.

On the other end of the phone, Detective Constable Stone picked up. *'Guv? You forcing bagpipes up a cat's bum in there?'*

Logan put a finger in his other ear. 'Stoney: where are we with Chris Browning?'

'Give us a chance, shift hasn't even started yet. Still waiting for the computer to boot up.'

'Soon as it does, get onto uniform – I want an update on my desk by five past ten. Then we're doing the briefing. And tell Wheezy Doug he's on teas.'

'*Guv.*'

Steel got to the big finale, and finished with her arms outstretched and head thrown back, as if she'd just finished running a marathon. Making hissing noises to mimic the crowd's applause. 'Thank you, Aberdeen, I love you.' Then let her arms fall at her side. Pursed her lips. And had a scratch. 'Pffff... What do you think, landslide?'

Logan clicked the handset back into its cradle. 'Don't you have a murder or something to solve?'

'Did it yesterday, while you were off. Had a cake to celebrate and everything.' She creaked the chair left, then right again. 'Bit quiet today, to be honest. I've got a Major Investigation Team with nothing major to investigate. Going to have to drag something out of the cold-case file if we're not careful.'

'Then go do something about that guy from Edinburgh who got the crap beaten out of him.'

'Not major enough.' She waved a hand. 'And the scumbag was a drug dealer. Probably deserved it. If they'd *killed* him, it'd be a different matter. But as it is? Pfff...'

'So find something else.' Logan pulled the top four sheets out of the folder and laid them side-by-side on the desk. The first one was the latest missing person poster: a photo of Chris Browning sat beneath the headline, 'MISSING PERSON ~ APPEAL FOR INFORMATION'. He wasn't exactly a Hollywood heartthrob – a middle-aged man with pasty skin and a receding hairline, little round glasses and sunken eyes.

Steel clapped her hands together, then rubbed them. 'Of course, being *referendum day*, there's bound to be frayed tempers and a bit of a barney, right? Might get ourselves a one-punch-murder or two.'

A knock, and Rennie was back. 'Sorry, Guv. BBC coverage starts at ten: we're sending Guthrie out for pizza. You two want anything?'

She pointed at him. 'Did you vote like I told you?'

'Guv.'

'Good boy.' The finger came round to point at Logan. 'What about you?'

'None of your business.' The next sheet was a list of the most credible sightings from the last week. Which wasn't saying much. 'Now if you don't mind, I've got a missing person to find.'

'Pfff. No' really a person, is he? A lawyer, a pervert, a wannabe politician, *and* a No campaigner? The more of them goes missing the better.'

'Yes, because dehumanizing people who don't agree with you always turns out well.'

'Don't care. Sick of his smug, dumpy wee face. Banging away on the telly and the radio and the sodding papers,' she put on a posh Aberdonian accent, '"Scotland's going to fall apart under independence.", "We're not clever enough to run our own affairs without Westminster.", "You're all chip-eating, whisky-swigging, heart-attack-having, ginger-haired, tartan-faced, teuchter thickies, and you should be glad the posh boys in London are prepared to look after you."' She sniffed. 'Tosser.'

'You made that last one up.' Sheet number three held a photocopied article from the *Aberdeen Examiner*. 'Missing Campaigner "Paid For Sex", Claim'. The journalist had got statements from a pair of working girls down on Regent Quay. Logan pulled out a pen, wrote the word 'Names?' and underlined it twice.

'And who cares what Chris Sodding Browning thinks anyway? Only reason the slimy git's getting airtime is because he was on that reality TV bollocks. *Silver City* my sharny arse. You want to make decent telly? Follow police officers about, no' some ambulance-chasing unionist turdbadger.'

'You finished?' The last sheet was a photocopy of Browning's diary for the day he went missing. Every appointment checked, everyone he'd met with interviewed. And still no idea where he was or what had happened to him. 'Chris Browning's perfectly entitled to support whatever side he wants. That's democracy.'

'Oh – my – God.' Steel took her feet off the windowsill and turned to face him. 'You're one of them, aren't you?'

'Eh?' Rennie frowned at Logan. 'Thought you liked girls, Guv? Not that there's anything wrong with it, but— Ow!'

Steel hit him again. 'No' one of *them*, you idiot, one of them: a Better Togetherer.' She shuddered. 'And to think I let you get my wife up the stick!'

Logan closed his eyes and folded forward, wrapped his hands around his face. 'Will you both, *please* bugger off?'

Rennie didn't. Instead he sat down in the other visitor's chair. 'Was great though, wasn't it? You know, that feeling of coming out of the polling station and thinking, "This is it. We could actually *do* this." Right? Wasn't it great?'

There was silence.

'Guv?'

Logan peeled one eye open.

Steel was sitting bolt upright in her seat, mouth hanging open. Then both eyebrows raised like drawbridges. 'What time is it?'

Rennie checked. 'Quarter to ten.'

She scrabbled to her feet. 'Get a car, *now*!'

2

The pool car roared its way up Schoolhill – past the closed shops – lights flashing, siren wailing like a hundred angry pigs. It still managed to sound better than Steel's rendition of 'Flower of Scotland', though.

She sat in the passenger seat, hanging onto the grab handle above the door as Rennie floored it.

Logan had to make do with his seatbelt, clutching it in both hands as the car flashed across the junction outside the Cowdray Hall, its granite lion watching with a silent snarl and a traffic cone on its head. The streetlight gilded it with a pale-yellow glow. Logan raised his voice over the wailing skirl. 'HOW COULD YOU FORGET TO VOTE?'

'IT'S NO' MY FAULT!'

'REALLY?'

'SHUT UP.'

His mobile buzzed in his pocket, the ringtone drowned out by the siren. He pulled the phone out and hit the button. 'McRae.'

'*Guv?*' Stoney sounded as if he was standing at the bottom of a well. '*Hello? Guv? You there?*'

He leaned forward and poked Rennie in the shoulder. 'TURN THAT BLOODY THING OFF!'

But when Rennie reached for the controls, Steel slapped his hand away. 'DON'T YOU DARE!'

His Majesty's Theatre streaked by on the right – a chunk of green glass, followed by fancy granite, light blazing from its windows – then a church that looked like a bank, then the library. Granite. Granite. Granite.

'Guv? Hello?'

'I'LL CALL YOU BACK.' He hung up as the pool car jinked around the corner onto Skene Street, leaving a squeal of tyres behind. The headlights caught two pensioners, frozen on the central reservation, clutching each other as the car flashed by, dentures bared, eyes wide.

When Logan looked back, they'd recovered enough to make obscene gestures. 'STILL DON'T SEE WHY I NEED TO BE HERE.'

Steel waved a hand. 'IN CASE I NEED SOMEONE ARRESTED.'

Naked granite gave way to a shield of trees, their leaves dark and glistening in the streetlights.

Rennie pouted. 'I CAN ARREST PEOPLE!'

'COURSE YOU CAN. YOU'RE *VERY* SPECIAL. YES YOU ARE.' She turned in her seat and mugged at Logan. 'ISN'T IT SWEET WHEN THEY THINK THEY'RE REAL POLICE OFFICERS?'

'HOY!'

The pool car swept out and around a Transit van, then back in again. Slowed briefly for the junction outside the Grammar School, catching the lights at red, and back to full-speed-ahead, tearing up Carden Place. Granite. Granite. Granite.

She poked a finger at the windscreen. 'THERE!'

St Mary's Episcopal Church loomed on the left of the road.

A vast, grand structure with lancet windows and buttresses. No tower. It occupied the triangular wedge between two roads, with expensive-looking cars parked along its kerbs.

Rennie slammed on the brakes and wrenched the steering wheel left. The back end kicked out for a moment, then they were lunging through the narrow gap between two spiky granite posts and scrunching to a halt on the gravel beyond. He flashed his watch. 'You've got one minute.'

Steel scrambled out of the car, sprinting across the gravel and in through the door marked 'POLLING STATION'.

'Cheeky old bag. I *am* a real police officer.'

'Sure you are.' Logan climbed into the warm night. Pulled out his phone and called Stoney back.

A couple of Yes campaigners stood off to one side, a couple of No on the other. Both sets waving Scottish flags and smiling at him. As if a flash of dodgy teeth and a bit of plastic stapled to a stick was going to make a difference. Both sets marched toward him.

The Yes lot got there first – a young man with spots and a goatee. 'Good evening. Can I ask how you're planning to vote?'

'I'm on the phone.'

'Yes, but it'll only take a minute, won't it?'

His companion stuck her hands in the pockets of her tweed trousers. 'Going to have to get a shift on.' She pointed at the door. 'Polls close at ten.'

'*Guv?*'

Mr and Mrs No had appeared. One in a tracksuit, the other in a three-piece suit. Three-Piece turned his smile up an inch. 'Can we help?'

'I'm – on – the *phone*.' Logan turned his back and walked off a couple of paces. 'Stoney.'

Tracksuit sniffed. 'No need to be rude. We're only trying to help.'

'*Yeah, I've been quizzing the dayshift. Got a couple of sightings,*' *but don't think they're up to much. One's in Torquay, one's in Nairn, and the other's in Lanzarote.'*

Three-Piece folded his arms. 'That's the trouble with Yes people. No manners.'

'Well, Chris Browning didn't go to Lanzarote. Not without his passport.'

Mr Spots folded his arms too, saltire flags sticking up like offensive weapons. 'Wait a minute – what makes you think he's one of ours?'

'Yeah.' Mrs Tweed poked Tracksuit in the chest. 'He was rude to us first.'

'Don't you poke me!'

'How come I can hear fighting?'

'I'm surrounded by idiots.' Logan held his phone against his chest. 'Sod off, the lot of you. I already voted, OK? Go bother someone else.' Back to Stoney. 'Get onto the *Aberdeen Examiner* and find out who fed them the story – I want to speak to their sources. We'll trawl the docks and see if anyone else saw Chris Browning down there.'

'You going to be back for the briefing?'

Mr Spots pursed his lips. 'Can I ask who you voted for?'

'No, you can't: sod off.'

'Guv?'

'Not you, Stoney, this lot.'

'So you voted No, then?'

'It's none of your business!' Logan jabbed a finger in the direction of Three-Piece and Tracksuit. 'And it's none of *their* business either. Now, for the last time: SOD OFF!' Bellowing out the last two words.

The four of them backed off, chins in, eyebrows up.

Three-Piece: 'Well, there was no need for that, was there?'

Mrs Tweed: 'No there wasn't.'

Tracksuit: 'There's always someone who lowers the debate to name calling, isn't there?'

Mr Spots: 'Honestly, some people think shouting's the same as democracy.'

Logan screwed his eyes shut. 'Stoney, if I'm up for four counts of murder tomorrow morning, can you feed my cat for me?'

'Deep breaths, Guv, count to ten.'

A smoky voice cut through the night. 'Ta-daaaaa!' And when Logan opened his eyes, there was Steel, bouncing on the top step with her arms up, like something out of a *Rocky* film. 'They canna take our FREEDOM!'

The little knot of idiots transferred their attentions her way.

'You want me to slide the briefing back a bit?'

Logan checked his watch again. 'Fifteen minutes. Then we hit the streets.'

3

The bells of some far off church tolled out a dozen chimes. Midnight.

Water Lane was narrow and dark, half the streetlights blown and broken. The cobbles were slick beneath Logan's feet. Not that it'd been raining. No, they were all slippery with… Yeah, probably best *not* to think about what he'd just trodden in. Or on.

A tall granite building made a wall on one side of the lane, its guttering sprouting weeds, lichen on the lintels, broken windows. Boarded-up doors that opened onto nothing but fresh air on the second, third, and fourth floors. A couple of trees had burst out through the windows high up there, like slow-motion explosions.

The other side was more granite. Cold and unwelcoming. Not exactly the most romantic of spots for an intimate liaison. But then romance probably wasn't on the cards. Not even Richard Gere's character from *Pretty Woman* would have wheeched any of the working girls here off to a swanky hotel for pampering, shopping and semi-wholesome fun.

Two of them shuffled their feet, then looked away from the missing person poster in Logan's hand. One looked as if she'd never see sixty again, but was probably barely out of her thirties. Her friend hadn't been at the drugs as long, so she still had all her own teeth and nowhere near as many pin-prick bruises up the inside of her arms. But they were both pipe-cleaner thin.

Logan sighed and tried again. 'Are you *sure* you've never seen him?'

The older one shook her head. 'Now, any chance you can sod off, only we've got quotas and that.'

Sugarhouse Lane was even narrower. The Regent Quay end was quiet – probably due to the half-dozen security cameras protecting the office buildings at the mouth of the alley. Further in, it was a different story. Blank granite topped with barbed wire on one side, warehouse-style walls on the other.

A lack of streetlights left the doorways and recesses in shadow.

Logan hunched his shoulders and stepped into the gloom.

The young man couldn't have been much over eighteen. If that. His red PVC T-shirt was dusty across the shoulders, his jeans torn and grubby about the knees. Every bit as thin and wobbly as the ladies of one street over. He licked his lips and stepped towards Logan. 'You looking for a good time, yeah?'

Logan pulled out the poster again. 'Looking for this man. You seen him?'

He lowered his head. 'Never seen no one...'

After a while, all the alleys blended into one another. Granite walls. Shadows. The smell of furtive sex and shame and desperation and barely-concealed violence.

Logan held the poster up and the woman with the thinning blonde hair shook her head. Same as the last five people he'd talked to.

As she clip-clopped away down the cobbles, Logan pulled out his phone and dialled Stoney. 'Anything?'

'Nah. It's like a Dress-Slutty Party for amnesiacs round here tonight. No one's seen him.'

'Well we know *two* people saw him. Has to be others.'

'Early days though, Guv. Maybe Elaine Mitchel and Jane Taylor don't come out till the clubs shut?'

Logan curled his lip and wandered back onto Regent Quay, with its warehouses, fences, and massive supply vessels, caught in the glare of security lighting. 'Don't fancy hanging about here till the back of three. Get onto Control – I want home addresses.'

'Guv.'

Till then, might as well complete the circuit and try Water Lane again.

Two steps in and Logan's phone launched into 'The Imperial March' from *Star Wars*. That would be Steel.

He pulled the phone out. 'What?'

'Too close to call, you believe that?'

'What is?'

'The referendum, you moron. They're showing all the ballot boxes arriving at the counting stations. Exit polls are too close to call.'

'Glad to hear you're working hard.'

'Don't be a dick. This is important.'

'Well, while you're sitting on your bum, watching TV, and eating pizza, I'm out searching the docks for witnesses. So if it's nothing urgent and *police*-related, feel free to be a pain in someone else's backside for a change.' He hung up and wandered further into the alley.

'This it?' Logan stood in the street and looked up. The tower block loomed in the darkness – twelve storeys of concrete and graffiti, a few lights shining from the upper floors. Wind whipped a broken newspaper against the chainlink fence, punishing it for its headline, 'A DIRTY CAMPAIGN OF FEAR AND LIES?'

Stoney checked his notebook. 'Want to guess what floor?'

A groan. 'Top.'

'Yup.'

There was an intercom next to the double doors, half the metal cover missing, wires poking out. Didn't matter anyway – the door creaked open when Stoney nudged it with his foot. Then he flinched, nose crumped up on one side. 'Lovely. Eau De Toilette. Incontinence, *pour homme.*'

Deep breaths.

Logan marched inside. A faded cardboard sign was duct taped to the lift's dented doors. 'OUT OF ORDER'.

No Kidding.

They took the stairs. Dark stains clustered at every landing, the nipping reek of ammonia strong enough to make Logan's eyes water. And the further up they went, the worse it got.

When finally they arrived on the twelfth floor, Stoney was a coughing, wheezing lump. Dragging air in. And Logan wasn't much better. By rights, the top floors should've been less stinky, shouldn't they? People would pee on their way downstairs, or on their way back to their flats. No one headed *upstairs* to pee, did they?

Stoney wafted a hand in front of his face. 'God's sake, stairwell must run like Niagara Falls on a Saturday night.' He coughed a couple of times, then spat. Wiped his mouth. 'That's it at the end.'

Flat four still had its number attached to the red-painted door. The word 'HOORS!' was sprayed across the wood in three-foot tall letters. If it was advertising, it wasn't working. After slogging all the way up here, who'd have the energy to do anything?

Logan knocked.

Waited.

Knocked again.

Had a third go.

A voice came from the other side, thin and muffled. *'Go away, or I'll call the police! I know who your mothers are!'*

OK...

'I can save you the trouble – it *is* the police.'

Silence.

Stoney puffed out his cheeks. 'Can we not sod about here, madam? It's a long way to climb and it stinks of pish.'

The door cracked open an inch and a slice of pale skin appeared in the gap. The eye was grey, the iris circled in white. Chamois-leather creases across the cheek. 'How do I know you're policemen?'

Logan showed her his warrant card, then Stoney did the same. She peered myopically at them, then grunted and closed the door again. Unlatched the chain. A pink cardigan slumped over a thin, hunched frame. Liver-spotted scalp showing through thin yellowy hair. She turned and led the pair of them through a stripped-bare hallway into the living room.

No carpet. No underlay. A tatty brown couch against one wall, a pile of dirty washing against the other. And in-between, a panoramic window that looked out across Aberdeen. A sky of ink, the streetlights glowing firefly ribbons. It would have been breathtaking, if the climb and sudden smell of cat hadn't already taken care of that.

An overflowing litter tray bulged in the corner, like a heaped display of miniature black puddings.

A large ginger cat sat in the middle of the couch, bright orange with a shining white bib and paws, as if he'd been painted with marmalade and Tipp-Ex. How the cat managed to stay so clean in this manky hole was anyone's guess. It raised its nose and sniffed at the scruffy pair of police officers, somehow implying that Logan and Stoney were the ones responsible for the horrible smell.

The woman sat down next to her cat and stroked its back, getting a deep rumbling purr in return. 'Whatever they told you, I didn't do it.' She kissed the cat's head. 'Did I, Mr Seville? No, Mummy didn't do nothing.'

Stoney took out his notebook. 'Didn't do what?'

She sniffed and looked out of the window. 'They shout horrible things at me when I get my messages. I'm not well. They could kill me. One of the wee shites tried to kick Mr Seville! What kind of person does that? Should be locked up.'

Logan went to lean back against the wall, then caught himself and stood up straight again before he contracted anything sticky. 'Elaine Mitchel and Jane Taylor. They live here?'

Hard to believe that *anyone* lived here.

'I'm an old woman. I deserve better than this.'

A rat deserved better than this.

'Are they in?'

A shrug. 'They come and go, I'm not their mother.' She pulled up the sleeve of her cardigan for a scratch, and there they were: the tell-tale bruises and scabs of a long-term intravenous drug user. 'Ungrateful cows were supposed to get me some cider and ciggies.' She scratched. Licked her lips. Scratched again. 'You got any ciggies?'

Stoney dipped into his pocket for a packet of menthol, then cracked open a window, letting in the gentle hum of the city. Lit one of the cigarettes and handed it over.

She took it and pulled, cheeks hollow, the end glowing and sizzling. Holding the smoke in for a beat, before letting it out in a post-orgasmic sigh. 'They're good girls. They look after their Aunty Ina.'

Stoney put his cigarettes away. 'How long they been on the game?'

'Got to make ends meet, haven't we? God knows we get sod all off the welfare state.'

Logan opened his mouth, then closed it again. Her use of the plural there wasn't exactly conjuring up a happy image. 'We need to speak to them. They're not in trouble, we just need to ask them some questions about something they saw.'

The eyes brightened. 'There a reward?'

'No.'

'Oh.' She sat back again and stroked her pristine cat. 'Are you sure?'

'The Imperial March' blared out from Logan's pocket. 'Sorry,' he pointed over his shoulder at what looked like the kitchen door, 'can I take this in there?'

'Free country. Long as your pal gives us another ciggie.'

Logan slipped through into a galley kitchen that looked as if it'd been decorated by someone on a dirty protest. Though, presumably, it was food smeared up the walls. Please let it be food. A bin was heaped with ready-meal cartons and boxes, spilling out onto the floor and worktop. Cheap supermarket own-brand lasagne, burgers, sausages, shepherd's pie... Mystery meat and gristle with added sugar and salt.

The sink was buried under dishes and cutlery. A thick dusting of dead bluebottles on the windowsill filled the space between empty supermarket-whisky bottles. A single clean patch was reserved for a placemat on the floor with three bowls on it. One water, the others heaped with glistening brown food. Going by the empty pouches on the cooker, Mr Seville was eating better than the people. The cat's meals certainly cost a lot more.

Logan stood as far away from the units and surfaces as possible and pulled out his phone. 'What?'

'Sodding Clackmannanshire, that's what! Fifty-four percent voted "No", forty-six percent "Yes". What's wrong with people?'

He closed his eyes and massaged the bridge of his nose. 'Did you call me up to tell me that?'

'*First result and it's a "No". Half one and we've already got a sodding deficit of nearly three thousand votes to make up!*'

'Go away.'

'*Laz, have you got any idea—*'

He hung up, but the phone blared its Imperial theme at him again. He hit the button. 'I'm *working*.'

'*Dundee turnout's only seventy-nine percent. If every bugger had bothered their arse and showed up, that'd be another twenty-five thousand votes, right there! It—*'

He hung up again. Scrolled through the menu system before she could call back and blocked her number.

At least now he might get some sodding peace.

Back in the living room, Aunty Ina was well down her second cigarette, while Stoney leaned back against the windowsill. The cat paused, then went back to washing an immaculate pink-padded paw.

Stoney nodded at the kitchen. 'Something important, Guv?'

'No.' He stood in front of the couch. 'We any nearer?'

'Ina here says we can search Elaine and Jane's room for twenty quid.'

She smiled. 'Seeing as they're family, and that.'

4

Stoney had a wee shudder as he straightened up and made rubber spiders with his blue-nitriled fingers. 'I'm not even going to *try* to describe what it's like under the bed.'

Aunty Ina stood in the doorway, another one of Stoney's cigarettes poking out the side of her mouth, the big ginger cat clasped to her chest like a purring baby. 'Aye, they're a bit manky right enough.'

A *bit* manky?

The room was an open landfill site for dirty clothes, take-away containers, and abandoned gossip magazines. They made drifts in the corners, were piled up around the double bed, avalanched out of the battered wardrobe. It smelled like the inside of an old sock in here, one that had been marinated in cannabis resin and sweat.

Logan tried his luck with the chest of drawers in the corner. The top one creaked out with a groan. Nothing but cheap-looking frilly pants. Some of which hadn't been washed.

'Course, they take after their mum. Never met a bigger slag in your life than Morag.'

Next drawer: socks tied in tight little bundles.

'So Morag's up the stick with Elaine, and she and

Whatsisname get married. Registry office. Couldn't wear white, could she? Not when half the school'd had a go.' Aunty Ina took a drag and blew a lungful of smoke at the stained ceiling. 'Didn't last. Well, hard to be a dad when you've got a paper round, isn't it?'

Next drawer: baby toys. Rattles, dummies, shaky things in the shape of flowers, a stars-and-moon mobile still in the packaging. A pink fuzzy cat. A tiny romper suit with orange and black stripes like a tiger. He pulled the tiger costume out and held it up. 'Does Elaine or Jane have a child?' Because if they did, Social Services were getting a call to rescue it from this rancid hovel.

Aunty Ina stuck the cigarette back in her mouth and shifted her grip on her cat. 'Naw, that's Elaine's. Silly cow thinks she'll be a *wonderful* mummy someday. As if. Collects this crap the whole time. Got bags of it in the wardrobe.'

Yeah, because *that* wasn't creepy.

'Anyway,' Ina rubbed Mr Seville's tummy, 'then along comes Shuggie and sweeps Morag off her feet. Come with me, baby, we'll see the world…' A sigh. 'Real looker he was too.'

Last drawer. It was full of carrier bags.

'Course, she's full of herself. "Oh, he loves me. Oh, he'll do anything for me. Oh, we're so happy." And six weeks later, she's got a broken arm, a broken nose, she's pregnant – *again* – and Shuggie's shacked up with some other poor cow.'

Logan tipped the first bag out on the bare mattress. An assortment of watches spilled out onto the stained fabric. A few still had the price stickers attached.

'Eight years later, and she's overdosed in a squat and I'm lumbered with her bloody kids. Some sister, eh?'

The next bag contained cheap jewellery, the kind sold at the tills in Markies and BHS. All plastic and shiny bits. All still pinned to rectangles of cardboard.

'Lucky the wee buggers didn't end up in care.'

Logan looked around the horrible little room Elaine and Jane shared in the horrible little flat, with their horrible little aunt. 'Yeah, *really* lucky.'

Bag number three was full of cosmetics from Boots – own-brand stuff, probably snatched off the shelves while no one was looking.

Aunty Ina finished her cigarette and pinged the butt away into the piles of dirty clothes. Then rubbed her ginger baby between the ears. 'If you find any money, it's mine. They borrowed it.'

Bag number four was different. It contained a parcel of white powder – about the size of a mealie pudding – wrapped up in layers of clingfilm and secured with strips of parcel tape. 'Well, well, well.'

Little beads of dark red had dried on the plastic surface, like ladybirds.

'The lying wee shites!' Aunty Ina stamped a foot on the bare floorboards, making Mr Seville wriggle in her arms. 'They told me they didn't have any gear!'

The patrol car pulled up outside the tower block, lights spinning in the darkness, and sat there – doors closed.

Logan stepped out from the block's shadow and rapped on the driver's window. 'You planning on joining us?'

Constable Haynes smiled up at him, then fluttered her eyelashes. 'Wanted to make sure it was safe, Guv. I leave Wee Billy here unsupervised for five minutes, might come back to find someone's nicked his boots and truncheon. He's only new.'

Her partner, sitting in the passenger seat, blushed – gritting his teeth and saying nothing, like a big boy.

Logan pointed up at Aunty Ina's flat. 'Top floor. No lift. Make sure the auld wifie stays put till we get the Procurator Fiscal organised. Soon as you're *there*, tell DC Stone he's wanted back *here*. And while you're at it—' His phone launched into its anonymous ringtone. 'Hold on.' He pulled it out and pressed the button. 'McRae.'

'Seven morons in Clackmananshire voted "Yes" and "No" on the same ballot paper. You believe that? How thick can they be?'

He closed his eyes. 'It's you.'

'Couldn't get through on my phone. Had to borrow one. Sodding Glasgow's seventy-five percent turnout. Seventy-five percent! What sodding use is that? Even Aberdeen managed eighty-two.'

'Stop calling me with numbers, OK? I – don't – care. I'm *working.*'

'Seventy-five percent. How many thousands of votes is that lost? Eh? You know what I think? I think—'

Logan hung up. Barred that number too.

PC Haynes pulled her bowler down low on her head, leaving just the fringes of her bob showing. 'Let me guess, Detective Chief Inspector Steel?'

Her partner clambered out of the car, all sticky-out ears and chin. 'She's driving everyone mental back at the ranch. Stand still for two minutes and she'll get you working out percentages and stuff. Nightmare. Like being back at school.'

Logan punched the duty superintendent's number into his mobile and wandered over to the pool car he and Stoney had arrived in, settling back against the bonnet while it rang.

A large, sharp voice battered out of the earpiece. *'Superintendent Ward.'*

'Sir? DI McRae. Just found a block of what looks like coke in a flat.'

'You have a search warrant?'

'Permission from the householder. We were looking for the two women who said they'd seen Chris Browning on the fourth. Their aunt told us we could search the place if we liked.'

'Hmmm… Let me have a word with the PF. Everyone still in situ?'

'Left DC Stone with the aunt, sir. Uniform's just arrived.'

'Good. Right. I'll let you know.'

And with any luck, that would be enough to cover Logan and Stoney's backsides when it got to court. Logan slipped his phone into his pocket, and settled back to wait.

Langstane Place bustled with staggery groups of men and women, calling and whooping to each other. A handful of Temporary Public Urination Stations, AKA: Daleks, had been set up along the road. Big grey plastic things, with four semi-private bays for people to pee in. Not exactly classy, but it was better than them doing it in shop doorways.

Stoney checked his watch. 'Twenty to.'

Logan sucked on his teeth for a bit. 'Don't see them, do you?'

'I remember when this was nothing but houses and churches. Now look at it.'

'Showing your age, Stoney. Got to move with the times.'

The place was one long ribbon of nightclubs, all heaving with referendum-night parties. Blootered voters, looking to exercise their democratic right to hump a drunken stranger. Offering to stuff each other's ballot boxes.

Aunty Ina had named a couple of places where her nieces usually plied their trade on a Thursday night. Regent Quay was one of them, this was the other.

Logan pulled out another copy of Elaine and Jane's mugshots – both looking half-dead and sallow, with a height chart behind them. He held the printout up for the bouncer outside Sneaky Jimmy's – a slab of muscle with a number-one buzz cut and tattoos up her neck. 'You seen either of these women?'

She narrowed her eyes and peered at the sheet. Then turned and waved her companion over. He wasn't as big as she was, but his scalp looked as if a Rottweiler had been chewing on it, scar tissue showing through the severe haircut.

267

'Marky, you seen this pair tonight?'

He bared his teeth and sooked a breath through them. 'Aye.' A finger like a sausage poked the paper. 'This one was minesweeping. Nicking other people's drinks when they wasn't looking. This one,' he poked the other photo, 'got into a fight in the ladies. Had to throw the pair of them out on their arses.' He raised an arm, then pulled up his shiny black bomber jacket, exposing a circle of red across his ribs. 'Cow bit me, and everything.'

Stoney tutted. 'Better get that looked at, mate. Don't want to catch anything.'

Logan took the printout back. 'When was this?'

'About twenty minutes ago? Something like that?'

And they hadn't been into any of the other nightclubs, so that really only left one place. Back to the docks.

'Thanks.' He turned and his phone launched into 'If I Only Had a Brain'. That would be Rennie. He followed Stoney back to the pool car and hit the button. 'McRae.'

A smoky growl sounded in his ear. *'Are you avoiding me?'*

Oh God, not her *again*.

'Yes. Take the hint.'

'Orkney: sixty-seven percent "No", thirty-three "Yes". Bloody Shetland's no better: sixty-four, thirty-six. What are we—'

'Have you done any work at all tonight?'

There was a pause. *'Might have done.'*

'Yeah, well I've recovered about a quarter kilo of cocaine. Go do something productive for a change.'

'No point. Shift ends in fifteen. Fancy hitting the pub?'

For goodness sake. He drummed his fingers on the car roof as Stoney unlocked it. 'I'm on *nights*, remember? Don't get off till seven in the morning.'

'Aye, well, there'll still be places open. I'm going to hang about and inspire the troops.'

Oh joy.

5

'What do you think, Guv – call it a night?' Stoney stuck his hands in his pockets and drew a foot along the double yellow line on Shore Lane.

Logan pulled his sleeve back and angled his watch so the streetlight's sickly glow caught the dial. 'Better give it till four. Make sure everyone's had time to stagger down here from the nightclubs.'

Besides, with any luck, Steel would have given up by then and sodded off home, leaving everyone in peace.

Shore Lane stretched from Regent Quay to the dual carriageway on the other side, where the occasional lonely taxi drifted by on its way somewhere much nicer than this. A canyon of granite, punctuated by darkened windows and downpipes.

Stoney puffed out a breath – just visible in the night air – then shrugged. 'Might as well get on with it, I suppose.' He turned and wandered down the lane, making for the dual carriageway.

Logan headed back to Regent Quay instead. A couple of flats had their lights on, probably sitting up watching the results come in, but mostly it was darkness. On the other side of the harbour wall, the security lights blazed, making the vast orange vessels glow.

The Regents Arms was still open though, one of those harbour pubs with an all-night licence for the shift workers. The sort of place you could get a sausage buttie and a pint of Guinness at six in the morning. The sort of place you could get your head kicked in for looking at someone funny. Even if you *were* a police officer.

A figure stood outside the door, hunched over, one hand cupped around a cigarette as if someone was going to snatch it off him if he lowered his guard. Cardigan, jeans, slippers, a nose that could prize open tin cans. He nodded as Logan passed, setting a mop of grey hair swinging. 'Inspector.'

'Donald.'

More grey buildings, shut up for the night.

The *clang, clang, clang* of something metal getting battered with a hammer came from the harbour. A people carrier drove past. Somewhere in the distance, someone launched into a mournful and tuneless rendition of 'My Love is like a Red, Red Rose'.

Logan turned the corner onto Water Lane, for about the ninth time that night.

Halfway down, beneath a broken streetlamp, a couple of figures huddled in the gloom. One tall, one not so much. Little more than silhouettes, caught in the glow of the dual carriageway behind. Then the shorter one sank down to its knees while the taller one leaned back against the wall.

No prizes for guessing what was going on there, then.

Hopefully whoever was on their knees had been paid in advance, because unless the tall guy was a *really* quick finisher, there wasn't going to be time to negotiate afterwards.

Logan marched down the cobblestones. Reached into his pocket for his LED torch.

Got within thirty feet, then clicked it on.

A harsh cone of bright white stabbed through the darkness, catching a bald man with his trousers and pants around his ankles, head thrown back; and a skeletal woman kneeling in front of him, head bobbing at his crotch.

Logan took a deep breath. 'POLICE!'

Mr Tall jerked upright. Spluttering, mouth stretched out like a dying frog. 'Shite!' He shoved the woman away, and he was off, lurching and scrambling as fast as he could with his trousers hobbling him.

The woman hit the cobblestones with a crack.

And twenty seconds later, so did Mr Tall – betrayed by his treacherous trousers. He careened into the road with arms and legs flailing. Scrambled to his knees, pulled himself upright, hauled his trousers into a more acceptable position, and ran for it.

Logan let him go. Stood over the fallen woman and offered her a hand up.

She scowled at him. Her cheekbones were razor sharp, her eyes hollow and dark. Her body shook and trembled, as if she'd been stuck on the spin cycle. 'You think that was *funny*?'

'You get the cash upfront?'

'Could've killed me.'

'Look on the bright side: you got paid and you don't have to do the deed.'

Elaine Mitchel sniffed. Then wiped her nose on the sleeve of her jacket, adding to the silver trails. She turned her head, staring off down the darkened lane after her departed customer. 'True.' A strangler's ring of love bites encircled her throat.

Logan helped her up. 'Been looking for you all night.' Then pulled out the missing person poster. 'You recognise this man?'

Her eyes flicked towards the poster, then away again. 'Don't remember, like.' Heat radiated from her bony chest, taking with it a smell of stale perfume and sweat.

Logan shone his torch on the poster, so the picture was nice and clear. 'Come on, have another look'.

She did, but only for the briefest of beats. 'Don't remember.'

'Chris Browning, forty-two, brown hair, glasses, slightly posh Aberdonian accent.'

She took a step away. 'Got stuff to do.'

Logan grabbed her arm. It was barely there – just a length of bone, wrapped in snot-streaked material, burning into his palm. 'His family's worried, OK?'

Elaine looked down at Logan's hand, then up to his face. 'You want to touch me, you gotta pay.'

He let go. 'Come on, Elaine, no one's seen him for two weeks. You told Jimmy from the *Aberdeen Examiner* that you saw Chris Browning on the fourth. You said he was a regular.'

She stared at her shoes – high heels, the leather all scuffed and stained. 'Don't remember. Didn't talk to no journo.'

'Jimmy *named* you, Elaine. Gave up his source, just like that.'

Her thin lips disappeared inside her mouth, creases forming between her eyebrows. 'Don't remember.'

A pair of headlights paused at the entrance to the lane … and then drifted past. Not this time.

'OK. I understand.' Logan nodded. 'Elaine Mitchel, I'm detaining you under Section Fourteen of the—'

'No.' She backed up, until she was against the wall. 'I don't…' She threw her arms out to the sides. 'Could you not leave us alone?'

'Section Fourteen of the Criminal Procedure – Scotland – Act 1995, because I suspect you of having committed an offence punishable by imprisonment. You—'

'OK! OK.' A sigh. 'OK. I never met the man.' She pointed at the poster. 'Him.'

'You told Jimmy that Chris Browning was down here every Wednesday, paying for, and I quote, "Disgusting and unusual sex acts".'

272

One bony shoulder came up to her ear, then fell again. 'Never met him.'

'Then why say you did?'

'Money.' She smiled at Logan, all twisted brown teeth and beige gums. 'A *hundred* quid.'

The wall behind the bar was festooned with stolen apostrophes. Some were large and plastic, some small and metal, some neon, others designed to be illuminated by whoever paid for them in the first place, not knowing that some wee sod from Aberdeen was going to wheech up a ladder with a screwdriver in the middle of the night and make off with their punctuation.

The barman took one look at Logan and sighed. Then raised his voice, so the dozen people spread in ones and twos about the place could hear over the telly playing in the corner of the room. 'Detective Inspector, what can I get you?'

Subtle.

Logan pointed at Elaine Mitchel. 'You?'

'Double vodka.'

'And a tin of Irn-Bru.'

The barman clunked a glass up beneath the optic, twice, then dumped it on the bar. 'You want a glass with the Irn-Bru?'

And give him something to spit in? 'No thanks. Tin's fine.'

It was produced, and Logan paid the man, then led the way across to a table in the corner, away from the speakers. Sitting with his back to the wall, just in case.

He wiped a thumb across the tin's top, clearing off the sheen of dew, then clicked the ringpull off. 'A hundred quid's a lot of money.'

Elaine shrugged, then took a sip. Holding the vodka in her mouth with her eyes closed. Savouring it.

'Who paid?'

She swallowed. Sighed. 'A man. Same as usual.'

'You know who he is?'

Elaine shifted in her seat, looking back at the television with its array of BBC journalists and pundits sitting behind a big curved desk. 'Any idea how it's going?'

'Do you know who paid you? Did you get a name?'

'We did a postal vote. Just in case, you know? Wanted to make sure it counted.' Another sip of vodka.

Up on the screen, they were scrolling through the results so far. 'WESTERN ISLES: "No". 53% To 47%. INVERCLYDE: "No". 50.1% To 49.9%.'

Steel would *love* that.

'Elaine. I need a name, or I can't help you.'

She picked at the table, where someone had carved the initials DG into the wood. 'Who says I need help? Doing fine, aren't I?'

'We were at your aunt's place tonight. She showed us your room.'

Elaine turned back to the television. 'Going to be no, isn't it? Probably just as well.'

'Want to guess what we found in your chest of drawers? Right at the bottom, with all the shoplifted watches, makeup, and costume jewellery?'

'What'd happen to all the benefits, eh? Who's going to pay our dole: BP and Shell? My arse.'

'We found about a quarter kilo of cocaine, Elaine. About, what, a good ten, twelve grand's worth?'

'Then there's all the supermarkets putting up their prices, and the banks sodding off down south, and the other big companies...'

'That's possession with intent.'

'And they'll close the border. Be like, a big stretch of barbed wire from Gretna to Berwick-upon-Tweed. Guard towers and spotlights and Alsatians and ghettos...'

'You're looking at nine to thirteen years, Elaine.'

She sniffed. Polished off her vodka. 'Isn't mine. Found it.'

He sat back. 'Here we go.'

'Nope, it's the God's. Me and Jane found it, down the Green. Can't bang us up if it isn't ours.'

'You *found* a quarter kilo of cocaine lying about in the Green?'

'Na. Yeah.' The bony shoulders rose and fell. 'Kinda. This bloke was doing a runner, right? Battering it down Correction Wynd, under the bridge hell-for-leather into the Green. Got a nose like a burst ketchup bottle, blood all down the front of his shirt. He dumps this padded envelope in a bin and keeps going. Thirty seconds later, these three big bastards hammer after him. Caught him outside Granite Reef and pounded the crap out of him.'

Logan's eyebrow climbed up his forehead. 'When was this?'

'Dunno. Tuesday?'

It was the assault Steel couldn't be bothered investigating because an Edinburgh drug dealer getting beaten up wasn't 'major' enough. And it explained what the little dark-red spots on the package of coke were. Blood.

'You see who did it?'

'Depends. It worth something?'

'Nine to thirteen years. You help me, I help you.'

She stuck a finger in her empty glass and wiped up the last smears of alcohol. Sooked it clean. 'You know Alec Hadden: drinks in here sometimes?'

'He one of them?'

Elaine shook her head. 'He's the one gave me and Jane a hundred quid to say that Chris Browning was a regular. Told us to say the guy was into all kinds of filthy stuff, you know? Real pervert scumbag. Likes it rough up the bum and that.'

Logan looked over her shoulder, taking in the assembled slouch of wee-small-hours drinkers. 'This Alec in tonight?'

She checked. 'Nah. Doesn't usually come in till five or six, though. Think he works up the hospital or something, doesn't get off till then.' Elaine smiled at Logan, exposing a lopsided jumble of brown teeth. 'If we're waiting, any chance of another voddie?'

Something buzzed in Logan's pocket. 'Hold on.' He pulled it out: text message.

```
I love Dundee!!!

Yes: 57%!!! Wee dancers!

I'm never making fun of Dundee ever again.

Dundee! Dundee! Dundee!
```

That would be Steel, hijacking someone else's phone again. Well, at least she was happy for a change. The phone vibrated in his fingers.

```
Well, maybe not never ever, it is Dundee
after all.
```

And again.

```
Sodding Renfrewshire is No: 53%

Tossers.
```

How could she type so fast with her thumbs?

He put his phone on the table and Elaine jerked her head towards the bar.

'So… Vodka?'

'Nope: station.'

That brown smile died. 'But—'

'A quarter kilo of cocaine, remember?' He stood. 'You

276

need to make a statement, or you need to go to prison. Your choice. But either way there's no more vodka in it.'

She slumped right down, until her top half rested on the table. 'Noooo…'

'How about this: you help me catch the guys who beat up the drug dealer, and I'll buy you a whole bottle?'

There was a small pause, then she dragged herself to her feet. 'Better than nothing.'

6

There was a knock on the interview room door, then Stoney appeared. 'Guv?'

His moustache was slightly … lopsided. He had a scrape on his cheek and what looked like the beginnings of an excellent shiner spreading beneath his right eye.

Logan frowned. 'Detective Constable Stone enters the room.'

Sitting on the other side of the table, Elaine slumped to one side. 'Can I go for a pee?'

'In a minute.' Logan pointed. 'What happened to you?'

'Gah…' His mouth stretched out and down. 'Jane Taylor happened. Had to drop her off at the hospital, couldn't even stand, she was so drunk. Didn't stop her though.' He fingered the bruise beneath his eye. 'Like a blootered Mike Tyson.'

'Yeah, Janey always did take after her dad.' Elaine's feet drummed on the grey floor. 'Seriously, I'm *bursting* here.'

What the hell. 'Interview suspended at four twenty-two. DC Stone, can you escort Miss Mitchel to the bathroom and back again. Ten minutes.'

He backed off a pace. 'She doesn't bite, does she?'

That brown smile was back. 'Not unless you pay extra.'

*   *   *

Logan took a sip from his polystyrene cup on the way back to his office. The coffee from the machine wasn't great at the best of times, but there was something about drinking it out of expanded hydrocarbon foam that really classed it up. Could always sneak into the MIT office and help himself to their stash. After all, they'd all have gone home for the night.

He dumped the cup in the nearest bin and made for the stairs. Taking them two at a time up to the next floor. Pushed through the door into the Major Investigation Team's domain.

Stopped.

So much for sneaking a go on their fancy coffee machine in secret.

Half a dozen plainclothes officers lounged in office chairs, all facing the large flatscreen TV at the front of the room, watching the BBC's live coverage. The interactive whiteboard was divided up into a grid – percentages and numbers across the top, the name of each Scottish region down the side.

The office was easily six times bigger than the grubby hovel that CID had been relegated to. Here they had new desks. New chairs. New ceiling tiles. A carpet that didn't look as if a herd of incontinent sheep had rampaged across it for twenty years. New computers. State-of-the-art tech kit. And right at the back, one of those fancy coffee machines that took wee pod cartridges and produced something that didn't taste of boiled slurry.

Steel had pride of place, surrounded by her minions, a bottle of Grant's Whisky open on the desk beside her, next to a pizza box containing a couple of congealed slices. She took a sip and scowled at him. 'West Dumbartonshire: fifty-four percent "Yes", forty-six "No".'

'That's good, isn't it?' Might as well brass neck it. He wandered over to the coffee machine and plucked a cartridge at random. Stuck it in the machine.

'No' good enough. Sodding Stirling was sixty percent "No".
Sixty.'

The machine churned and groaned and chugged.

Steel pointed at a bloke in a stripy shirt and undone tie.
'Colin?'

He nodded, blinked in slow motion, then squinted at the
whiteboard. 'Midlothian fifty-six percent "No". East Lothian:
sixty-two percent "No". Falkirk: fifty-three percent "No".'

Steel waved a hand. 'Shut up, they're doing Angus. Come
on Angus, do it for Aunty Roberta…'

Up on the screen, a man with almost no hair above his
ears stood behind a podium, in front of an Angus Council
display board. '… *the total number of rejected votes was sixty-six
and the reasons were, for rejection, were as follows. Seventeen for
voting for both answers—'*

'How? How could anyone be that stupid? It's a yes or no
sodding question!'

*'The total number of votes cast in relation to each answer to the
referendum question, in this area, was as follows…'*

'Stop milking it and read the sodding result!'

*'"Yes": thirty-five thousand and forty-four. "No": forty-five thou-
sand one hundred and ninety-two. That concludes this evening's
count.'*

'Noooooooooooo!' Steel buried her head in her hands.
'Sodding hell.'

Logan grabbed his coffee and slipped out before she resur-
faced.

Elaine yawned, showing off those crooked brown teeth again.
Most of them boasted a shiny grey chunk of dentist's jewellery. She sagged in her seat. 'We about done?'

'Just a couple more things.' Logan turned the ID book
around so it faced her. 'Can you identify the fourth man?'

She sighed, then jabbed a finger at the page, selecting a

hairy man with tiny squinty eyes and a nose that pointed at his left cheek. 'Him.'

'And you're certain?'

'Said so, didn't I?'

'Right.' Logan copied Captain Hairy's name into his notebook. 'For the record, Miss Mitchel has identified Dominic Walker as the fourth assailant. And that's it?'

She nodded. 'Can I sod off now?'

'One more.' Logan closed the book, then checked his notes. 'I need an ID for Alec Hadden – the guy who paid you to lie about Chris Browning being one of your regulars.'

Elaine shrugged. 'Tell you what, Regents Arms is open till nine. How about we go back there and wait till he turns up?' She licked her lips with a pale, dead-slug tongue. 'Get a couple of drinks. Get a bit friendlier...?'

Sitting next to him, Stoney flinched. 'Gah!'

Logan frowned at him. 'You OK?'

Colour rushed up his cheeks. 'She's playing footsy under the table, Guv. Came as a bit of a shock.'

Took all sorts. 'Interview suspended at four forty-five so Constable Stone can assist Miss Mitchel with the production of an identikit picture of Alec Hadden.' Logan switched off the recorder and stood. 'No funny business.'

'Guv, it wasn't—'

'Now: none of that. You keep your galloping hormones to yourself.' He left them to it, pulling out his phone and dialling with his thumb as he made his way back to the office. 'Guthrie? It's Logan. My office: I want you to run some PNC checks.'

'Guv.'

By the time he got there, PC Guthrie was already waiting, like an expectant golden retriever. Logan scribbled down names for each of the four thugs Elaine Mitchel had IDed then added 'ALEC HADDEN' at the bottom. 'Full check on the lot of them. Then get onto the hospital and see when they think Jane Taylor will be sober enough to interview.'

'Guv.' He stood there, clutching the sheet of paper.

'Run along then.'

'Oh, right.'

Logan settled behind his desk and pulled over the phone. Put in a call to Aberdeen Royal Infirmary. But no one there had heard of Alec Hadden. Was he sure he'd got the name right? Not really. Ah well, better luck next time.

Worth a try though.

He logged back into his computer, getting the paperwork started for a warrant to arrest the guys who'd battered the drug dealer from Edinburgh. Assuming they could get Jane Taylor to corroborate her sister's IDs, that was. Be hard to convince a sheriff to give them a warrant on the say so of a single addict. Two: yes, one: no.

There was a knock on the door, and Stoney stuck his head in. The shiner was darkening nicely beneath his eye. 'Guv?' He held up a printout. 'Alec Hadden.'

Wow.

'That was fast.'

'Used my initiative, Guv, and googled him.' Stoney put the printout on the desk. It was a photo of a thin man with shoulder-length brown hair and a broad grin, underneath the headline, 'LOCAL MAN IS WORLD PORRIDGE CHAMPION'.

'*World* porridge champion. La-dee-dah.'

'Bet he keeps the trophy where everyone can see it too. Looks the type, doesn't he?'

'OK. He's supposed to be at the Regents Arms sometime after five. Probably better keep it low key – last thing we need's a brawl kicking off in there.'

Stoney grimaced. 'You sure we can't call in the Riot Brigade? Regents Arms isn't exactly cop-friendly.'

'Low key does *not* mean shields, battering rams, and

crash helmets. We'll go with you, me, and Wheezy Doug… What?'

'Wheezy's got court tomorrow. Went home at midnight, remember?'

'OK, when Guthrie's done with the PNC checks, tell him to change into civvies. We're going down the pub.'

7

'Dear God, it's Action Man!' Stoney rocked back on his heels as PC Guthrie appeared in the corridor.

He'd changed out of his police-ninja black into a pair of cargo pants, green jumper with patches on the elbows and shoulders, and finished the ensemble off with a pair of big black boots. 'What?'

'Go on, do the kung fu grip thing.'

Logan hit Stoney. 'Don't mock the afflicted. Everyone ready?'

All three of them produced their handcuffs, and wee CS gas canisters. Then Guthrie dug into one of his many trouser pockets and came out with a canister of Bite Back. 'Just in case.'

'Good boy.' Logan put his cuffs away. 'Right, let's do it. We can… What?'

Stoney was staring over his shoulder. 'Guv?'

A smoky voice of doom grated out behind. 'Gah! It's all *ruined*.'

Logan didn't bother turning around. What was the point? 'Detective Chief Inspector Steel, I presume.'

She sniffed. 'Sodding Aberdeen City. How *could* you?' The words were a little slurred at the edges. 'Cowardly bastards.'

Stoney winced. 'More "No"s?'

'The sodding BBC have called it. Twenty-six out of thirty-two local authorities so far, and only four voted "Yes". *Four*. Two hundred and thirty *thousand* votes down. No way we can come back from this. It's over and Scotland bottled it!' A hand slapped down on Logan's shoulder. 'Laz, I think we need to go get very, very drunk.'

Stoney grinned. 'Funny you should say that, we're off to— Ow! You kicked me!'

Logan kept his eyes on Steel. 'We're away to pick up a suspect.'

She narrowed her eyes. 'You're a lying wee sod.' She poked him in the chest and leaned in, enveloping him in second-hand whisky fumes. 'Where are you off to?'

Guthrie stuck up his hand. 'The Regents Arms. Going to arrest someone.'

Steel beamed and threw her arms wide. 'Perfect! I'll come supervise.'

'Oh no you don't.' Logan backed towards the exit. 'You're off duty, and you've been drinking. You're supervising nobody.'

'Fine.' She dropped her arms and narrowed her eyes. 'Be like that.' Then she turned and marched off down the corridor. 'But don't say I didn't warn you.'

Wonderful.

The same auld mannie was standing outside the Regents Arms, smoking another furtive cigarette, in his slippers. He nodded as Logan stepped up to the door. 'Inspector.'

'Donald.'

Inside, the number of patrons out for a pre-dawn booze-up had swelled to twenty. All nursing drinks. Their sour faces turned to watch as Logan, Stoney, and PC Guthrie marched in. Then slowly drifted back to the TV.

The usual suspects were up there on the screen, pontificating as the ticker crawled along at the bottom of the picture. '"No": 1,402,047 – "Yes": 1,171,708'

Stoney had a quick look around. 'No sign of Hadden. Maybe he's been and gone?'

Guthrie pulled up his combat trousers. 'Might be in the bogs?'

Logan pointed. 'The pair of you go check.' Yes, it might look a bit odd, the two of them going in together, but this way they were more likely to make it out again alive.

As they marched off, Logan wandered up to the bar. 'Two tins of Irn-Bru, and one Diet Coke. Don't need glasses.'

The barman sighed, then turned and took their drinks out of the fridge. Placed them in front of Logan. 'You vote today?'

'Yup.' He pulled out the photo Stoney had downloaded. 'You seen this guy?'

A pause. Then a raised eyebrow. 'World porridge champion?'

'Has he been in?'

'Don't remember.' The barman turned and picked up a tumbler. Pressed it against an optic of Bells. Placed the whisky in front of Logan, along with the tins. 'That one's on the house for participating in the democratic process.' Delivered without a hint of a smile.

OK…

Logan paid for the other drinks and carried the lot over to the same table he'd had last time. Back to the wall. Good view of the rest of the bar and the entrance.

Two minutes later, Stoney and Guthrie emerged from the toilets and joined him.

'What took you so long?'

Guthrie twisted a finger through an imaginary lock of hair. 'Doing our makeup and talking about boys.'

Stoney shifted in his seat, having another look around. Then cracked the tab on his Diet Coke. 'Don't look now, but: six o'clock. That not Kurt Murison?'

'Where?' Guthrie turned right around and stared.

Stoney hit him. Dropped his voice to a harsh whisper. 'I said, don't look!'

'How am I supposed to know if it's him if I don't look?'

Logan scanned the interior. Six o'clock. Even sitting down the man towered over the table. Broad shoulders. Shaven head. Ears that looked as if they'd been designed for someone a third the size. Huge hands.

He looked up and for a moment their eyes met.

Not romantic.

Logan glanced at the television instead. Kept his voice low. 'Yup, that's Kurt Murison.'

'Crap.' Deep breath. 'What do we do?'

'Nothing. We sit here and we drink our fizzy juice and we wait for Alec Hadden to turn up.' He had a sip of Irn-Bru. 'And if Kurt makes a move, the two of you follow him and arrest him.'

Guthrie pulled a face. 'You sure? Because I remember what happened the last time someone tried it. DS MacEachran was in traction for six weeks.'

'DS MacEachran is an idiot.'

'True.'

They sat. And they waited. And they drank their fizzy juice.

Up on the TV, someone in an ill-fitting suit was going on about the new political landscape and how great it was everyone had come out to play.

Stoney checked his watch. 'What if Hadden's a no show?'

'Then you and Guthrie still get to arrest Kurt Murison.'

'Oh joy.'

The ticker ran the latest scores again. '"Yes": 54.47% "No": 45.53%'

'You know what?' Stoney turned his Diet Coke round in a circle. 'Maybe it's for the best? I mean, if we'd got independence, we'd just be swapping one load of shiftless thieving useless bastards for another lot, wouldn't we?'

Guthrie sniffed. 'Yeah, but they'd be *our* shiftless thieving useless bastards.'

Logan polished off the last of his Irn-Bru, 'And, to be fair, we're already paying for two lots of them... Uh-oh – we've got movement.'

Kurt Murison scraped back his chair and got to his feet. Dear God, he was even bigger standing up. His arms were too big to hang loose at his sides, instead they stood out from his huge chest, as if he was carrying an invisible barrel under each one. He turned and lumbered towards the toilets, leaving a half-empty pint and an open packet of crisps behind. Safe in the knowledge that no one would *dare* touch them.

Guthrie pushed his tin away. 'Probably off to coil a Douglas, or, perchance, a Thora.'

'Don't be daft.' Stoney rolled his eyes. 'Tell him, Guv: men do Douglases, women do Thoras. Basic biology, isn't it?' He peered over his shoulder. 'Maybe we should go after him? Catch him with his pants down.'

Logan shook his head. 'We're police officers, Detective Constable Stone, not monsters.'

That got him a sigh. 'You know what I think?' Stoney dunked a finger off the tabletop. 'I think Scotland, England, Ireland, and Wales should all get their own parliament, and then once a week they do this big joint videoconference to decide stuff that affects everyone. That way we could fire half the buggers and save ourselves a fortune.'

Guthrie shook his head. 'Better idea: performance-related beatings for all politicians. Could put it on TV and charge people to phone in with suggestions.' He had a half-arsed attempt at a Geordie accent. 'It's day two in the Westminster house, and the Prime Minister's trying to weasel his way out of a kick in the nads.'

Stoney mimed picking up the phone, joining in with an OTT Cockney. 'Cor blimey guvnor, Oi'm gonna bid fifteen quid to see him battered wiv an *'addock*!'

'And here's the leader of the opposition, still dressed in a rubber gimp suit after making a prick of himself on Monday.'

'Luv a duck! Twenny quid if ye paddle his arse wiv an electric *saaaaaandar*.'

Guthrie grinned. 'See? You could wipe out the deficit in a single season.'

'This is genius, we should call Channel Four.'

Logan leaned back in his seat and left them to it.

Still no sign of Alec Hadden. Assuming, of course that Elaine hadn't made the whole thing up in the first place. Maybe Chris Browning *was* one her regulars? Still, why would she lie about being paid to slander him? What was in it for her? Didn't make any... Hold on.

The front door barely creaked as a thin man slipped in. Had to be a regular, because no one looked up from their drink. Shoulder-length brown hair, pointy chin. This year's World Porridge Champion. Alec Hadden.

So Elaine wasn't lying after all. Wonders would never cease.

Hadden had a quick peer about, then made for the bar. Stood there with his back hunched, in conversation with the bartender. Got himself a pint of Export.

Stoney and Guthrie had extended their brief to take in the United Nations and nipple clamps. Logan leaned forward and hushed them. 'Alec Hadden. At the bar. Right now.'

Guthrie slipped a hand into his pocket and pulled out the cuffs. 'You want to grab him straight away, or let him settle in?'

'Ah...' Stoney licked his lips. 'Might be an idea to get it over with while Kurt's in the toilet? If he sees us slapping the cuffs on someone, it'll kick off.'

True.

'OK.' Logan pushed back his chair. 'Let's go see what Mr Hadden has to say for—'

The front door banged open and the whole bar did its *Deliverance* impersonation again. Silence. Stare.

Then Logan groaned.

Sodding DCI Sodding Steel. She stood in the doorway, wobbling slightly. One eye screwed shut, the other roving the place.

'Oh *great*.'

She lurched across to the bar and dug a hand in her pocket. Came out with a handful of change and a few notes. Clacked them down on the bartop. A couple of pound coins rolled off along the front of the taps. 'Grouse. Make it a … a brace.' She grabbed onto the wood with one hand, keeping herself upright.

The barman nodded. 'Double Grouse, coming right up, *Chief Inspector*.' Raising his voice on that last bit, just to make sure everyone heard.

Over at the next table, a large woman with a tattoo of seagulls flying around her thick neck rolled her eyes. 'Not more sodding cops. Like a bloody masonic lodge in here tonight.'

Steel took her drink and wacked it back in one go. 'Again.'

Then she turned, new drink in hand, and squinted around the room. Wobbled in place. Pointed up at the TV where a bloke in a suit stood before a big display banner with views of Aberdeenshire on it. 'Shhhhhh…! Turn it up, turn it up.'

The barman sighed, then did.

'… *turnout is eighty-seven point two percent. The total number of votes cast for each answer to the referendum question in this area are as follows. "Yes": seventy-one thousand, three hundred and thirty-seven. "No": one hundred and eight thousand, six hundred and six.*'

A roaring cheer erupted from the telly.

And when it had died down, *'I'm not quite finished.'*

Laughter.

Steel clenched one fist, the other wrapped around her glass, and bellowed up at the TV. 'YOU BUNCH OF UTTER BASTARDS!' Whisky slopped onto the wooden floor.

The barman cranked the sound down again.

Everybody stared at her.

The bathroom door clunked shut again, and there was Kurt Murison, wiping his hands on his jeans. 'Who's bastards?' His voice was unusually high for someone who looked as if they could eat rusty nails.

Stoney closed his eyes and swore. 'It's going to kick off, isn't it?'

Kurt loomed over Steel. 'Come on then. Who's bastards?'

She twirled round, more whisky joining the spillage. 'Aberdeenshire. All of them: *bastards*.' She jabbed her free hand at the screen. 'Look at it! Over sixty percent "No".'

A shrug. 'Their prerogative, isn't it? Democracy and that. Will of the people.'

'The people are dicks.' She raised the glass to her mouth and swigged, but there wasn't a lot left. 'Oh...' She clunked it down on the bar. 'Again.'

'Got to respect the outcome, don't matter what side you voted. All still Scotland.'

'They can respect my sharny arse.' She rocked a little, then frowned up at him. 'Here, do I know you?'

Hadden inched away down the bar. Putting a bit of space between himself and the coming storm.

Kurt jabbed a thick, meaty finger into Steel's shoulder. 'People like you make me sick, with your "Remember Bannockburn" and quotes from sodding *Braveheart*.'

Guthrie got to his feet and pulled out his wee canister of CS gas. Tightened his grip on the handcuffs. 'Here we go.'

Steel poked Kurt back. 'What's wrong with that?'

'I don't remember Bannockburn, 'cos I wasn't sodding there. And neither were you. We forgave the Germans for bombing Clydebank flat – that was only seventy-three years ago – and you're holding a grudge from Thirteen Fourteen!'

Her eyes narrowed, then widened. 'I know you! Kurt "The Mangler" Murison. You've got warrants out on you.'

He flexed his shoulders. Loomed some more. 'Who's asking?'

Stoney swore again. Stared at Logan with a pained expression. 'Tell Sonja I loved her...' Then he got out his CS gas and stood shoulder to shoulder with Guthrie. Put a bit of steel in his voice. 'Alright, that's enough.'

Everyone in the place turned to stare at him.

He cleared his throat. 'Kurt Murison, I'm detaining you under Section...'

But Kurt didn't explode. Instead he turned and legged it, battering out through the pub's double doors.

Guthrie grinned. 'Yeah, you better run!'

Logan thumped him. 'Don't just stand there, you idiot, get after him!'

'Right.' And they were off, the pair of them charging after Kurt, CS gas and handcuffs at the ready.

8

Steel grabbed hold of the bar again. Burped. 'Was it something I said?'

Everyone else went back to their drinks as Logan joined her. 'You're a disaster, you know that, don't you?'

'Maybe it's my perfume?'

Alec Hadden had eased himself closer to the door. Another five feet and he'd be gone.

Logan grabbed a handful of his collar. 'Oh no you don't.'

Hadden bit his bottom lip. Didn't struggle. 'Sod.'

'Think you and I need to have a little chat, don't we, Alec? Maybe you can share your world-beating porridge recipe?' He dragged the thin man back to the table. Pushed him down in to a seat. 'You want to make this easy, or difficult? I'm happy either way.'

Thin fingers drifted across the tabletop. 'I don't know what you're talking about. Maybe you've got me mistaken for—'

'Chris Browning.'

'Ah…' He stared down at his wandering fingers. 'Right.'

Steel lurched up to the table and thunked three large whiskies down. Rocked in her chair. 'What we talking about?'

'Mr Hadden is about to tell me why he paid two prostitutes

to lie about Chris Browning being a regular. Weren't you Mr Hadden?'

Silence.

'Or would you like to do this down the station?'

He shrugged one shoulder, curling into it until his ear was pinned against his jacket. 'It was ... you know ... to counteract the lies?'

'The lies.'

'For months, that puffed-up frog-faced git's been on the telly and the radio and in the papers, giving it doom and gloom, yeah? We're going to have no jobs. No currency. No defence budget. All the big companies are going to leave us. We won't be able to pay our benefits, or pensions, or doctors. Got kinda ... fed up of it.' His shrug swapped sides. 'Thought it'd even the scales a bit if everyone thought he liked getting it rough from a pair of hoors.'

Logan stared at him. 'And that passes for grownup political debate where you come from, does it?'

Steel threw her head back and laughed. A proper full-throated roar that set everything jiggling. 'You wee dancer.' Then she slapped Hadden on the back and pushed one of the whiskies in his direction. 'You earned that.'

He pulled on a lopsided smile. 'Thanks.' Then a sigh. 'Didn't help though, did it?'

She gave his shoulder a shoogle. 'Cheer up. Always next time. None of this once-in-a-generation bollocks, we've got what...' She turned and blinked at the TV for a bit. 'Laz?'

'Forty-five percent.'

'See? Forty-five percent. All we need's for one person in twenty to change their minds, and it's fifty-fifty!'

The smile grew a bit. 'Suppose.'

'Damn right.' She held up her glass. 'Slàinte mhath.'

Hadden clinked his drink against hers and they drank.

Logan took the glass off him. 'So you're saying you had nothing to do with Chris Browning going missing?'

'God, no. No, all I did was slip a couple of quid to Elaine and Jane. Told them to phone the *Examiner* and say Browning liked it rough and kinky. Honest. Ask them. And that wasn't till after he went missing.'

Logan just stared at him.

'*Honest.* I mean I know it was childish and that, but I wanted... It didn't seem fair they were always trying to scare people and ... it ... the "Yes" campaign needed... I...' Pink spread across his cheeks. 'Sorry.'

'You do know defamation is against the law, Mr Hadden?'

'Meh, it's civil, no' criminal.' Steel pushed Logan's free, untouched, thank-you-for-participating whisky across the table to Hadden. 'Our wee friend here wasn't trying to hurt anyone, was he? Just wobble the balance *our* way a bit.'

'Please. I'm really, really sorry.'

'There you go: he's sorry.' She knocked back her Famous Grouse. 'Didn't even work in the end.'

Their shoulders dipped.

Up on the TV screen, they called the Fife results. "No": 55.05%, "Yes": 44.95%.

Only one more local authority to declare and that was it.

Hadden gulped down the free whisky. Huffed out a breath. 'Look, can I ... I don't know ... buy you a drink or something? As an apology.'

Steel beamed. 'Course you can!'

Logan shook his head. 'Going to need you to come back to the station and make a statement.'

'Don't you listen to him, Haddy. You go get your Aunty Roberta a nice double Macallan and we'll say no more about it.'

'Thank you.' Hadden got up and went to the bar.

Logan watched him go. 'You know he'll try to do a runner, don't you?'

But he didn't. He bought three whiskies and he brought them back to the table. Shared them out. 'I'm really, really sorry. I am. It was just … I dunno, stupid.'

Steel helped herself to a double and wheeched it down. 'Ahh… Nice.' She pointed at Logan's. 'You're on duty, right?' Then helped herself to that one as well.

'Whoops…' Steel's legs didn't seem to be working any more. Probably due to the fact that they'd be knee-deep in whisky on the inside. 'M'fine…' Her smile spread and faded and spread and faded, as if it was out of focus. 'Cldn't be brrrrr.'

Half six in the morning and the bar crowd had thinned out again. Now, only the hardcore remained – clinging to their drinks in much the same way that Steel was clinging to the table. 'Whhhsssssssski.'

Hadden nodded towards the bar. 'Should I…?'

'No chance.' Logan stood. 'Whatever hangover she's got in the morning will be punishment enough.'

Steel peered up at him. 'Wanmorrrr.'

'Don't care. You're going home.'

'Awwwww…'

He dug his hands into her armpits, but it was like trying to pick up a pile of loose socks. Every time he got one bit upright, another bit collapsed.

Hadden hurried round to the other side. 'Let me give you a hand.'

Between them they wrestled her to her feet. Then caught her before she hit the ground. Turned and frogmarched her out through the front doors and onto Regent Quay.

The first hints of dawn curled pale blue at the corners of the sky, doing nothing to overpower the docks' spotlights.

Half six, and Aberdeen was waking up. The sound of traffic picking up on the dual carriageway.

Hadden shifted his grip on Steel's other arm. 'Where to?'

Closest place would be Logan's flat, but if she was going to puke she could sodding well do it somewhere else. Station, or her house? Hmm…

'Back to the station.' That way Steel's wife wouldn't be left wading through a lake of pizza-and-whisky vomit. She could owe him one.

'You got a car?'

'Nope. Walked.'

High overhead, a seagull screamed.

'Going to take a while then.' Hadden frowned. 'We could take my car? Got vinyl seat covers, in case she… You know.'

And Steel 'you know'-ing was very likely indeed. Plus, the sooner he could make her someone else's problem the better. 'Yeah, that'd be good, thanks.'

Hadden led the way with the left-hand side of Steel, while Logan followed with the right. She just dangled in the middle, making burbling noises.

'I'm really sorry about Chris Browning—'

'It's OK. Enough. I get it.' Logan puffed out a breath. 'You screwed up.'

'I know, but—'

'She was right, it's a civil law matter, not criminal. If Chris Browning wants to sue you for defamation when he turns up, that's his business. Hold your hand up and settle out of court. It'll cost you a lot less than paying for his lawyers *and* yours.'

A little smile. 'Thanks.'

They half-walked-half-carried Steel along the road, then left into James Street – another claustrophobic little alleyway that connected Regent Quay to the dual carriageway. Alec Hadden's rusty Volvo sat at the end, with most of its rear end sticking out over the double yellows.

Logan leaned Steel against the car's back door. 'Right, you'd better give me the keys.' He held his hand out to Hadden. 'You've been drinking.'

'Yes. Right. Of course.' He took out the keys, complete with little tartan fob, and passed them over. 'That's what I meant.'

'Good.' Logan plipped the locks open, and they wrestled Steel into the backseat.

'Erm...' Hadden pointed. 'Think we should put her in the recovery position or something? Just in case?'

He had a point.

Logan rearranged her arms and legs, till it was as close as he could get given the space. She could barf away to her heart's content and not choke on the chunks. The footwell was going to end up in a hell of a mess, though. 'OK, let's get—'

Something hard battered into the back of his head, sending him sprawling, filling his skull with the sound of burning and the smell of broken glass...

A voice in the distance. 'Sorry.'

Then another thump and everything went—

9

Steel slumped back against the pillow and groaned. 'How could you do it? To *me*?'

'How could I?' Logan reached over and poked her in the shoulder. 'What about you?'

'Don't you even dare.' She clacked her lips open and closed a couple of times, then shuddered. 'Tastes like a badger threw up in my mouth…'

He looked around the room: embossed wallpaper painted a vile shade of pale pink. Polished floorboards with a knotted rug. Dresser in the corner with a mirror above it. Flatpack wardrobe. One window, and a door. And, of course, the bed. All shiny and brass with a barred headboard and foot-board, little sceptre things on the corner posts. 'Where are we?'

Steel puffed out her cheeks. 'Susan's going to kill me when she finds out.'

The view through the window was nothing but blue sky and clouds.

'What happened to our clothes?'

'I mean, bad enough cheating on her, but with a man? With *you*?'

'Will you shut up and focus? We didn't do this – Alec Bloody Hadden did.' Logan reached up with his spare hand and ran his fingers across the back of his skull. Winced as a hundred needles tore through his scalp. There was a lump back there that felt the size of a hardboiled egg, the hair spiky and stiff. Probably dried blood. 'Ow…'

She scowled at him. 'Who the hell is Alec Hadden?'

'He was the scumbag buying you whisky last night.'

The expression on her face didn't change.

'The Regents Arms? Remember? You staggered in half-cut and tried to pick a fight with Kurt Murison?'

Steel curled her top lip. 'Kurt "The Mangler" Murison? God, I *must* have been drunk.'

'Had to carry you to the car. Then sodding Alec Hadden battered me over the back of the head.' And when Logan got his hands on him, he'd repay the favour with a stiff boot in the testicles. Hadden was going to come down with a bad case of resisting arrest. There was a second bump, beside the first. More needles. 'Ow…'

'Well stop poking at it then!' She raised her head from the pillow and grimaced. 'Look at it: pink! No' even a nice pink – *Barbie* pink. Who paints a bedroom Barbie pink? What are they, six?' A sniff. 'Where's my clothes?'

'How would I know?' He nodded to himself. 'Right, we need to get out of here.'

'*Really*? Gosh, whatever made you think of that? You must be some sort of genius!'

'Shut up and think. How do we get out of the cuffs?'

'Don't look at me. Only time I've ever been handcuffed to a bed there's been spanking and safewords.'

'Yeah, thanks. That's a *lot* of help.' Logan stared at the end of the bed, where their feet poked out from under the duvet. His right ankle was shackled to the bars, but Steel's weren't. 'Why didn't he cuff your legs too?'

She pulled her feet in, hiding them. 'Got a verruca. Maybe he's squeamish?'

'That, or you're too short and your legs don't reach.'

'I am no' short! Perfectly normal size for a Scottish woman.'

'Keep telling yourself that.' Logan stuck his free leg out of the bed and put his foot on the floor. Pushed. Nothing happened. A second time, harder this time, and the bed frame creaked, then shifted half an inch to the right. Big brass bed with two fully grown adults in it – of course it was going to be a sod to shift. Especially with only one leg.

'Hoy!' Steel hit him. 'Stop shoogling about. Sodding handcuff keeps digging into my wrist.'

Again. Gritting his teeth and shoving.

'Ow! What did I just tell you?'

He stopped and stared at her. 'I'm trying to move the bed, that OK with you?'

'No' if I end up with a broken wrist, it isn't.'

'God's sake… Fine.' He took hold of her hand, lacing the fingers together. 'Happy now? This way it won't tug at your *delicate* skin.' Logan dug his heel in and pushed.

She peered over the edge of the bed. 'What *exactly* are you trying to achieve?'

'If we can get to the wardrobe, there'll be clothes. That OK with you?'

Another shove. Another half inch. And already the muscle in his thigh was shouting at him. One more shove and it was screaming.

'Going to take all sodding week at this rate.' She stared at the window. 'What time do you think it is?'

'How should I know…' A final push and he slumped back, panting, leg dangling. Just have to take it in stages. They'd probably moved about as far as a fun-sized Mars Bar.

'Supposed to be back on shift at five.'

'Good for you.' He dug his heel in and pushed again.

'Someone's going to notice we're missing.'

If anything it was getting harder. 'Come on you wee sod...' Maybe the rug was bunching up under the bed's legs?

'And then they'll come running. Batter the door down. Barge in here with their...' She slapped a hand over her eyes. 'Nooooo. They'll see me in the nip. In bed. With *you*.'

'How? How will they even know where we are? You were half-cut to start with. They'll think you're just hungover and copping a sicky.'

'I *am* hungover.'

'And whose fault is that?'

'Oh shut up.'

'You shut up.'

Another push. More panting. One more ... and cramp tightened like a fist around his calf, twisting the muscle into a burning knot trying to rip its way free of the bone. 'Aaaaaagh.'

'Oh for God's sake. Stop it.' Steel thumped her other hand against his chest. 'Not getting anywhere.'

The pain tightened again. He had to force the words out between clenched teeth. 'Well I don't see *you* doing anything.'

She stared at the ceiling. 'Fine.' Then a deep breath. 'Close your eyes. And keep them closed till I tell you. Because if you even *think* of peeking...'

'Why would I want to peek? Bad enough imagining it, never mind seeing it for real!'

'Close your sodding eyes!'

He did, and the duvet shifted as Steel slipped out of the bed. He grabbed hold of his half and held on tight before it slipped and everything was on show.

Her feet made a soft slapping sound as they hit the floor. 'Stark, bare-arsed naked and handcuffed to a man. Never been so embarrassed in my *life*.'

Then there was some grunting. Some swearing. And finally

302

the bedframe shifted, moaning in time to Steel's heaves. Groan. Squeal. Groan. Squeal. Groan—

A clunk from the other side of the room and a man's voice. 'What...?'

Logan's eyes snapped open.

Alec Hadden stood in the doorway, mouth hanging open, a newspaper tucked under one arm and a bottle of water in the other.

'Aagh!' Then Steel leapt back into bed, burrowing under the duvet as if her life depended on it. But not quick enough to protect Logan from an eyeful.

He shuddered. Oh God...

Her cold skin slapped against his leg, then she recoiled to the edge of the bed, taking as much of the duvet with her as possible.

Logan held on for grim death.

She let go of his hand.

'What are you doing?' Alec stepped into the room. Closed the door behind him.

Steel stuck her head above the covers. 'WHERE THE HELL ARE MY CLOTHES?'

'Ah.' He settled down on the edge of the bed, shoulders drooped, head bowed. 'They're in the wash. You were sick, like, *everywhere*. I mean on the car seat, in the footwell, on yourself, on your friend here. Everywhere.' A shrug. 'So I bunged everything in the washing machine.'

'YOU SAW ME NAKED!'

'Only for a little bit.' A sigh. Then he took out the newspaper and held it up. The headline 'UNION BACK' sat over a big Union Jack flag. A shocked Salmond in one corner, a smug looking Cameron in the other. Hadden gave another big, theatrical sigh. 'Forty-five percent "Yes", fifty-five percent "No", and they're calling it a *decisive* victory. How? How is that decisive? Yeah, it's a *decision*, but that's all it is.'

303

Steel jabbed a finger in his direction. 'You just abducted two police officers, sunshine. You think that's a good idea?'

'Now they're talking about backing out of all that Devo-Max stuff they promised. "It's rash.", "It was unwise.", "England won't let Scotland have anything if it doesn't get what it wants first." Can you believe that?'

'Listen up, chuckles: you're no' getting away with this. They'll already be out there looking for us. How long do you think it's going to take them to kick in your door, eh?'

'They lied to the Scottish people. They laid out this bowl full of promises: more power, more influence, more money, and now Westminster wants to take it all back.'

Logan shuffled as far up the bed as he could. Which wasn't far with the handcuff fastening his right leg to the frame. 'Politicians lie, Alec. It's what they do. Not exactly a shocker, is it?'

'We could have been free...'

'I know it's disappointing, but it's the way it is. This is what democracy looks like. You just have to accept it, put it behind you, and move on.'

He turned and stared out of the window. 'Why should we? Why shouldn't we arm ourselves and take back our country? Referendum didn't work. It's time for revolution.'

Steel grabbed a pillow and battered it off Alec's head. 'Don't be so sodding wet.'

'Don't—'

'Unlock these handcuffs, *now*.'

'You'll arrest me.'

She looked at Logan. Then at Alec, eyebrows up. 'Of course we'll sodding arrest you! What did you think was going to happen? You abduct two police officers, you strip them, and you chain them to the bloody bed, did you think we'd bake you a cake?'

Logan held up his other hand. 'OK, OK, let's all calm

down. No one's starting a revolution, and no one's arresting anyone.' He pointed at the handcuffs around his ankle. 'Alec, can you unlock that, please? It's cutting off circulation to my foot.'

'I don't understand why everything went wrong.' He dropped the paper on the bed. Ran a hand through his long brown hair. 'I didn't want any of this. I just wanted...' His bottom lip trembled. 'I didn't mean to hit you. I just ... I panicked. I didn't...'

Steel rolled her eyes. 'Oh in the name of the wee man. Don't be such a big girl's blouse.' She shook her fist, making the handcuffs rattle against the brass bars of the headboard. 'Unlock these things and we'll talk about maybe getting you into a nice low-security prison.'

Alec licked his lips. Opened his mouth...

Whatever he was about to say, it was stopped by the sound of a doorbell somewhere on a lower floor.

Alec stood. 'I have to go.'

'Unlock these sodding handcuffs!'

But Alec didn't. Instead he stood. Chucked the paper onto the duvet. 'In case you get bored.' Then he grabbed Logan's side of the bed and dragged the thing back into the middle of the room. 'Don't move it again. You're scratching the floorboards.' He turned and marched out, closing the door behind him. The thump was followed by the *click* of a key turning in its lock.

Logan thumped back into his pillow. Then winced as the lumps on the back of his head got squished. 'Oh very clever. That was a spectacular bit of hostage negotiation, that was.'

'Kiss my—'

'You don't threaten the person you're negotiating with! Yeah, let us free so we can arrest you.'

'Of course we're going to arrest him.'

'You don't have to tell *him* that!'

305

'Close your eyes.' She grabbed his hand again, then slipped out from beneath the duvet. There was grunting, creaking, and swearing again as the bed moved. But they weren't going towards the wardrobe this time, they were going in the direction the bed was pointing.

'What are you doing?'

'I said no sodding looking!'

'I'm not looking.'

More grunts. More creaks. More swearing. Then *clunk*.

The mattress springs twanged as Steel climbed back on the bed. 'Keep them closed!'

'Tell me what the hell's going on.'

'Looking out the window… Down there. Can just see past a bit of roof, there's a car parked at the kerb.'

'Thrilling.'

'Shut up. Want to see who's visiting.'

'Open the window and shout for help.'

'Hold on…' Thump. Bang. A growling noise. Then, 'Open you wee sod…' More straining noises. 'Gah. It's locked. We… It's Rennie! And DC Stone. You wee dancers!' She banged on the window. 'BUGGERLUGS, UP HERE! HOY! UP HERE! LOOK UP YOU PAIR OF MORONS!'

'What are they doing?'

'NO! DON'T GO BACK TO THE CAR! WE'RE UP HERE! HOY! RENNIE YOU SODDING IDIOT!'

Silence.

'What?'

A long, rattling sigh, and then Steel collapsed back on the bed beside him. 'They drove off.'

'Oh, that's just *brilliant*.'

'We're going to be stuck here for ever, aren't we?'

10

Logan stared up at the ceiling as Steel climbed under the duvet again. 'How could they just drive off?'

'Because they're idiots.' She groaned. Covered her face with her free hand. 'No' that this situation isn't dramatic enough, but it's about to get worse.'

'What now?'

'I need a pee.'

Breath whooshed out of him. 'You are *not* peeing the bed.'

'I'm peeing in, or on, something, whether you like it or not.'

'Well … pee in the wardrobe then. Or better yet: tie a knot in it.'

She frowned at him. 'How am I supposed to "tie a knot" in it? Have you no idea how a woman's body—'

'Shhh…'

Logan stared at the door.

Click.

It swung open, and there was Alec Hadden back again. With a length of chain in one hand and a padlock in the other. His mouth tightened and his eyes widened. 'What did I tell you about moving the bed? You've scratched the hell out of the floor! Look at it. LOOK AT IT!'

307

'Think it's bad now?' Steel sniffed. 'Wait till I pee on it.'

He dropped the chain and the padlock. 'You horrible... How...' He clenched a fist. Took a deep breath. Nodded. 'I see. What we have here is a lack of respect.' Alec unbuckled his belt.

Steel stuck her chin out. 'If you think you're putting your dick anywhere near me, you've got another think coming!'

He pulled his belt from his trousers. Curled one hand around the buckle, and wrapped the leather around his fist a couple of times, leaving the end dangling. 'I didn't want to do this. You made me.'

'You sodding *dare*!'

Logan held his hand up again. 'Come on, we all need to calm down here. This isn't going to solve anything. We...'

Alec lunged, swinging the belt overarm at Steel, teeth bared.

She dodged to the side, grabbed the belt and yanked him towards her. Then slammed her forehead into his face.

There was a wet crunch and he went sprawling across the bed. Steel was up on her knees, everything airing in the breeze – pale, swinging, and wobbling – as she hammered her fist down into Alec's head. Once. Twice. Three times. He struggled up, and she mashed her fist into the bloody mess of his nose.

Thunk.

Alec wobbled. Rocked. Then his eyes crossed and he slid backwards off the bed. Thump onto the floor. Lying spread-eagled on the scarred floorboards. Not moving.

Steel let out a shuddery breath. 'God, now I *really* need to pee.'

'So search him again.' Steel pulled the duvet up beneath her chin. Her free hand was swollen and curled, the skin darkening from red to purple. Probably broke something.

Logan heaved Alec over onto his back again. It was cumbersome and awkward, but nothing compared with the effort of hauling him up onto the bed in the first place. 'It's not here.'

'Then where the hell is it?'

'I don't know, do I? Maybe he doesn't keep the handcuff key on him? They're not his handcuffs, they're ours. Maybe he doesn't even know what the handcuff key *looks* like?'

'Oh this is just great. Thank you very much.'

'How is this my fault? You're the one who battered him.'

'What was I supposed to do?'

Lying on the bed, Alec groaned. His face was a mess – swollen and bloodied, a couple of teeth missing. Most of his nose wasn't where it was supposed to be any more.

'He's waking up.'

Steel sooked a breath through her teeth. 'You hit him this time. My hand hurts.'

Logan rolled him into the middle of the bed, getting scarlet smears on the duvet cover, and stuck his free leg out. Reaching with his toes for the dropped chain. Holding his breath and stretching for it. The handcuff dug into his other ankle. 'Got it.'

He wrapped his toes around the cold metal and pulled it, clinking back to the bed. Reached down and grabbed the end.

Steel looked over his chest at the floor. 'What about the padlock?'

'Give us a chance...' His foot reached, and reached, and reached. Logan's tongue poked out the side of his mouth.

But there was no way he could even come close.

'You need to push the bed closer so I can reach.'

'For goodness sake. Do I have to do everything?'

'Yes. You have to do everything. I'm contributing absolutely *nothing* here.'

'You're such a whinge. Close—'

'I know. Close my eyes.' He shuddered. 'Trust me, some sights I never want to see again.'

'Oh: ha, ha.' She slipped out and the bed groaned and

creaked and gouged its way across the floorboards. 'This …
was … easier … when … there was … just … your fat …
arse on … there.' The bed came to a halt and Steel climbed
beneath the duvet again. 'Right, you can open your eyes.'

He grabbed the padlock with his toes and together they
chained Alec's hands behind his back. Then wrapped the rest
of it around his ankles, before pulling it tight and padlocking
the two ends together. Leaving him trussed up like a turkey.

Steel put her foot on his shoulder and shoved him over
the edge of the bed.

Alec tumbled to the floor with a thump and a groan.

'Serves you right.' She wriggled down into the bed and
scowled up at the ceiling.

'What now?

'Still need a pee.'

'Wardrobe?'

A sigh. 'Wardrobe.'

'What do you mean there's no clothes in there?'

Steel's voice came out muffled from inside. 'I mean, there's
hundreds of clothes. Millions of them. It's like a branch of
Markies in here. What do you think I mean?'

'Wonderful.'

'Hey, I'm not enjoying it much either…' A pause. 'Urgh.
I've got pee on my feet!'

'I spy, with my little eye, something beginning with "B".'

Lying next to him, Steel sniffed. 'Better no' be "boobs". You
promised no' to peek!'

'It's not "Boobs". And one glimpse was enough to scar
me for life, thanks.'

'Blinds?'

'No.'

*   *   *

'Don't stop!' Steel gripped his hand, the cuffs digging into his wrist as the bed moaned and creaked beneath them. 'Harder!'

Logan grunted and put his hips into it as the whole frame swayed and clanged.

'Come on, come on, come on...'

'Argh...' He slumped back against the mattress, sweat prickling between his shoulder blades. 'It's no good.'

'We can *do* this!'

'No we can't. The frame's not going to fall apart. Doesn't matter how much we shoogle it.'

'Sodding hell.'

'Because I'm thirsty, OK?' Logan wriggled as far as to the left as the cuffs around his wrist and ankle would let him, right hand groping at the floorboards. 'Little more...'

'Sodding hell.' Steel grunted and groaned, and the bed gouged its way across the floorboards again.

'Come to Logan...' The bottle of water Alec dropped was just out of reach.

More grunts and groans.

'Got you!'

'OK...' Steel frowned at the ceiling. 'Shoot Gordon Brown, shag Nick Clegg, marry David Cameron.'

Logan raised an eyebrow. 'You'd marry a Tory?'

'He's worth millions, isn't he? Soon as we're married, there's going to be an unfortunate accident and I'll inherit the lot.' A grin. 'An unfortunate accident with a wood chipper. Hello Daveyboy, I've made you a lovely cup of tea. Come out into the garden and drink it next to this dirty big chunk of machinery. Whoops! Shove. Grrrrrrrrrrrrrrrrrrrrind!'

'Urgh.' She curled her top lip. 'Your hand's all sweaty.'

'So stop holding it, then.'

'Can't. Every time I let go you shoogle about and I get a chafed wrist. You're like a ferret in a carrier bag. A sweaty ferret. That can't hold still for two minutes.'

'This is hell, isn't it? I've died and I've gone to hell...'

'I'm bursting, OK?' Logan crossed his legs. Didn't help though, was still like a spaniel dancing on his bladder.

Steel pulled a face. 'Serves you right for drinking all that water.'

'I was thirsty.'

'So go pee in the wardrobe.'

'How?' He levelled his voice, weighed out each word as if talking to a very small, very stupid child. 'My ankle's handcuffed to the *bed*. I can't get *off* the bed like you can. If I *could* we wouldn't be in this sodding mess.'

'You're a dick, you know that, don't you?'

'Going to have to pee off the edge of the bed.'

'Oh great. So I widdle in the wardrobe like a civilised human being, and you just pish all over the floor like some sort of animal. And then we get to lie here marinating in the stench.'

He turned and stared at her. 'You don't exactly piddle rosewater yourself.' Then he jerked his head at the other side of the room. 'Shove the bed over there and I'll pee in the corner. Well, corner-ish.'

'Oh God, I can hear it splashing!'

'Will you shut up? This isn't exactly a precision instrument at the best of times.'

'Urgh...'

'Something beginning with "D"?' Logan glanced around the room. 'Door?'

'Nope.'

'Dresser.'

'Nope.'

Hmm… Ah, of course – dangling from the side of the blinds. 'Drawstring.'

'Nah. Give up? It's him on the floor: "Dickhead".'

The little creases deepened between Steel's eyebrows. 'It's just, sometimes, I really miss my dad, you know? He'd have loved Jasmine.'

'He OK with the whole gay thing?'

'Course he was. What's not to like?'

'Fair enough.' Logan frowned up at the ceiling, making patterns from the light and shadow. 'Never really knew my father.'

'Oh aye, Mum put it about a bit, did she?'

A laugh barked out of Logan, setting the mattress vibrating. 'Can you imagine?' Then a shudder. 'Actually, better not. No, he was in the Job. Constable Charles McRae. Went to pick up a bloke on a warrant for aggravated burglary in Stonehaven. Only the guy had a sawn-off shotgun and wasn't cool with going back to prison again. I was five.'

Steel reached across the duvet with her spare hand and gave his shoulder a squeeze. 'Sorry.'

'Why do you think I joined the force? Couldn't think of anything that would hack my mother off more.'

'Pfff… Curtains?'

Logan shook his head. 'Nope.'

'Carpet?'

'That's not a carpet, it's a rug.'

'Oh.' She chewed at her top lip. 'Cushions?'

'Give up?' He pointed at the window. 'Clouds.'

'What? It has to be *inside* the room, you idiot. Who taught you how to play?'

* * *

'Oh-ho, Chuckles is on the move.'

Logan peered over the edge of the bed. Steel was right: Alec Hadden was twitching. Then a groan. Then a cough that left a smear of red-flecked sputum on the floorboards.

Steel raised her eyebrows. 'Thought I'd killed him for a bit there.'

A tremble ran through Alec, wrists and ankles still firmly chained and padlocked behind his back. 'Gnnnnnnngh...' And then he went limp again.

'Serves you right, you wee shite. That's what you get for abducting police officers.'

11

'Well?'

Logan's fingers walked along the brass tubing, tracing the corner where the headboard joined the main frame. Smooth metal, slick and cool. There – a hexagonal lump. 'It's a nut.'

'So undo it!'

He grabbed the sides and twisted.

Nothing.

Tried again. Gritted his teeth. 'Come on you wee sod...' Fire raced through his fingers, up into his palm. Then wrist. Then, 'It won't budge. Too tight.'

'Right. So we need to loosen it. OK.' She sucked at her teeth. 'Don't have a spanner, just have to go back to shoogling. Clockwise shoogling.' A breath. 'Come on Roberta, you can do this.' She poked Logan in the shoulder. 'Eyes. And *keep* them closed.'

He scrunched them shut. 'OK.'

She folded the duvet back on top of him, then there was some grunting.

The handcuff around his wrist twisted. 'Ow, ow, ow, ow!'

'You think that's bad?' Her weight settled on top of him, one knee on either side. 'How do you think I feel?'

He slapped his hand over his eyes as well, just in case.

'I swear Laz, if you get a stiffy during this—'

'Just get on with it.'

'Deep breath, Roberta. Think of Natalie Portman.' Then the thrusting started. Back and forward. Harder. Making the frame creak. Then Steel added a side-to-side thrust of the hips, getting the bed to make little circles. Harder and faster.

Logan pulled his head further into the pillow, out of the way of anything that might be swinging about up there.

Creaks, groans, pinging noises, grunting.

This would be a *really* bad time to be rescued.

Ping, creak, groan, grunt, then thumping joined the mix. Probably the bed's legs banging on the scarred, piddled-on floorboards. Her voice was laboured, squeezed out between breaths as she kept on grinding. 'Try now!'

Oh God. Don't look. Don't look.

He slipped his hand back beneath the bed, feeling for the nut.

The whole thing rocked and wobbled, joints opening up and closing with each thrust. Be lucky if he didn't lose a finger.

The nut was cold and hard in his hand. Logan grabbed it. Squeezed. Twisted... 'Come on!'

And it gave. Not much, but a tiny twist. Again. As long as he timed his turn with the right point in the rotation, the nut loosened. Again. And again. And again. 'It's coming! Yes! It's coming! Yes! Yes! Yes!'

Then it wasn't coming any more. The nut jolted out of his grasp and the whole side of the bed collapsed as he snatched his hand out of the way.

'You wee beauty!'

'Ow...' If anything it was even more uncomfortable than being handcuffed to the unbroken bed. Now the whole frame was out of alignment and the cuff around his wrist and ankle were pulling him apart.

Steel scrambled off him. 'Keep those sodding eyes shut.' Then there was more grunting and groaning. But thankfully no thrusting. 'Come on... Agggggghhhhhh... Break you wee—'

Clang.

And the other side of the bed collapsed too.

'Woo-hoo!'

The scuff of bare feet on floorboards. Then she let go of his hand. 'Right, I need you to sit up.'

Logan did as he was told, struggling in the darkness, dragging the headboard with him.

'Keep going. Forwards. Grab your ankles.'

'This better not be more kinky stuff.'

'Just do it.' Then another bout of grunting as the head-board shifted. 'Going to wedge the bars over the corner post... There you go. Might want to grit your teeth for this bit.'

'What? What are you— Aaaaagh!' Pain ripped through his wrist as the handcuffs tried to bend it in a way it really hadn't evolved for.

'One more go.' A grunt.

'Are you *trying* to kill me?'

Then a *ping* rang out and the pressure on his wrist disappeared.

Logan risked a peek. She'd used the corner post as a lever to snap one end of the bar out of place. And now the hand-cuffs were free. He shut his eyes again before he saw anything else.

'HAHAHAHAHAHAHA! I'm a sodding *genius*!' Steel slapped him on the back. 'Told you I'd get us out of here. Now we do the same crowbar trick with the footboard, and we're good to go. Brace yourself.'

Groan. Strain. *Ping*.

Logan slid backwards down the mattress.

317

They were free. Naked and still handcuffed together, but at least they weren't attached to that bloody bed any more.

'OK, you can look now.' Steel stood and raised her free hand like the Statue of Liberty. The duvet cover was wrapped around her in a makeshift toga. 'Tres stylish, nes pa?'

'I feel like a complete dick.' Two floral pillowcases, tied together, didn't make a great loincloth, but it was better than nothing.

'Look on the bright side – I can't see yours, so we're good to go.' She paused to nudge Alec Hadden with her foot. 'We'll be back for you, Chuckles. Don't get too comfy.'

As if that was possible, lying on a pee-stained wooden floor, trussed up with chains.

Logan led the way over to the door, the other handcuff dangling from his ankle – scrapping along the boards.

'Hoy!' Steel hit him. 'What did I tell you about shoogling and these sodding cuffs?'

He closed his eyes. Counted to three. 'Fine.' Then took her hand again. 'OK?'

She looked down at their hands, then up at his naked torso, then down at his makeshift loincloth and the pale, pasty legs poking out underneath it. 'Don't think George Clooney's got much to worry about.'

Why bother?

He opened the door. Peered out. A stairway reached down two storeys, new looking, with magnolia walls and framed prints of wildflowers. That would make this an attic conversion then. Another doorway opened off the small landing onto a room crowded with boxes.

Steel sniffed. 'What if there's another one of him?'

'Think they might *just* have heard us destroying the bed.'

Down the stairs, carpet soft and warm underfoot. A

window looked out on the back garden. A whirly washing line sat in the middle of a square of green, heavy with clothes. *Their* clothes. Getting dark out there, the sky heading from clear blue to navy.

First floor. Three white-panelled doors led off the landing.

'Shhh!' Steel stopped, head cocked to one side as something growled. 'Starving.' She pointed downstairs. 'Kitchen – food. Then out the back door and get our sodding clothes.'

'Think you can keep your stomach in check for five minutes while we get dressed? Not that much to ask, is it?'

'Hungry.' She straightened her toga. 'And in case you're wondering: Detective Chief Inspector still outranks Detective Sergeant.'

'Detective *Inspector*.'

'Acting Detective Inspectors don't count.' She took a step down the stairs, hauling him with her. 'You want to play with the big girls? Get a proper promotion.'

God's sake…

He followed her down to the ground floor. Didn't really have any option with his wrist still cuffed to hers. Holding hands as if they were on some sort of horrible, deviant date.

The kitchen lay at the end of the hallway – a pristine expanse of shiny tiles, stainless steel, and polished-wooden work surfaces.

Steel made straight for the fridge. 'Sandwich would do… Oh.' Her shoulders drooped. 'All they've got is a carton of fake butter and an onion. And that doesn't look too fresh.'

Logan stretched out an arm and opened the bread bin. Pulled out a loaf of sliced white and dumped it on the counter next to the toaster. Stuck a couple of slices in and pushed down the handle. 'OK? You happy now?'

She sniffed. 'Think if you're going to abduct someone, the least you could do is get a bit of cheese in. Some smoked ham. Few eggs.' Steel grabbed the butter and clunked the fridge shut again. Tried one of the cupboards. 'Pot Noodle would do at a push.'

Steel chomped on her toast, melted buttery-spread glistening on her chin. 'Hurry it up, going full-on football studs here.'

Gloom enveloped the back garden. Two small patches of light spilled out through the kitchen window and the open back door, just enough to make their breath shine in the cool evening air.

Logan unpegged his pants from the whirly. 'Close your eyes.'

Steel raised an eyebrow. 'In this cold? It'll be all shrivelled up like a half-chewed wine gum anyway. Get a move on.'

He hauled his pants on, then took his trousers off the line and pulled them on too. Then ditched the Laura Ashley loincloth. The shirt was more of a challenge – could only get it on over one arm, buttoning it up across his chest as far as possible, the other sleeve hanging limp at his side. Same with the jacket.

Steel popped the last chunk of toast in her mouth, then sooked her fingers clean. 'Where's mine?'

'You were eating.'

'Make with the bras and pants, you unchivalrous wee sod.'

He passed her the underwear, trying *really* hard not to see how red and lacy it was. Then stood there, cheeks like barbecues, as she struggled into both. Shifting around, hand-cuffed wrist twisting so she could fasten her bra behind her back.

Don't touch her bare skin, don't touch her bare— Agh ... too late.

The figures reflected in the kitchen window looked like something from a Cohen Brothers movie. Steel with her

320

random hair – fully suited, except for the one bare arm and shoulder – Logan her taller, slightly less scruffy, mirror image.

She scowled, then scratched at her naked armpit – where the rogue bra strap dangled. 'Off-the-shoulder's no' a good look for you. No' with those pasty arms.'

'How am I supposed to know what he's done with our keys?'

'Still,' she shrugged, 'on the bright side: there's no risk of you flashing your horrible man bits any more. Thank heaven for tiny wrinkly mercies.'

'Yes, because you're Keira Knightley meets Marilyn Monroe, aren't you?' He tightened his grip on her hand and pulled her through into a utility room, just off the kitchen. It smelled of warm laundry. The contents of their pockets were piled up on the work surface above the washing machine: phones, keys, cash, wallets, warrant cards, and all the other bits and bobs. 'Yes!' He grabbed the keys and flicked through them. 'No.'

She peered at the silvery collection in his hand. 'No what?'

'No handcuff key.'

'Must be. Give.' She did exactly the same thing that he had. With exactly the same result. 'Bugger.'

'I told you, didn't I? Honestly.'

'Blah, blah, blah.' She picked her e-cigarette from the pile of stuff and clicked it on. Sooked hard on the mouthpiece. Closed her eyes and sighed. 'Ooooh, God, that's better…'

Logan powered up his phone. 'I'll give Stoney a ring and—'

A thump came from somewhere above.

They both looked up at the ceiling.

Steel curled her free hand into a fist. 'If that wee scumbag's wriggled free, he's getting a flying lesson out the nearest window.' She dragged Logan back into the kitchen, then out into the hall.

His left thumb skiffed across the screen, never hitting the right button. 'Would you slow down?'

'No.' Up the stairs to the first landing.

'How am I supposed to—'

'Shhh…' She put a finger to her lips. 'Listen.'

Another thump. Not overhead this time, but off to the left.

She pointed at one of the three doors. Mouthed the words, 'Three. Two. One.' Then a nod.

Logan grabbed the handle and twisted. Threw the door open. 'POLICE! NOBODY… Oh.'

It was a single bedroom. And there was a man on the bed. Well, not so much 'on' as 'chained to' by the arms and legs. Naked except for an adult nappy, with a ball gag in his mouth. Middle-aged, pasty skin, with receding brown hair, wide sunken eyes, and a stubbly beard.

Steel pursed her lips and raised an eyebrow. 'Aye, aye, someone's been naughty.'

He writhed on the bed, mumbling behind the ball gag.

Logan hauled her over to the bed. Then glanced down at his own half-on-half-off clothing. 'I know it doesn't look like it, but we're police officers. I'm going to unbuckle the gag, OK?' He reached forward, pulling Steel's arm with him, and fiddled with the buckle.

'Gaaaah!' Red weals cut across his cheeks, where the leather strap had been. The man coughed a couple of times, then spat. Hauled in a breath. 'Oh God, you have to get help! Please! He'll be back soon!'

Logan frowned down at him. Take away the beard and… 'It's Chris Browning, isn't it? We've been looking for you for *weeks*.'

'Guv? Hello?' Stoney's voice came through the locked door. His silhouette rippled through the patterned glass on either

side. Probably trying to see into the house. *'Hello?'* Then he knocked. *'Guv, you there?'*

Steel squatted down and levered up the letterbox flap. 'Give me your handcuff keys.'

'Guv? Can you unlock the door?'

'You deaf or something, Constable Stone? Keys, now.'

He stepped back. *'Someone's there with you, aren't they Guv? Are you being coerced? Stand back, I'm breaking the door down!'*

Logan slammed his free hand into the glass at the side, setting it booming. 'Just post your sodding keys through the letterbox!'

'But—'

Steel poked her hand through the nylon brushes. 'Give me the keys, or I'm going to reach down your throat, grab your pants, and haul them back out through your gob!'

The second ambulance pulled away from the kerb, lights spinning in the sunset. Steel pulled her e-cigarette from her pocket, clicked it on, and took a deep drag. 'Ahhh. That's better.'

Logan rubbed at the thick red line encircling his right wrist. 'There you go, we just saved an influential "No" campaigner.'

She shrugged. 'Win some, lose some.' She sniffed, then spat into the neat front garden. 'Anyone asks, the naked thing didn't happen. Understand?'

Goose pimples raced up Logan's arms, coming together at the back of his neck. 'Ack... I'm probably going to need therapy.'

'Official report, we were handcuffed to a radiator or something. No naked. No bed. No piddling.'

'Agreed.'

She turned and stared up at the building. 'So, come on then – how did you vote?'

'None of your damned business, that's how.' He lifted his chin and walked toward the waiting patrol car. 'Now, if you'll excuse me, I'm off to get very, *very* drunk.'

She shambled along beside him. 'Good idea.' Then reached out and took his hand again. 'You're getting the first round in, though.'

And however bad the hangover was, they'd just have to deal with it tomorrow.

READ THE ENTIRE SERIES FROM

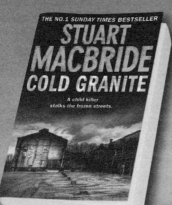

THE NO.1 SUNDAY TIMES BESTSELLER
STUART MACBRIDE
COLD GRANITE
A child killer stalks the frozen streets.

THE NO.1 SUNDAY TIMES BESTSELLER
STUART MACBRIDE
DYING LIGHT
She's just the first. How many more will die?

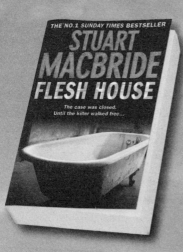

THE NO.1 SUNDAY TIMES BESTSELLER
STUART MACBRIDE
FLESH HOUSE
The case was closed. Until the killer walked free...

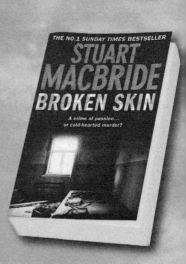

THE NO.1 SUNDAY TIMES BESTSELLER
STUART MACBRIDE
BROKEN SKIN
A crime of passion... or cold-hearted murder?

LOGAN McRAE
THE BEGINNING...

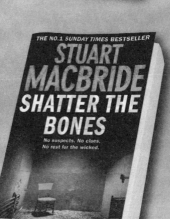

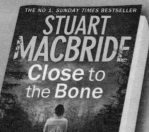

The Ash Henderson novels

Five years ago DC Ash Henderson's daughter, Rebecca, disappeared on the eve of her thirteenth birthday. A year later the first card arrived: homemade, with a Polaroid stuck to the front. Rebecca, strapped to a chair, gagged and terrified. Every year another card – each one worse than the last.

The tabloids call him 'The Birthday Boy'. He's been snatching girls for years, always just before their thirteenth birthday, killing them slowly, then torturing their families with his homemade cards.

But Ash hasn't told anyone what happened to Rebecca – they think she ran away – because he doesn't want to be taken off the investigation. He's sacrificed too much to give up before his daughter's murderer gets what he deserves...

Eight years ago, 'The Inside Man' murdered four women and left three more in critical condition – all with their stomachs slit open and a plastic doll stitched inside. And then he just ... disappeared.

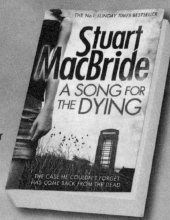

Ash Henderson was a Detective Inspector on the investigation, but a lot has changed since then. His family has been destroyed, his career is in tatters, and one of Oldcastle's most vicious criminals is making sure he spends the rest of his life in prison.

Now a nurse has turned up dead, a plastic doll buried beneath her skin, and it looks as if Ash might finally get a shot at redemption. At earning his freedom. At revenge.

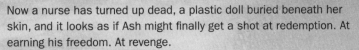

⬇ ebook · audio